E

TERROR

Walter R. Turney

A JAKE SALAZAR INTRIGUE

Shakehouse Productions

Epitaph in Terror
published
by
Shakehouse Production, LLC 2024

ISBN 979-8-218-44541-6 (paperback)
ISBN 979-8-218-44612-3 (e-book)

Cover Design by Michael Turney

To my loving wife, Charlene, and son, Michael.

To save your world you asked this man to die.
Would this man, could he see you now, ask why?

Epitaph for the Unknown Soldier
W.H. Auden

When a book, any sort of book, reaches a certain intensity of artistic performance it becomes literature. That intensity may be a matter of style, situation, character, emotional tone, or idea, or half a dozen other things. It may also be a perfection of control over the movement of the story similar to the control of a great pitcher over the ball.

From a letter written by Raymond Chandler to
Earl Stanley Gardner

Baseball has the largest library of law and love and custom and ritual, and therefore, in a nation that fundamentally believes it is a nation under law, well, baseball is America's most privileged version of the level field. No one man is superior to the game.   For me, baseball is the most nourishing game outside of literature. They both are re-telling of human experience.

A. Bartlette Giamatti
President of Yale University and
Seventh Commissioner of Major League Baseball

My heartfelt thanks and deep appreciation to my cousin, Mark Macrae, without whose knowledge and expertise I couldn't have written this novel. Epitaph in Terror takes place in that grand summer of '49 when baseball fans on the West Coast, far from the East Coast rivalry between the Yankees and Red Sox, held their breath and rooted for their favorite home team. By mid season, Californians, north and south, were placing their bets as the Hollywood Stars and the Oakland Oaks fought tooth and nail for the Pacific Coast League Pennant.

Contents

Chapter I

Outlawed Pitches and Stealers of Home

I missed the "Banner" and the "Play ball!" and didn't arrive until the top of the third. The Stars were already down six runs. When I left Hollywood, three days before for a high stakes poker game in Vegas, the Twinks were four games up on the Oaks. I sure didn't figure walking in on this! Even the kid on the mound didn't look familiar.

My roommates, Hilo Dominici and Angelico Mercado, knowing I was going to be late, had saved me a seat.

When I reached our box, Hilo introduced me to his latest catch. She was a curvaceous knockout, by the name of Healani, who'd just arrived from the Islands. He informed me that the Oaks had hit the crap out of Pinky Woods in the first. I was just about to get comfortable between Hilo and Angel when Smitty Teste, one of the three Brooklyn Dodger scouts sent west by Branch Rickey, put in his own two cents. The old, opinionated scout had been a constant complaint at our backs from the beginning of the season.

"Six years ago, when Pinky was with the Red Sox," said Smitty, turning the page of his New York Times and snapping it to attention on the column of his choice, "none of these Oaks, not even this Martin kid, could have touched his fast ball!"

"I prophesize he wins twenty games this season." Angel's Filipino intonation and razor sharp sibilance cut through the afternoon sunshine and Smitty's eastern pomposity with all the deadly feminine grace of his native short sword and dagger – Espada y Daga – that once sliced through the flesh of the Japanese.

"Nah, not a chance; these days he's a bum among bums," insisted Smitty. "Takes one to know one," I added. Despite my total opposition to the rumored possibility of the Stars becoming the first major league team on the West Coast, as far as the Big Show was concerned, Smitty knew me to be a diehard New York Yankees fan.

"I'm not talkin' glorified Brooklyn bum or Boston bum," Smitty scoffed in his familiar know-it-all aloofness. "I'm talkin' straight out hit the showers bum among bums!"

Smitty was an old boy the Dodgers sent west to keep tabs on Fred Haney, the Stars manager, and his players. This, after Rickey, the Dodgers big shot, and Bob Cobb, the Stars front office guy, cracked a deal to make the Stars a farm club for the Dodgers. So, not a week after Smitty arrived from back east, what do you think this "senior judge of youthful talent" believed to be his major duty as a scout? Every morning, he made it a habit of driving over to the newsstand on Melrose and buying up yesterday's *New York Times*, *Herald Tribune*, and *Washington Post*. Then, he'd sit his fat ass down beside this pile of eastern rags and proceed to lecture Hilo, Angel, and me about the current state of the postwar political world. On one side, were the Nazis still rumored to be mustering up a Fourth Reich in the jungles of South America and, on the other, evidence of an imminent threat of clandestine Reds creeping around our sterling halls of Washington and tinseled studios of Hollywood. The grand design of the baseball diamond provided the suspendered and potbellied scout with a perfect field of analogies for his scrutiny of a world politically split in two. Smitty's weird and obnoxious gospel belonged in a loony bin, not on the ballfield. For example, when he caught sight of some old-timer with nothing left him but a de-escalating fastball and a piece of emery cloth in his back pocket, before you knew it, he was going on about baseball's outlawed spitball and equating it with Hitler's dishonest fascistic "pitch" to the German people. "Trust me, boys, it can happen here. It can happen here!" Or, say, if a hitter stretched a double into a triple and was known to be fast enough to steal home, Smitty would start going on about how "that threat on third" reminded him of "those commies walking around the State Department!" As far as Smitty was concerned, these Stalinists were ready to subvert our democracy and steal the whole damn show right out from under us – "just like Pepper Martin back in the Series of '31!" Oh yeah, Smitty's world was a colossus traffic jam of pre and post war realities. Rumor had it, he'd gone around the bend when he lost his son on D-Day. The way I saw it, he wasn't much different than the rest of the nation. In one way or another, the war had changed us all. In that year of '49, we all qualified as our own sign of the times. Unfortunately, Smitty's once keen eye for horseshit on the field had become impaired by the bullshit political arguments that had filled the pages of our newspapers since the end of the conflict in '45. Looking back at the game that day, I suppose I was pretty much expressing the commonsense of most Americans, at the time, when I went to envision Professor Teste's epitaph:

Here Lies
Smitty Teste
Ever a watchful eye for
"Outlawed Pitches" and "Stealers of Home"
The former, he ravenously judged. The latter, he helplessly feared.
ALL IN THE NAME OF CAPITALISM'S GREATEST GAME

Truth of the matter, I wasn't about to argue with Rickey's old hidebound crony.   Hell, the Dodger's boss probably shipped him west just to get him out of earshot. Anyway, we were both technically working for Bob Cobb. Considering the fact that before Bob asked me to fill in here and there on security issues around the park, paying me a bill a week off the books, Hilo, Angel and I had spent the entire last season in the bleachers.   Now, with choice box seats, free of charge, third base side, we were all the beneficiaries of tickets to paradise.   Not bad for a returning vet and a couple of his old pals.   All three of us insatiable baseball fans.

Still, that last crack of Smitty's, describing Pinky as a "hit the showers bum among bums," was nothing short of a slight against the quality of play in the PCL.   I was about to turn around and give the old professor a piece of my mind when the Oaks rookie, Jackie Jensen, hit a scorcher down the third base line that proved to be untouchable for the Stars rookie, Jim Baxes.   The fact that the Cal All-American easily turned the blast into a double took me back to the question I asked myself when I had first entered the park that afternoon.   Who the hell was the kid on the mound for the Stars?

"Cup of coffee, up from the bush, that Haney picked up in Frisco a month or so back," said Smitty, more than willing to change the subject having caught sight of the look on my face.

"I say he got good stuff and up for more than one cup of coffee," said Angel.

Hilo reminded me that I'd seen this kid Bachman – Joe Bachman – pitch a couple of weeks back against the San Diego Padres.   Come to think of it, I did remember this tall, blonde, strong German-looking kid who had a damn good fastball that slid away on righties.   I mentioned to

Hilo that the last time I saw him pitch, he wore his glove with his index finger on the outside like he'd played shortstop or second base before becoming a pitcher. I even commented on it at the time. Hilo put me straight as to why the kid's index finger was now inside his glove. "There was a line shot off the bat of Martin in the second. I swear, it would have taken Bachman's head off if he hadn't gotten his glove hand up to protect his face."

This sudden death reality reminded me of all of us who had volunteered for three-man patrols in the Philippines. Considering the constant pain in my right leg and remnants of shrapnel in my back, I couldn't help but sympathize with this bush-leaguer deciding to change, for the moment, his old infielder habits and keep his index finger of his left hand hidden and out of sight. After all, if he was to survive on that daily, yet tentative, cup of coffee, and not the secure rookie status of an official contract with the Dodger organization, a functioning index finger on his glove hand was an absolute necessity.

After Jensen's double, Bachman was able to retire the side. Not bad for a hopeful up from the bush.

In the bottom of the third, Frank Kelleher, the Stars right field slugger, hit a three-run blast over the centerfield bleachers. The Stars were on the board and every one of us in Cobb's third base box rejoiced in the possibility of a rally. Smitty put his East Coast newspaper down, hooked his thumbs under his suspenders, and, chomping intently on his half-smoked cigar, assumed the role of an old scout truly concentrating on the progression of the game at hand. As for the rest of us, we all relaxed into the beautiful afternoon sunshine and the anticipation of yet another win for the Twinks.

We were quite the snazzy gathering. Hilo, crowned in his duckbilled green eyeshades, sported his newest, direct from his aunt in the Islands, Malihihi Aloha shirt. He possessed a closet full of these short sleeved, silky, sexy conversation pieces. I had to admit, his newest arrival was the most alluring of his entire wardrobe. On a pure black lustrous background, on either side of the shirt's centered pearl buttons, were the eternally combative Asian symbols of Yin and Yang. Pictured on the left side of the shirt was a yellow bodied, black striped, vicious, and earthbound tigress. She was actively intertwined in combat with a mythical, all-powerful, fire-fringed ascending dragon, on the right side of the shirt. The latter winged beast was believed to reign in heaven. Hilo said the image reminded him of my Tai Chi Quan exercises with Angel, in particular, our martial practice of push hands. However, that afternoon, when Hilo went to interpret the images for Healani, it became another story altogether. He bypassed the martial arts interpretation and went straight for the pleasurable entanglement he foresaw between Healani and himself. "Tigresses go down; dragons rise up." The fact that Hilo was underwearless, in his Bermuda shorts, and sockless, in his size 13 tennis shoes, just enhanced her fascination with his interpretation of his shirt's classic Hawaiian motif. As fate would have it, the star-struck Healani had first encountered Hilo years before in Honolulu. She was a teenager and he was a featured star with Harry Owen's Royal Hawaiian Review. At that time, he had predicted that they would meet again. Hilo, the ever charming playboy, always had the ability to explain to his latest potential conquest just how fate worked in the world of an accomplished lothario such as himself. In Healani's case, their current reengagement, considering she was no longer underage, would result in a night in the sack.

While Hilo's livery bespoke his native Hawaiian roots, Angel fashioned himself the palpable expression of his fellow Filipino's rebellious stance in a postwar America. With both of us off fighting the Japanese in the Philippines, he had missed the infamous L.A. Zoot Suit Riots of '42. However, once Hilo and I convinced Angel that he should return with us from the Islands to become a U.S. citizen, the very idea of L.A. cops and stateside G.I.'s ganging up on Filipinos, Latinos, and Blacks for wearing Zoot Suits, did nothing less than increase his determination to wear his "riot gear." Once Angel was able to secure a longshoreman job, he mentioned to me his intentions to don the slick, stylish attire of the Zoot culture for his social outings. Determined that he should take a measured look at a decision that could lead to some dangerous confrontations, I jokingly quoted from my favorite author, Jack London: "The whole world went to hell when three men went to make one pair of pants." Without a pause, Angel replied, "So now that one Filipino can afford three zoots, things must be looking up to heaven." Although every inch of Angel's fashionable image provided evidence of his allegiance to the sartorial rage of his fellow pinoys and pachucos, his attire did contain some personal touches. On any appropriate well starched shirt, Angel proudly displayed his distinguished service medal that he received from the hands of General MacArthur, himself. His second stylistic choice was in no way merely decorative. The wide, untraditional, 20-inch cuff on any of his impeccably tailored slacks veiled an instantaneous accessibility to a sharpened lethal bulge just above the ankle of the outer portion of his right leg. How can I put it? You can popularize, all you want, the idea of fashionably lifting the damned Zoot off the docks, but you'd best think twice about taking the docks off the damned Zoot.

I suppose I'd have to admit to being the least fashionable among the crew. Brown penny loafers, army issued khaki pants, and olive drab pocket T-shirt remained my constant. However, there was a bit of dash to my attire that afternoon. On summer days such as this, in honor of my old man (bless his soul), I always wore my Borsalino Panama straw fedora. And did I mention my Baush and Lomb, Air Force issue AN631, gold-plated, teardrop lensed sunglasses that Angel bought for each of us last Christmas from an ad in Popular Science magazine? That afternoon, Hilo, obviously preferring to maintain eye contact with Healani, left his at home. Angel and I were both sporting our flyboy Ray-Ban shades.

With old Smitty at our napes, to keep us focused on the big picture, we were one nifty box of post war eye candy. We had nothing more to do than enjoy the Sunday afternoon's first game of a doubleheader. For the moment, all looked well with the world. Hilo had just begun to form a new band and was (as far as I could see it) about to shack up with his latest hearts' desire. Angel was making the best money he'd ever made in his life and didn't have to kill anybody in the process. As for myself, I'd just returned from Vegas with one hefty bankroll. Pop had taught me to play one hell of a game of poker, and it looked like I could pretty much measure up to any pro in Reno or Vegas. Honestly, from this third base box, so bright and early in the game, it sure looked like I'd successfully returned to the life I'd left behind before the war. But then, homecomings for a vet can be tricky, mine had already provided me with a much darker revelation than a bad night at the table or a tough break on the diamond. For the moment, I was hoping for no more surprises.

The following inning, Haney provided the right hander with another sip of coffee. Damned if he didn't strike out the side. Unfortunately, the Stars remained scoreless in the bottom of the fourth. With the Oaks having already batted around twice, the top of their order was due up in the fifth. I excused myself and headed down toward the Oaks on- deck-circle for a word with a couple of East Bay buddies that I hadn't spoken to in some time. One of them I hadn't seen since my return to Oakland and my convalescence in '46, the other was an older high school friend and competitor I hadn't been in contact with since I shipped off to America's War in the Pacific in '42.

Descending towards the lush green grass and pale brown dirt of a ball diamond always sent me back to when I was a kid. I must have been around six when Pop first took me and my older brother, Jimmy, to the Oaks Park in Emeryville. I was an East Bay boy born in Frisco and raised up in Oakland. It was after the war when I decided to move to the Hollywood, L.A. area. Sure, the Hollywood Stars Gilmore Field was a beautiful ballpark, but it was no Oaks Park. Pop used to call it "the Stradivarius of ballparks" because of the way the crack of the bat resonated in its masterfully constructed Orpheum of aging wood. Of course, a mere glance behind home plate, at Gilmore, revealed something that I would had never found at Oaks Park. Television cameras had been permanently in place since '39. Cobb insisted that TV coverage would provide the Stars with "a great new audience of baseball fans." As for myself, if I wasn't in the park, I preferred listening to the game on the radio. Still, aside from that old time wood-on-wood crack of the bat and the presence of TV cameras, the greatest difference between watching a game in Oaks Park, back in the day, and watching one now at Gilmore is the appearance of the batters at the plate. Just this season, Cobb introduced the first use of pliable plastic batting helmets, protective equipment that would have been laughed at back in the merciless hardball '20s.

Turning to my right, I caught sight of some of the Hollywood celebrities who were in the grandstand that day. Cecil B. DeMille was sharing popcorn with Victor Mature the star of his latest Biblical epic, *Samson and Delilah*. Further up the grandstand was William Powell. He was enjoying a hotdog and chatting away with a New York newcomer to Hollywood, Shelley Winters. Both stars were topping the bill of a B movie about to be released in the fall by Universal, entitled *Take One False Step*. If you're wondering why I was up on all this Hollywood gossip, I suppose I had gotten it into my head that Cobb, who owned both the Stars and the Brown Derby franchise, was going to invite me and my buddies to his iconic restaurant to rub shoulders with all the stars and starlets.

Squinting in the direction of the shadowy seats at the high end of the grandstand, I caught sight of Lucille Ball and Desi Arnaz sharing a smoke and some popcorn with William Holden. Talk was, Lucy and Desi were ready to crack a deal for a TV show that was about to send this new medium into a whole new sphere. Cobb always wanted to keep things on the square with the Hollywood community ever since he and his then-wife, Gail Patrick, bought the Stars franchise some ten years ago and built Gilmore Field. They wisely sold shares of the organization to a large number of Hollywood celebrities. Not one of its stockholders, not even Gene Autry (the richest dude in town), would be allowed to hold a major portion of the stocks. Back in '39 when Gilmore Field opened, the L.A. Times expressed this sentiment. This PCL team that had wandered for years in search of a hometown had come to rest under the sheltering auspices of "a Chamber of Commerce activity on the part of a group of people who want their little corner of the world to be better than all the other corners." It was a comfort that some fashionable

Hollywoodlanders would take the time and money to recreate their own little diamond shaped corner of the world that confirmed their belief in the common spirit of our national game. As a Californian, I felt my affiliation with the Stars was something to be proud of, to maintain, secure, and protect. On that sunny Sunday afternoon, I couldn't help but envision myself a humble little gatekeeper for one damn good ball team on its way to its first pennant in close to twenty years.

When I reached the railing that separated the field from the stands, I took off my shades and shouted at the Oaks second baseman in the on-deck circle, "Hey Martin, you don't really think you're going to hit this cup of coffee a second time around!"

Billy turned to me with that familiar *are you looking to have your lights punched out* sneer that I'd seen him give hecklers during that season of winter ball he played at Bushrod Park in Oakland back in '46.

When I took off my fedora, Billy recognized me and his sneer turned to a smile.

Leaving the on-deck circle, he walked over to me and shook my hand. "Jake Salazar!" he said. "Great to see you up and about."

"And look at you making your mom so proud that her son is well on his way to the Big Show."

"And as for this Bachman kid," he confessed, tightening the grip on his bat, "I swear, he's a bit of a magician. But I think I've got his number; got a hell of a slide to his fastball. Say, how's your brother Tommy, still playing semi-pro in Oakland?"

"Pick-up games now and then. Fact is, he's getting married."

"Oh no, not that," grimaced Billy.

"Nice Italian girl."

"Well then, he's doing something right," he said. Turning in the direction of the Oaks dugout, he shouted to Lavagetto, who was in the hole. "Hey Cookie, you recognize this bum!"

Cookie turned in our direction. A look came over his face as if he'd seen a ghost. He put his bat down and hurried to embrace me.

"Well, if it isn't 'everything's just Jake in the old town hall tonight,'" he said, as we embraced after so many years. "I hear you tangled with some Japs since the last time we saw each other."

"Yeah, and I came out on top."

Squeezing both of my upper arms, in the vice-like grip of a journeyman infielder, he said, "You sure as hell did, Jake. You sure as hell did!"

Billy said, "As I remember, Jake always comes out on top. Just like that day he was pitching for University High and you were playing third for McClymonds. And..."

"...And Jake struck me out three times," admitted Cookie.

"It just wasn't Cookie's lucky day," I said.

"Yeah, like two years ago in the Series; can you imagine the luck of this guido to hit that double off Bevens?" quipped Billy.

Turning to Billy he said, "Don't knock it, kid. I'm nothing short of history, now."

"I suppose, as far as fame goes, I'll just have to settle for my moment in that newsreel when we retook Bougainville," I said. There was a poignant pause among the three of us. Suddenly, all our youthful days of summer darkened under the knowing look that Billy and Cookie gave me; they knew I would never play ball again.

Laviggetto looked as if he was about to burst into tears. He reached out his hand and we shook. "God bless you, Jake," he said. Then he turned and headed back toward the dugout. Billy just stood there at a loss for words.

I said, "It was good talking with you guys."

Billy said, "Same here."

"I'll see you, Billy."

He turned to walk to the on-deck circle, then turned back and said, "Say hello to Tommy for me."

"I will."

"Oh, and tell him not to give up those pick-up games. That winter ball season in Oakland, Tommy and I were the best damn double-play combination in the league."

"I'll tell him, Billy."

Billy hadn't yet reached the on-deck circle when I heard a voice behind me.

"Mr. Salazar."

I turned and said, "That's the name."

It was the college kid, Norris, who'd been working for Cobb over the summer.

"Mr. Cobb wants to see you in his office, pronto," he said.

"Sure, I'll be up in a minute," I answered.

"That's *right now*, Mr. Salazar," he told me. "Mr. Cobb said I'm to bring you up myself."

"His wish is my command," I said, as I signaled to Angel that I was heading up to Cobb's office. He had helped me with some of the security issues that came up in the last few months, so he pointed to himself, as if to ask, "do you want me to come along?" I waved my hand in the negative and followed Norris up the grandstand steps in the direction of the semi-hidden door that led to Cobb's office.

I noticed that Bachman left the dugout after the bottom of the fourth and figured that was it for the kid. Surely, Haney was going to relieve him in the fifth. As I followed Norris up the steps of the grandstand, a big cheer went up. I turned toward the field and damned if Bachman wasn't taking his glove off the top of the Stars dugout and walking out to take the mound.

It looked like this cup of coffee was having his day in the sun. I took a moment at the top of the stairs. This kid, Bachman, was having a day equal to the one I'd had when I led University High to a 6 to nothing win over McClymonds. That day, I struck Cookie Lavgetto out three times and pitched my perfect game.

My days in the sun were over, but it appeared that Bachman's had just begun.

Leaving the afternoon sunshine and the lighthearted enthusiasm of the game, I followed Norris through the camouflaged door, at the top of the grandstand, and began to climb the dimly lit staircase that led to Cobb's office.

Chapter II

The Limited Space of an Infinite Definition

Over the last year, I climbed the three tiered staircase to Cobb's office several times, but never during a game. The strange muffled cheers of the crowd, penetrating the wooden and steel reinforced walls of the grandstand, sounded a bizarre counterpoint to the determined, regimented echoes of Norris' and my ascending footfalls. I was trying to remember when I'd last experienced such a contrast of natural sounds. After a moment, I realized where I'd heard it before. *Determined boots climbing in mud and that gentle breeze through the palm trees that day on Guadalcanal. And then there was the red-headed kid with bad teeth who was one of the five of us about to take on the Japanese in the cave at the top of that rained-soaked hill. "What da ya figure they got up there, Sarge?" he asked. I'd seen the look before. A kid who couldn't hurt a soul let alone kill somebody. He never made it to the cave to find out what in hell they had up there.* I stopped for a moment to catch my breath. Suddenly, I was that red-headed kid wondering what Cobb had in store for me up there? A cold, uninviting shiver was running up my spine.

When we reached the door to Cobb's office, the cheers of the fans faded like that sea breeze through the palms.

Norris knocked and Cobb told him to come in. The kid opened the door and said, "Mr. Cobb, I found Jake Salazar."

I always remembered Cobb's office, one of several overlooking the field, to be bathed in sunlight. This afternoon, however, its blinds and curtains were drawn. All the photos of the past PCL greats, lining the walls, were now veiled in the shadows created by the green shaded postal lamp on Cobb's desk.

When I recognized the unmistakable sound of a woman in tears, I knew something was up, all right, and I could only figure it wasn't all that good.

Stepping out from the shadowy corner of the room, Cobb reached into his pants pocket and pulled out his keys. "Norris, here's the keys to my car. You know where it's parked; do me a favor and drive Miss Patrick home."

Taking the keys in hand, the kid said, "Sure, boss."

Gail Patrick, the movie star, stood up and wiped the tears from her eyes with a laced handkerchief. Turning to Cobb she said, "My god, Bob, what am I going to tell his parents?"

"No phone calls until we work this whole thing out. I'll come by tonight, and we'll discuss what's to be said and to whom," answered Cobb.

I could have sworn I'd magically found myself on an RKO set as Patrick turned to make her exit in my direction. She played the sad and jilted bride of Cary Grant in *My Favorite Wife*, the last screwball comedy I'd seen before shipping off to the Pacific to kill Japanese. I'd seen her from a distance around the park, but we'd never been formally introduced. This, sure as hell, was not the moment to fill her in on how those larger than life close-ups of her high cheekbones and oval faced beauty had gotten me through many a lonely night in the tropics. Christ, always been a sucker for brunettes. I figured she'd leave the room without a glance in my direction, but she stopped and turned to me before leaving and said, "I've heard a great many good things about you, Mr. Salazar. My only prayer is that you'll do your best to help us through this dreadful situation." For a moment I forgot my lines. Then came the helpless look on her aging, beautiful face. It surprised the hell out of me. It was a close-up of a woman in distress, the Gail Patrick I'd never seen on the silver screen.

"I'll do anything I can to help, Miss Patrick," I said.

She left the room followed by Cobb's trained puppy, Norris.

There was an awkward pause between the boss and myself. Then, I looked him squarely in the eyes like a battle worn sergeant demanding some crumb of info on an imminent advance and blurted out, "What in hell's going on?"

Cobb, always the dandy to the last, hurriedly donned his seersucker sports coat. He walked right past me and said, "Follow me and you'll know soon enough!"

And I did just that.

As we descended the stairs, on our way to the Gilmore exit, I contemplated the fact that, just like so many times in the army, I'd done myself the disservice of forgetting my place. Whatever the hell was going on, I'd best keep in mind that Cobb was my paycheck. After all, it wasn't that irresistible brunette movie star but Cobb who was the real haughty dollar sign that had drifted in my direction. If I wasn't careful, I was going to end up a sign all my own, a detour sign - bright and flashing neon through the rain - that read: Jake Salazar, always a sucker for an alluring temptress and a misleading poker face at the far end of the table.

Passing through Gilmore's exterior ticket booths, we walked north toward Beverly Boulevard. Norris and Patrick, ahead of us, had turned in the opposite direction and were already entering the boss's Chrysler.

Cobb turned and reassuringly shouted to his ex: "No phone calls; I'll get back to you as soon as possible!"

As we made our way through the rows of cars jamming the Gilmore parking lot, the roar of the distant crowd seemed to break like cooling waves over the hot pebbled asphalt.

Crossing Beverly and speeding south on Genesee Avenue, a Gilmore Field maintenance truck entered the parking lot and immediately sped out of view around the curvature of the stadium. It was apparently bound for the field crew's entrance on the other side of the wooden structure. Well aware of the speed limit on Genesee, Cobb momentarily stopped in his tracks, turned in the direction of the speeding truck, and said, "Remind me to do something about that."

By the time we reached Beverly, I was so hopped up on adrenaline that the pain in my leg had disappeared. I also realized our destination. A couple of months back, it had been rumored that Cobb and his celebrated shareholders bought a six unit Spanish Style group of bungalows just across from the Gilmore parking lot on Beverly. Seemingly, he had turned one of them into an office space.

As we crossed Beverly, I noticed a couple of Ford LAPD squad cars parked in front of the bungalows. It appeared as if I was walking into a situation worse than anything I could have imagined. SNAFU: Hollywood style! There was a tall, bull-shouldered, uniformed officer standing at the entrance to the adobe styled cabanas. Strangely enough, he looked familiar. By the time we reached the palm tree entranceway to the units, I recognized him. It was Richie Goodman. We'd played football and baseball together at University High. He had been my quarterback when we won the city championship in '30 and my catcher when I pitched my perfect game in '31. The sight of him quickly brought to mind our youthful goodbyes when his parents decided to move south our senior year.

As I approached Richie, I took off my shades and hat.

"Well, I'll be damned," he said, as we shook hands, "if it isn't Jake Salazar!"

"Long time, Richie," I said.

"Hell of a long time, if you ask me." His answer was accompanied by that knowing look of a fellow vet. "So, are you some gumshoe in with the Chief on this one?"

"All I know is, I work for Bob Cobb over at Gilmore Field." I nodded in the boss's direction. Cobb, believing I was still right behind him, continued walking toward his new office space.

"Right," Richie said, looking a bit confused.

"So, what's going on here?" I asked.

"Hell if I know. The Chief and his homicide crew were right around the corner, mopping up on some down-on-her-luck dame's suicide, when we got the call. Seems the manager heard the shot, opened the door, and found the body. Whole damn thing went down less than a half hour ago."

"Murder?" I stupidly reiterated.

"On the killing grounds of war, it's legal; not so much in the States."

"Tell me about it."

Cobb had reached the steps to the bungalow. Realizing I'd stopped to chat with god-knows-who, he shouted angrily down the pathway. "You coming or not!"

"I'll be right there," I said. Then turning to Richie, "We'll catch up."

"Damn straight; once a quarterback, always a quarterback."

"Thirty-one on six, that was the best of them," I joked. We both smiled, a strange and sudden recognition of things that would never be again.

I caught up with Cobb as he was opening the front door of the bungalow.

It had been several years since I'd been in the presence of the dead; I wasn't looking forward to this.

The bungalow was typical of those built in the '20s. Upon entering, a small living room was right off the hallway to your right. Walking further back was a bathroom, then a bedroom about the same size of the living room.

As we entered the unit, it was obvious that Cobb had spent a pretty penny on remodeling. He had added custom-made, inset oak bookshelves, and filing cabinets to the bedroom, turning it into an office space. The newly stained wood lining the walls, top to bottom, gave an odd English manor ambience to the bungalow's inner and outer Spanish shell. On the back wall, there were three huge pointed arched, interconnected windows illuminating the room. In the center window, Cobb had installed a stained glass representation of the Hollywood Star patch worn by his players on the team. With the sun casting a shadow of the insignia over the oak desk in front of the window, the office had the atmosphere of a sanctum sanctorum of handshakes, secret deals, and capital confidences of great import. With the corpse, slumped over the antique desk, the gravitas of the room turned terrifying and sinister.

As I walked in the direction of the young man's corpse, a totally irrational thought came to mind. Maybe this guy isn't dead. I remembered that kid floating in the waves, with his leg shot off, on the beachhead at Cebu. He had looked dead, but he wasn't. It was only the force of Cobb's commanding voice, introducing me to the two members of the forensic squad, that stopped me in my tracks.

"Jake, I think you know Nash," said Cobb, motioning to the photographer moving around the crime scene popping off flashbulbs. I was first introduced to Nash as a sports photographer for the *L.A. Examiner*.

"I thought you only covered sports," I said.

"Actually, I moonlight for the *Examiner*. This is my day job; it pays the bills."

"And this is…" Cobb pointed to the guy with the rubber gloves dusting for prints. It was obvious, he didn't know his name.

"Name's Coleman, Mr. Cobb, John Coleman." Looking at both of us, he said, "I'd shake your hands but I don't think either of you would want me dusting you for prints."

"I can assure you that anybody I've killed isn't in this room," I said.

Brush and powder in hand, Coleman took a long, contemplative pause and looked reverently at the corpse lying across the desk. "'If one had to live on some high rock, or so narrow a ledge that he had only room to stand, if he had to remain standing on a square yard of space all his life, a thousand years, eternity, it were better to live so than to die at once!'"

"Amen to that," added Cobb.

Staring down at the corpse, I thought it appropriate to complete the quote. "'Only to live, to live and live! Life, whatever it may be!'"

Coleman looked surprised, turned to Cobb and said, "It's not every day I run into a gumshoe in a GI issued T-shirt who's read Dostoevsky."

"I'm not a gumshoe. I'm a baseball fan."

"Sounds to me, Jake, like it's about time you made a more adult career choice," came a rumbling, gravelly declaration from behind my back. The voice, though deeper and older, was a strangely familiar one.

"I understand you and the Colonel are old friends," said Cobb.

Suddenly, as often as it does in poker, I was the chump on the ledge unable to turn around for fear it would lead to my demise. Not about to fold, I took a deep breath, lifted my eyes off the corpse in front of me, and turned to confront the hidden figure I'd missed when I first entered the office. It was him all right, 20 years older and a hundred pounds heavier than the six-four, trim, blonde haired California Highway Patrolman and nemesis of my youth. The huge bloated bullfrog of a man seated in the ornate burgundy velvet club chair at the dark corner of the room had apparently reached the zenith of a checkered career in law enforcement. The Colonel was at last enthroned. Like some shadowy monarch in the last act of a Jacobean tragedy, with a dimly lit green Tiffany to his right and a courtly wall of black and white autographed photos of the famous and infamous of Hollywood at his back, there he sat: the crowned, sovereign, gray eminence of law and order in a city of scandal and sin.

"What the hell are *you* doing here, Longdown?" I asked.

"Oh, I thought you knew, Jake. The Colonel's been Chief of Homicide, in the Fairfax Division, for well over six months," said Cobb.

I couldn't help but look surprised.

Longdown laughted. "Didn't you get my postcard, kiddo?"

I shot back. "Must have been lost in the mail. And I'm no longer your kiddo!"

Longdown lifted his massive bulk from the club chair. Like some old steam driven locomotive taking in coal, tempered by the huffs and puffs that articulate a forward movement all its own, he lit his half smoked cigar and said, "Fair enough, Jake. After all, kiddos steal cars, but the Jake Salazars' of this world receive bronze stars for gallantry at Bougainville and silver stars at Cebu."

I looked from Cobb to Longdown and said, "So what's the deal here?"

The Colonel walked past me and bumped my shoulder on his way to the corpse sitting at the desk. That bully move couldn't help but remind me that he was still the natty, silent presence who had allowed his immaculate CHP uniform to speak for itself the night he pulled me and my next door neighbor over for stealing my uncle's car. My neighbor had gotten off with a slap on the wrist, but yours truly, the mastermind behind the theft, got a week in juvie. Foolishly, when I saw the 10 caret gold Rotarian pin on Longdown's uniform, I thought I was in for a free ride. Pop was a Rotarian. Boy, did I get that wrong! From my 13th year, when I stole the car, to my 16th year, they remained in touch with each other in order to keep me in line. They worked in tandem to keep me off the streets and on the ball field. Longdown had even shown up at a few of the games I pitched, one of which was my perfect game. While I understood my parent's good intentions, they were unaware of what I experienced that night I spent in the CHP lockup at Sacramento. I never told either of them what it was like to witness the Colonel practically beat a vagrant to death just because he'd spoken out of turn. Frankly, I never thought much of cops after that night. I suppose you could say that both Pop and Longdown had the right idea in trying to keep me on the straight and narrow, but the day I graduated University High, I went downtown, bought a fake ID, and enlisted as a merchant seaman. I said, "to hell with both of them" and went to sea. When I returned in '37, Pop informed me that the Colonel had killed a guy. The authorities had managed to hush it up insisting it was self-defense. Who knows, maybe it was. With a cop like Mason Longdown, it's damn hard to separate the good intentions from the bad ones. By the time the Japs bombed Pearl Harbor, rumor had it that the lifetime enforcer had moved south and taken a policing job in a small town outside of L.A. When I returned from the Pacific, Pop had already passed away and I lost track of Longdown. Obviously, I had caught up with him this afternoon. More to the point, he had caught up with me.

The Colonel had traded in his CHP uniform for an ash stained, beige cotton suit. Baggy and oversized, its wide padded shoulders (only accentuating his humongous bulk) confirmed the fact that this 300 pound gorilla was back in my life. Still, there was that Rotarian pin on his lapel. Only now, at its center, a big fat diamond in recognition of a lifetime of service. Hell, I read the papers, it seemed the Rotarians were having as good a year as the Stars. Something or other to do with the formation of the United Nations. This was big time international stuff, all in the name of good men, good will, and good times on Wall Street. Nothing wrong with that, right?

Having reached the dead man, Longdown paused to contemplate the crime scene. He wrinkled his memorable broken nose, now grown to a bulbous turnip red, and turned in my direction. The band on his Hamburg shimmered in the afternoon light like a rotating lighthouse scanning the outer seas for a vessel in distress.

"Death: the irreversible moment when time stops and you're nothing more than space," he said.

"You a poet these days, Longdown?" I asked.

"I take it, it's been sometime since you've looked upon the end all," he said.

The bastard already knew the answer to that question, so I remained silent.

"Over the years, I've come to look upon the sight of death as 'the limited space of an infinite definition.' Of course, cops like me have the lousy job of turning the infinite into the finite."

Looking from Longdown to Cobb, I said impatiently, "Again I ask, what's the deal?"

"When Bob mentioned you were working for him on a part time bases, I knew you were the man for the job."

"And exactly what job is that?"

The Colonel turned to Cobb and said, "Show him the letter, Bob."

Cobb took a piece of folded gray stationary out of the breast pocket of his sports jacket and handed it to me. "I got this about a month ago."

It was one of those anonymous and threatening type of letters constructed out of words cut from newspapers. The writer declared himself to be the member of a Fifth Column of Nazis active in the L.A. area. As far as he saw it, the war against the "Jew capitalists" and their decadent lapdog organizers of games like baseball were about to experience a new type of warfare built on terror and sabotage. All in the name of the Fuhrer, who was not dead as long as he lived in the hearts and minds of the German people. The lower right corner of the letter was stamped with a large red official like swastika and signed "Avengers of the Third Reich."

"I figured it was nothing but a lot of nonsense," added Cobb. "But in the last few weeks, I've been getting these strange, threating phone calls…"

"That's when Bob mentioned you, and we agreed that you'd be the perfect man to…"

I handed the letter back to Cobb, and bluntly interrupted them both.

"I'm not looking for trouble! Just a few honest poker games in Vegas and a humble means by which to maintain my third base line seats for me and my buddies."

"Don't worry, Jake, if you're uncomfortable being in on this…," said Cobb, "you can still keep your job over at Gilmore."

"Here's the *deal,*" said Longdown. "Cobb will pay you four hundred bucks a month on the books. I'll supply you with a license and a piece. I'll even throw in a badge to make things comfortable. You'll be under my command and report back to both of us."

"Trust me, Jake," said Cobb, "if we didn't think you were the right man to help us get to the bottom of this thing, we wouldn't have taken the trouble to bring you here."

"Come on, Jake," encouraged the Colonel, "gird-up your fuckin' loins and walk over here. Have a second look at this kid. Shot through the back of his neck by some cowardly Nazi!"

The unforgettable look on the face of that aging beauty, Gail Patrick, and the promise I'd made to her suddenly crossed my mind. After a pause, I found myself walking toward the dead kid at the desk.

"Tell me what you see, Jake," prompted the Colonel.

There was a small detectable bullet hole at the back of the kid's neck. There was a stream of wet blood from the bullet's exit wound at his throat. As well, some coming from his mouth and nose.

"What was his name?" I asked.

"Howard Story," answered Cobb. "Newly arrived from the mid-west. He was introduced to me by an old hand from the silent era. I hired him to straighten out some problems with my books."

I looked at the opened arched window to the right of the stained glass middle one and concluded: "Close range... relatively powerful small caliber... something like a Mauser."

"Right you are, Jake," said Coleman, brandishing a small caliber slug between his thumb and forefinger. "Found this Selbstladepistole 7 mm embedded in the back wall. It went clean through a photo of Myrna Loy."

"Two for the price of one," joked Nash, who'd just finished up his photo session of the corpus delicti with a snapshot of the glass-shattered photo of Loy.

"Our perp, no doubt, shot this unfortunate young man through the open window," continued Coleman. "I found this handwritten note by the window, just now." Coleman held up a perfectly cut, oblong piece of a brown paper bag. It read: 'Begin with this one.' "I have a feeling the murderer meant to leave this little curiosity beside Story's body. He probably ran away when he heard the landlady pounding at the door. Our Nazi must have spent some time in a scriptorium."

It wasn't so much the message that took me by surprise but the familiar precision and style of its calligraphy. I must have looked like I was about to faint.

"You all right?" asked Longdown.

"Yeah, I'm all right. I suppose all of this is just a bit too much."

"For Christ's sake, Mason! In the blink of an eye, we take the guy from a ball game into a crime scene. I think Jake's had enough for today," suggested Cobb.

"Yeah, I'd like to get back to the game if I could."

"We've got to know your decision as to whether you want to join us in this investigation as soon as possible," demanded Longdown.

"I'm going up to Oakland, next weekend, for my sister's birthday. I'll let you both know when I get back on Monday."

"Of course, there's not to be a word of this to anyone," warned Cobb.

"Absolutely," I said.

I turned to exit the room and was halfway down the hall when I realized the Colonel was right behind me.

"It's Service above Self, Jake. The only way to approach life as I see it."

I turned to him and said, "Spoken as a true Rotarian."

"I was sorry to hear that your dad passed away."

"Thanks, Mason."

"You know, I think you should seriously consider the job offer we've made you. I'm not trying to tell you how to live your life, but the hell you went through in the Philippines is no excuse for making your way as a gambler. Don't fall into the same rut that you found yourself in when you didn't make the cut for the Oaks in '39. Twenty years from now, you don't want to turn around to the sight of nothing but burnt bridges."

"Better I should be a private dick for the LAPD," I said, sarcastically.

"At least you'd be up to some good. Serve some purpose in life outside of covering your own ass for the price of a prostitute on Market Street."

"You've really kept book on me over these years."

"Just like your old man, I really care. Remember, Jake, *service* is the supreme commitment of life."

I was on my way out the door when I yelled back at him, "Tell it to the Marines!"

Exiting the complex, I reassured Richie that we would find some time to catch up on things.

Making my way back to Gilmore Field, a strange sense of urgency came over me as I crossed Beverly and hurried through the cars in the parking lot. It was the same feeling of desperation I felt to get back stateside after experiencing all the slaughter and death in the Pacific. I was frantic to be back home to those normal, everyday things like a baseball game on a Sunday afternoon. The closer I got to the field and the cheering crowd the farther I was from the reality of death in Cobb's office.

By the time I was back in my seat I'd calmed down a great deal. Angel sensed there was something wrong, but I reassured him I was all right.

It was the top of the ninth. Wouldn't you know it, Bachman was still pitching up a storm. It appeared as if he'd changed gloves. The one he started the game with was still atop the Stars dugout. I assumed his index finger was still hurting and that he decided to put on a glove that gave him more protection. Moreover, the Twinks were losing in a big way.

In the bottom of the ninth, Kelleher's double gave the Stars another run, but the Oaks won the game 12 to 4. Haney had to have seen something in the kid because he kept Bachman in for seven innings even with the Oaks getting another six runs off of him.

The clubhouse boys were moving up and down the stands selling sandwiches when Angel said he, Helani, and Hilo were going to run over to Herbert's Drive-In to pick up some hamburgers for the second game. He asked me if I wanted one.

"Tell you the truth, I'm really not feeling well. I'm going to catch a cab back to Venice," I said. "I'll see all of you later."

He didn't question me and said, "We see you back at the house after the second game."

Sitting alone, among fans anxiously anticipating a possible Twinks victory in the second game, I attempted to piece together the events of what was one hell of an afternoon. The day had begun with me returning from Vegas and going to the ballpark where I witnessed a rookie pitcher experiencing an opportunity to show his stuff. After I had spoken with Billy and Cookie, this kid's chance of a lifetime couldn't help but get me to thinking back to my own greatest day on the mound in high school. Then there was the call to Cobb's office and the march backward into the land of the dead where I encountered Longdown, the well-meaning monster of my youth, and his job offer that was bound to turn my life upside down for good. However, despite this series of unexpected events, there was one thing I confronted on this sunny afternoon that remained a baffling enigma. How was it possible that the unmistakable beauty of my father's matchless hand at calligraphy, the singular precision by which he formed his capital B, found its way onto the threatening brown paper bag note left by a murdering rout of Fifth Column Nazis?

After about five minutes of reflection, I exited the park and caught a cab outside Gilmore for Venice Beach.

Despite the fact that the following day was the 4th of July, a holiday that the three of us (since the end of the war) had turned into a ritual of attending a baseball game together, I wasn't up for celebrating. I didn't even take the time to read the morning and afternoon sports columns. I just remained at home and finished off a bottle of scotch. Disappointed at my unwillingness to celebrate the 4th and bewildered as to exactly what was bothering me, Angel decided to attend the 4th of July doubleheader alone. Hilo and Healani remained in bed all day; the dragon and tigress engaged in their own form of fireworks.

Though they won the second game of the doubleheader the day before, 4 to nothing, the Stars lost both games to the Oaks on July 4th, 2 to 1 and 6 to 5.

So much for the Twinks four game lead over the Oaks.

Chapter III

Royal Hawaiians and the Long-knives of Filipinos

For over a month, Hilo, Angel, and I had been planning a party in celebration of our move to the Venice Canals. I wasn't about to let this latest development over at Gilmore Field spoil the festivities. Not only that, my trip to Oakland was coming up after our party on Friday. It could prove especially important if I was going to find out how Pop's calligraphy wound up on a threatening note left by some Fifth Column Nazis at a homicide. Besides, if I decided to take Cobb's offer, this information would give me something to throw into the pot right from the top. The sure bet was if I came up with a fat zero in Oakland I'd fold the whole damn deal and remain the gambler Pop had masterfully made me. Looking at the situation from the odds-on judgment of a ace-high hopeful who knew little more than the fact that there were six ways to seven for crap to roll to heaven, I wasn't about to easily forego the freedom of a card shark for a lifetime dedicated to 'Service above Self!' No, I wasn't going to take the plunge without some clue as to why Pop's handwriting was found on a note beside the body of Howard Story.

Tuesday morning, after Bachman's impressive performance on the mound, I caught up with Frank Finch's Monday column in the *Times*. He had high praise for the rookie. "Haney's willingness to keep Bachman in for the duration allowed the young pitcher to display a great deal of confidence on the mound and a surprising variety of pitches for his age. Had the Stars bats kicked in by the sixth and their infield not committed errors in the seventh and eighth, allowing the Oaks four more runs, the outcome of this game would have been another story altogether."

There was no denying that the kid had something on the ball. Finch's brief interview with Billy offered an honest assessment of the kid's abilities by the Oaks second baseman. "When he came into the game, in the second, his fast ball was sliding away from me. By the seventh, it was cutting in on me so hard that it broke my favorite bat. His first variation I pounded right back to the mound at him. The second, I couldn't do anything with." Knowing Martin, I'm sure the phrase wasn't "anything with" but "a damn thing with."

There was no mention of the murder of Howard Story in the *Times* that Monday morning. I was sure there wouldn't be. Until Cobb and his primary shareholders came up with a cover story, far from the realities of a Fifth Column of Nazis out to undermine America's national game, this murder wasn't about to go public. After all, any lie could ring closer to a plausible truth than the truth itself.

With Angel, Hilo, and Healani still asleep, I woke up early that Tuesday morning, made some coffee, grabbed my two editions of the *Morning Times*, and sat out on our porch that overlooked the canal. The wind was blowing from the north and the oft-present petrol stench from the oil rigs to our south vanished to a whiff.

It had been well over a year since the three of us had decided to give up our separate apartments and move in with each other. Our new address was 214 Carroll Canal. We'd been warned against the move from the beginning. Forty odd years had passed since the tobacco millionaire, Abbott Kinney, envisioned and financed his unprecedented public works project that combined an amusement park with adjacent canal side esplanades. The greater portion of Kinney's original state of the art amusement park, made up of sideshows and thrill rides, had by now been demolished. With the onslaught of the automobile and its inseparable oil business, by the late '20s, seven of Kinny's original canals had been filled in, covered over in asphalt, and turned into streets named after the old dreamer's waterways. Today, his pleasure garden community of interlinking canals was pretty much forgotten and left to ruin. Still, Hilo, Angel, and I loved the idea of living on the water.

Whether it was the pristine beaches of Hilo's half-moon Hanalei Bay, Angelico's surging Davao River of his native Mindanao, or my teenage adventures of sailing from Sausalito to Big Sur, we all lived close to the water in our youth. We all liked the romantic atmosphere of living on a canal within blocks of a beach. Considering the fact that the rent was some of the cheapest in L.A., it was agreed that we could all benefit. For Hilo, who was tired of the endless pickup gigs with Hawaiian orchestras and wanted desperately to start up his own band, the affordable digs would enable him to buy that legendary tear-drop Gretsch electric guitar made from the late '30s on. Here was the instrument he felt would identify him as a leader of a musical ensemble. "This is the guitar with the perfect neck for rhythm, one that is long and straight like a beautiful woman's; that's where you must begin, you know, if you want to make beautiful music." There was an old man in San Diego who was willing to sell him this masterpiece at a reasonable price. Hilo just needed the three hundred bucks. Angel, on the other hand, wanted to save some money that would provide him with the free time to take advantage of the GI bill and attend business school at night. Maybe even work less on the docks. His ultimate plan was to open a Tai Chi Quan school that would allow him to couple his knowledge of the so-called 'Supremely and Ultimately Balanced and Harmonized Fist' with his native Filipino skills at knife fighting. As for myself, I always figured that someday I'd try writing a novel. I'd won a prize for a short story in high school and had been encouraged by my English teacher to keep it up. With a low rent and some consistent bankrolls from high-stake games in Vegas, I just might be able to take the time to write.

All of this projection sure sounded good especially when it meant living cheap and saving money. However, when it came down to the moment of truth and the three of us actually moving into 214 Carroll Canal, we wouldn't have had the confidence to do so without me stumbling onto my job and friendship with Bob Cobb. The owner of the Stars and The Brown Derby chain, always looking for another tourist angle to draw people from around the country to Hollywoodland, had been in negotiations with City Hall to take another stab at cleaning up the remaining six Venice Canals. By utilizing the fact that a couple of returning vets, like Angel and me, actually wanted to take up stakes in the Venice Canal system, Cobb was able to put a human face onto his pet project of rejuvenating Kinney's original pleasure garden. Within a month's time, arguing that here might be an opportunity to house veterans, he convinced the powers that be to form a committee to look into an engineering project that would aide in the recurring of fresh water into the canal with the incoming tide from the Pacific at Plaza Del Ray. Not only that, Cobb sent over an electrician from Gilmore Field to rewire our spacious, two storied Swiss Chalet styled bungalow. He made sure that L.A. Power and Light didn't drag their heels when it came to turning on our water, gas, and electricity. Unfortunately, in spite of Cobb's sincere efforts at settling us into the canal, his engineering project never got off the ground.

Knowing that all of us were pretty handy, I decided to front the two hundred bucks for the paint and lumber to get this unique piece of L.A. real estate ship shape and up to code. It took about two months and there she was a bright yellow and green waterside Chalet, a veritable beacon of hope amidst the ruins of Kinney's paradise.

Within a week of our arrival, we were welcomed by many residents of the Venice Canals. There appeared to be a few aging holdouts who, in spite of the fact that the oil industry had invaded their idyllic surroundings, refused to move from their once pristine environs. They defiantly remained to live out their lives in their own personal deteriorating dreamscape. These days, aside from the residences literally abandoned, a small portion of the canal's dwellings were occupied by Mexican and European squatters. The Mexicans had deserted their livilihood as migrant workers in the central valley of California to take their chances working as domestics and dayworkers in L.A. The European refugees, most of whom were well-educated, had dreamed of taking up their old professions in the States, but quickly realized that wasn't possible and wound up working as custodians and night watchmen.

Angel's Spanish was better than mine so I had him approach the Mexicans with the idea of forming groups of individuals willing to walk the canals, at low tide, and clean up some of the garbage gathered over the years. Though a few were eager for the task, the majority, obviously illegal immigrants, weren't all that enthusiastic to show their hand publicly. I had better results with the Europeans. A Polish couple, in their early 60s, by the name of Kowalczyk, were more than willing to help organize a community clean-up. Aleksy had been a professor of political science in Warsaw, before the war, and his wife, Emilia, was a leftist journalist. Both, under the threat of Hitler's camps, had gotten the hell out of Warsaw, by '37, and made an Atlantic crossing to New York City. There, they lived on the lower eastside for the duration of the war. Two years ago, they decided to travel west. This choice hadn't proved to be a bad one. Emilia obtained a job as a translator for a Polish publishing company and Aleksy had been able to secure a position as an associate librarian in the L.A. school system. They both spoke excellent English, Spanish, French, and Polish. They were quite successful in organizing the clean-up between their own compatriots, the Latinos, and the old timers. Cobb was even able to arrange a weekly garbage pickup. From garbage to electricity, he had his finger on the pulse of the wheeler-dealer in-crowd society of Hollywood and L.A. Within a month or so, the canals were looking better than they had in twenty years.

That Tuesday morning, Angel was picked up by some of his fellow dock workers. An hour later, Hilo drove Healani home in our shared '35 Packard sports coupe. I reminded both of them about the party that was coming up on Friday. If they wanted to invite anyone, they'd better do it now. I whispered this specific information in Hilo's ear not knowing whether Healani was anything more than a two night stand.

It was about an hour after they left that I received a phone call from Cobb. He preferred that I stay away from the field and not attend the six home games of the Stars with the Seals that week. He wanted me to take some time to consider my decision about joining the investigation. A couple of the regular security guys would don some plain clothes and move about the stands. Cobb reiterated that I was not to tell a soul about the murder and then conveyed his apologies as to why he would not be attending our party on Friday.

"I remember you telling me that you invited Smitty. I don't need that nosy crony of Rickey's asking me all sorts of unanswerable questions. I think I'll stay out of sight for the next week until we can sort out how we're going to approach this investigation. I've already contacted a few of our most trusted shareholders about how we will proceed if knowledge that Howard Story's murder took place at our property on Beverly. Since I haven't made any announcements or had anyone of note into the new office, I doubt that the newspapers are aware of the Stars connection with the real estate."

"That's a positive."

"Not only that, the whole Nazi thing may just be a way of throwing us off the scent. You never know, this murder might be the result of something personal. You might not be privy to this, but Story was a handsome, new gay 'Gentleman' in town, if you know what I mean. He may have found himself embroiled in something over his head."

"That's certainly possible."

"Anyway, tomorrow there'll be a brief mention of the murder in the press. Story's parents have been notified and they'll be here by the end of the week. The coroner's inquest will take place sometime in the next few days. Due to the 'unnatural causes of death' his report won't be made public."

"I understand," I said. "I was thinking this morning how great you've been to the three of us and I can't help but feel I'm being unfair by not…"

"No, no; no obligation there. So far, we're even steven. Remember, Jake, nobody in Hollywood does a damn thing for anybody without looking for something in return. If you're not going to get something out of this for yourself, forget about it. Frankly, I have to agree with the Colonel, I think you'd make one hell of a lawman."

"A regular Wyatt Earp," I said.

"Don't knock it. I've spoken with some of the old timers who knew him when he came to live out his last days in Hollywood. He was just courageous and corrupt enough to provide a square and fair deal all around."

"What more can you ask for?"

"I'm going to need that answer from you by Monday the 11th."

"You'll have it, boss."

"Enjoy the time off. Talk to you then."

He hung up.

On Wednesday morning, a short column appeared on page three in the *Examiner* covering the murder. The paper reported the tragic and mysterious death of one Howard Story shot through an open window of his office residence at 7715 Beverly. "The 21-year old had recently arrived in our city. Though murdered on Sunday the 3rd, the police have withheld information about young Story's demise due to his only relatives – mother and father – living in Kansas City. They have since been notified and are on their way to Los Angeles to identify their son's body."

I decided to do as Cobb had suggested. I relaxed, took the week off, and got the party together.

When I thought about it, this was the first party I'd hosted since before the war. Mom and Pop had always encouraged us to be popular in high school. My brother, James, my sister, Millie, and I had successfully pulled off some great get-togethers back then. Of course, Friday night's party would be much more of a mix than a mere group of 1930's high schoolers getting together for fun and games.

Hilo and his three piece band would provide the dance music, and when they ran out of tunes there were always the Swing 78s on the phonograph. Angel invited several of his fellow dock workers; Hilo asked seven or eight of the bar girls he knew from working the clubs in

L.A. Hopefully, there would be a balance between male and female. Aleksy had introduced me to a couple of black veterans, Ben Forman and Willie Grant, who'd been squatting in the southern most Sherman Canal ever since their returned from overseas. We hit it off right from the top, and they promised to come to the party. I felt certain that we were going to have a great mix of people. I was quite sure that the younger ones could take care of themselves; as for the elders, they probably knew each other and would engage in conversation or not. Perhaps even old enemies could become new friends.

Aleksy and Emilia were the two exceptions amongst the old ones. After all the help they gave me, I felt they deserved some new drinking and conversational companionship. So when Aleksy informed me that they'd both become fanatical Yankee fans, while living in New York, there was no question about it. They had to meet the good professor, Smitty Teste. The way I saw it, these three well educated ancients would be capable of talking and arguing baseball and politics from Outlawed Pitchers to Stealers of Home and Beyond.

Just as Cobb had honestly confessed that nobody in Hollywood does a damn thing for anybody else unless there's something in it for them, I had to admit there were some invitees to this party that I was most anxious to meet and converse with. In particular, a poet named Perkoff, and a couple of his friends, I believed would prove to be of great value to me, in the long run.

About a month ago, I met Stuart Perkoff at the old Townhouse Bar on Windward Avenue in Venice. We'd been sitting next to each other at the bar and after a couple of rounds, and some intermittent exchange of ideas, we realized that we shared a love of fine scotch and American literature. An hour or so later, after moving to our own booth and buying a bottle of Glenmorangie, we were so engrossed in conversation that there appeared no end to our insatiable desire for more booze and more combative exchanges about our favorite writers. We must have spent several hours talking about Melville, Hemingway, and so many other literary masters.

That night, Stuart informed me of what was really "going down" in my own backyard. While I looked upon Venice Beach as a cheap and out of the way escape from the hustle and bustle of the L.A. scene, it was fast becoming a Mecca for the Beats, a post-war Avant-Garde movement of artists with a whole new vision for American art. "Painters, sculptors, musicians, playwrights, novelists, and poets, they're coming from all over the country!" he declared. "I tell you, Jake, this idea of American Literature as an East Coast thing is over and done with. California's leading the pack these days!"

"Have you ever read Robinson Jeffers?" I asked.

"A few poems, why?"

"Jeffers had the same idea about California. He said it was going to set the pace in literature, poetry, politics, and any damn thing you can think of."

"I'm surprised that Jeffers had that awareness, because as far as his poetry goes, he's just the last of the old boys writing in an antiquated classical form."

"Really," I said.

"For real, man," whispered Stuart, leaning in my direction in a somewhat secretive manner.

I didn't know how to respond to Perkoff's criticism of Jeffers; he had always been one of my favorite California authors. Until my sister, Millie, gave me a Modern Library edition of Jeffers' collected poems, when I'd returned home on shore leave in '34, I'd been mostly interested in reading novels. Fact is, it had taken quite an effort to even get into Jeffers' poetry. I must have read "Roan Stallion" close to ten times before I really got hold of the beauty and primitive insight of Jeffers' uniquely crafted story-poem. And that was because of my love of California, the sea, and my frequent visits south to Big Sur when I was younger. Recently, I read his *The Double Axe* and couldn't help but reflect upon a day I'd spent with Jeffers and his wife before the war. The epic, novella length, anti-war poem is about a casualty of war turned zombie who claws his way out of the grave and, returning to his native Big Sur, kills his father in an act of revenge. For me, this horrific act of patricide gave a voice to all those men I had seen die so helplessly in the war; avenging their nation's patriarchal past sadly remained the only supernatural solution capable of absolving their knowing souls of their own untimely deaths. A line in the poem, "Two summers from now (I suppose) we shall have to take up the corrupting burden and curse of victory," pretty much summed up the present political situation that had developed since the end of the war. Jeffers' simple, straight forward, penetrating insight had personally cut deep into my wounded body and soul. Though the post-war evangelical public and highbrow critics, alike, couldn't stomach a line like "...I'm the only dead body that has had the energy to get up again Since Jesus Christ. His whip was, they say, love. Mine...fury," I had no problem, whatsoever, opening my mouth wide at that altar of truth.

When Stuart and I stumbled out of the old Townhouse Bar that morning, around 2 a.m., I decided to invite him to our party. He readily accepted my invitation and asked if he could bring along a couple of his friends who would be arriving from the East Coast about the time of the party.

"Sure, with more 'Beats' to the bar, we'll dance out the evening in an atmosphere of utter 'cool,'" I drunkenly joked. It was fun ending a sentence with a word that was now an attitude and not just my ability to keep my temper.

"I think you'll like them. Jack's just about to publish his first novel and Allen's had a revelation that he's going to write the greatest poem of his generation. There's only one hitch, Jack's got to sneak him out of a New York Psyche Ward to get him here."

I thought to myself, this is going to be one hell of a party.

I wrote down my phone number and address on a bar napkin and handed it to Stuart. We shook hands and both of us turned and headed in the direction of our homes. Never got a better night's sleep in my life.

Friday morning, I received another phone call from Cobb. Seems Bob Hunter, who covered the Stars for the *Examiner*, had gotten wind that the Stars owned the property where Howard Story had been murdered. Cobb admitted to owning the bungalows but insisted that he had no knowledge of the murder other than what he read in the newspaper. Hunter was one of the best sports writers in the city, but he worked for the biggest muckraking tabloid scandal sheet in L.A. Cobb had a suspicion that it could have been Nash who was responsible for the leak. "If Hunter calls you, you don't know from nothing. Understand!" ordered Cobb with all the resonance of a Mafia boss. He had introduced me to Hunter at a game back in April and remembered that we'd exchanged numbers.

"Understood," I said.

By Friday afternoon, everything was in place for the party that night. We had enough booze and soda to drown a school of fish. Hilo had ordered several chicken, pork, and fish chafing dishes from The Tahitian over on Ventura Blvd. Angel managed to borrow a coffee machine from the docks. On the other side of the buffet we had towers of paper plates and cups. The Kowalczyks promised to supply us with some Polish pastries. I asked Emilia if she knew how to make a Polish doughnut that I remembered our neighbor, in Oakland, always bringing over to the house. "It's called paczki. I'll bring you them," said Emilia. "But I also bring makowki and mazurek. These will be a surprise!"

The party was set for 8 o'clock. Hilo's band showed up at 7:30 along with a number of beautiful Hawaiian, Polynesian, and Japanese bar girls all wearing some bright fashionable variation of their native dress. By a little after 8, Angel's friends from the docks had arrived; moments later, the Kowalczyks and most of the locals from the canals showed up. Ben and Willie breezed in soon after with a couple of six packs. By 8:30, Hilo started his first set, with his hapa haole styled trio (himself on the guitar and ukulele, Mitch on bass, and Quincy on steel guitar), playing a few Hawaiian favorites, "Sweet Leilani" and "My Little Grass Shack in Kealakekua." These were tunes made famous by his mentor Harry Owens and His Royal Hawaiians. One of Hilo's favorite come-ons was that he was of Royal Hawaiian blood straight down the line from one of the thirty wives of King Kamehameha the 1st. According to Hilo, the dead giveaway of such an illustrious ancestry was his thirteen inch shoe size. "You need the big, wide feet of a King to ride the surf," he'd often confess to his latest temptation. Such philandering was on hold, however, when Healani turned up with her friend, Leonor, a beautiful Portuguese girl who'd joined Healani on her trip from the Islands to the mainland. Leonor had these wide placed, almond shaped, deep green eyes, and jet black hair.

Along with that, she had an intelligent face and a body that you only wished might show up in your dreams some night. Once Healani introduced us, Hilo called me over to his makeshift bandstand. Pointing in Leonor's direction, he whispered in my ear, "Not bad for a Haole, hey!" Hilo was always trying to set me up.

After Hilo finished his first set, around 9:15, Angel put on some Benny Goodman. Ben and Willie decided to take stage with a couple of bar girls, who ditched their traditional dress for some jitterbugging short skirts, and proceeded to cut a rug.

It was about this time that Smitty Teste dropped in for a looksee on the festivities. I immediately introduced him to the Kowalczyks and, in no time, they were deep into a conversation ranging from the latest atrocities of Stalin to whether or not Ted Williams was going to win the American League MVP.

By 11, Hilo finished his last set, and Ben had run home to get his 78 album of Charlie Parker's *Bird at the Roost*. Most of the old timers, from the canals, had already said their goodbyes. The Kowalczyks, having found their perfect conversation mate, chose to remain.

It was going on 11:30 when I realized Perkoff and his eastern friends hadn't shown up. Considering that the party had turned into a patchwork of overall calm and intimate conversations, I decided to forego my position as host and concentrate on learning more about Leonor. I was about to exit to the porch, with this Portuguese beauty, when our backdoor burst open and I heard the familiar drunken voice of Stuart Perkoff.

"This is the place, is it not!" shouted the surly, bearded mountain of a man.

Suddenly I was a host again. Offering my apologies to Leonor, I crossed the room to greet Stuart and his two traveling buddies. I noticed that Perkoff was nipping at a close to empty bottle of Goslings 140 proof Black Seal Bermuda Rum. One of his sidekicks, a rather frail looking young man with curly hair and wearing glasses, was clutching an unopened bottle of the same precious poison. All three appeared to be several sheets to the wind.

"Jake Salazar, I'd like you to meet Jack Kerouac and Allen Ginsberg," said Stuart, mustering all the good manners possible, considering the fact that he and his fellow travelers had just chugged the better portion of a bottle of 140 proof black label rum.

I shook Jack's hand first. He had the solid masculine grip of a day laborer that demanded an equally empowered response on my part. "Pleasure," he said. He turned his muscular frame and handsome face in the direction of the few unattended bar girls. Allen's grip, on the other hand, was as limp as a wet noodle and could have passed as a parting gesture of a corpse in a coffin.

I introduced the threesome to my remaining guests and suggested that they grab a paper plate and partake of what was left of the repast. Perhaps even add some Coke to their rum.

"This one's for all of you," declared Allen, raising the bottle of rum as an offering to his now fellow partiers.

The three gathered some eats, advisedly added Coke to their witches' brew, and edged their way into the various points of conversation around the room.

Jack checked out the lineup of bar girls and decided that none of them was his type. He segued into a conversation with Ben about the Parker tracks on the phonograph.

"You know, there's this cat named Miles Davis who's about to turn jazz in a completely new direction," Jack informed Ben.

"Tell me about it. It's called 'Cool Jazz,' more mellowed out than the Bird's Bebop thing."

"Yeah, I hear Miles is working on an album of 'Cool Jazz' at this very moment in New York City."

"Mark my word...what's your name again?

"Jack."

"Jack, I'll be the first dude to listen in on that shit."

"I'll be right there with you, brother."

Allen found a comfortable spot on the sofa between Smitty and the Kowalcyzks and was filling in these ex-New Yorkers on the current state of affairs on the Lower East Side.

"And what do you do in New York, Allen?" asked Aleksy.

"Well, at the moment, I'm heavily involved in psychoanalytic therapy."

"What did I tell you, Emilia," said Aleksy, turning to his wife. "The moment he walked through the door, I said, 'there is a young man studying to be a psychiatrist.'"

"Not exactly. Fact is, for the last two months, I've been a patient at an institution in New York City for the criminally insane."

A deafening silence came over the conversation.

Then, with a motherly smile, Emilia broke the ice with a question. "You are on leave from this institution, yes?"

"No, three nights ago I escaped with the help of my angel over there," he said, pointing to Kerouac. "Unbelievable; 72 hours on the road, and before we know it, we're across the States in a flash."

"But for your own good, you're going to return to this institution, right?" asked Smitty, as if he were suggesting the young man spend a few more years in the minors before attempting the Big Show.

"I'm on the fence about it."

"Is it that you don't agree with their therapeutic approach to your illness?" asked Aleksy, in a fatherly manner.

"You could say that."

"So what's the problem?" added Smitty.

"They want to turn me straight, but I'm a lover of men not women," said Allen. He winked in the direction of Angel who'd been listening in on the conversation from a chair next to the sofa. Ginsberg's wink was answered with nothing less than a stone-cold stare from my dangerous Filipino friend.

Angel had spent the greater portion of the party drinking with his buddies from the docks. Here and there, he had joined in on a dance to a Goodman tune. In full Zoot riot-gear, his martial arts moves afforded him a strong second to Ben and Willie's more natural, graceful, and imaginative jitterbugging.

To say that Angel's sexual propensity was simply that of a homosexual would be far from the truth. As a youth, he traveled from his native Philippines, south to Indonesia, then north into the heart of China, all in pursuit of the spiritual truths of Tantric Buddhism and the hidden powers and secrets of the primal martial art of Tai Chi Quan. It was during these travels that he would learn it was possible to enlist one's passions (his desire for sex with men) as a means by which to accelerate both his knowledge of earthly things and his quest for enlightenment. Such intensified passion would, as well, eventually allow him to transcend cycles of terrestrial bondage (Samsara). Strangely enough, Angel believed it was this same impassioned path to wisdom that would eventually even enable him to cure himself of his homosexuality. His mother and father, who were murdered by the Japanese, had wished him to marry and have children. Over years of diligent meditative practice of Tantric yoga, Angel had successfully envisioned his sexual consort, his partnered Karmamudra, in the form of a female. He believes that by practicing this advanced, spiritual exercise he will ultimately be able to marry and add to the Mercado family tree. In order to rationalize his homosexual relationships, while desiring to marry a woman, he has made it a policy of always paying for sex with men.

I had a feeling that Ginsberg, far less groomed in the knowledge of his own sexuality, was about to find himself chin deep in the shit of his own insane ignorance. I was well aware that my naïve guest just might be capable of believing the impressive bulge between his legs was equal to the steeled and deadly resolve strapped to Angel's right ankle. I found myself bent on turning the conversation in another direction rather than chance an unfortunate misunderstanding between partygoers.

I decided to ask Stuart about the promise he made to read some of his poetry at my party. Sure enough, he remembered to bring a work in progress with him.

Ben suggested a ballad track from the Bird album to accompany the reading of Stuart's poem.

The working title of the poem was *Feast of Death, Feast of Love*. Stuart explained that it was far from a final draft and probably a lot shorter than it would be when completed. He read extremely well in a deep and commanding baritone. Everyone clapped when he finished and there followed all sorts of questions as to the source of his inspiration. If Stuart's poem was any example of the new artistic vision of his Beat generation, I had to admit, I never heard anything like it. But then again, except for my resolute and repetitious readings of Jeffers, I was no damn student of modern poetry. Still, to my taste, Stuart's poem lacked heart and was little more than a bizarre sequence of conceptual snapshots transitioning between visions of free love and the perplexing and inescapable question of why six million Jews had to die.

Granted, we'd all come out of the war with our own psychological scars. However, to my mind, after hearing Stuart's poem, I could only rejoice at the fact that I'd thankfully escaped my generation's conflict without a dependency on the abstract.

No matter what I thought of Stuart's poem, my original intent for having him read it, in the first place, had succeeded. Angel got out of his chair to say goodbye to some of his friends from the docks, and Allen lost any immediate interest in him and returned to his conversation with Smitty and the Kowalczyks.

Of course, like a good host, I congratulated Stuart on his eloquent reading of the poem and quoted his perfect transition from youthful images of free love and the imponderable reality of genocide: "wake up! to a morning sun shining thru even newspaper headlines, sun on men in sand wading thru blood."

"You liked that, didn't you. I knew you would," he said. Catching Leonor's eye, from across the room, he started in her direction. "Excuse me, Jake, but I'm about to reap a poet's reward."

"So what did you think of Stuart's vision of love and death?" asked Kerouac, who was approaching me for the first time since we'd been introduced.

"Different."

"He's our leader, you know," said Jack, slurring his words a bit. "He's the Beat who's going to set the pace for all our futures."

"Stuart tells me we're brothers of the sea, Mister," I said, changing the subject.

"Merchant Marines? Not really my thing," he said, looking around the room and refusing to look me in the eye.

"Why is that?"

"They wouldn't let me be who I am."

"And who is that, exactly?"

"That, Jake, is something I know and you, my friend, have yet to find out."

I'd seen his type before in Basic. Too many fucking things on his self-aggrandizing mind to take the time to cover a buddy's back or take out a target for the betterment of all.

"Mentally unfit, right?" I was really angry!

He turned and stared me right in the face. I knew he was about to belt me one. At that very moment, Ginsberg let out with an incredible wolf-like howl. We both looked in the direction of the sofa. Angel was back in that chair opposite Allen. They were deep in conversation.

"No man, it's the name of the poem I'm working on," said Allen to Angel.

"What kind of poem is called Howl?" responded Angel.

"A poem that's about beautiful beings, like you and me, who have gone through hell in search of their beloveds," confessed Allen.

"Holy shit," whispered Jack. "I swear I can't take this cocksucker anywhere."

Advancing toward his wayward and outspoken friend, he said: "Allen, some other time and place for the Howl poem. OK!"

"No, no, no, my dear angel Jack. This is the perfect time and place to try out those few blessed fragments that have come to me from the light in the darkness," insisted Allen.

"I killed many Japs. Not one of them howls for mercy before I cut their throats," said Angel.

"I'm not talking about war," said Allen. "I'm talking about love."

"I would like to hear this poem," said Aleksy.

"I make love to a man, I pay for it," said Angel. I'd heard him give the same warning to a fellow homosexual coming on to him in a Hong Kong dive.

"My poem is an attempt to free love from the chains of Molach, the god of capitalism who has frightened me out of my natural ecstasy!"

Jack turned to me in confidence. "It's impossible to help a man who wants to be a monster one minute and a god the next."

I knew he was talking about Allen, but I'd come to the same conclusion about Angel ever since we first met as merchant seamen back in '33.

Ben turned off the phonograph, and our remaining guests focused their attention on the mental institution escapee who was about to give us a preview of what he believed would become the greatest of his poems.

"'I have seen the best minds of my generation destroyed by madness, starving hysterical naked, dragging themselves through the negro streets at dawn looking for an angry fix…'"

Willie, who'd hardly said a word all night, suddenly chimed in, "You draggin' your cracker ass down my negro street at dawn, lookin' to cop some fix, you'd best be movin' like some greyhound on fire!"

His comment got a laugh from damn near everyone.

"But who is it that is driven to such madness if it isn't men like you and me?" said Allen directly to Angel.

"And who are these mysterious men like you and me?" asked Angel.

"Let it go, Angel. Drop it," I said.

"We are those," said Allen, in a drunken, strange, and loving way, "'…who let themselves be fucked in the ass by saints of the open road and scream with joy when they are blown by sailors, seraphim of Atlantic and Caribbean love…'"

Angel rose slowly to his feet; his eyes were ablaze with rage. "And where is the hero in this pile of filth?"

"Oh, I get it now. You're like some of those fools over at the hospital who really believe they can go straight and…"

"Where in your poem is the feeling you get when you are willing to die for something you believe in?"

"I can't think of one thing I'd be willing to die for. I only want to live and be free to love and write as I wish."

Angel gracefully reached under his right pant leg, and pulling out his stainless steel Bowie, he drew it back behind his right ear in rediness to throw it. He declared, "And what if God would have you die this very night?!"

"Jesus Christ!" yelled Jack. Allen, and the nearby guests on the sofa, stood up and backed away from the sudden threat.

"Put it away, Angel!" I pleaded.

"I put it where my art may serve the truth!"

As Angel's Bowie sailed through the air, Ginsberg fainted. The weapon, thrown far afield of any living creature, whizzed across the room to penetrate the bungalow's newly painted standard. Bending down to help his friend, Jack shouted, "You fucking crazy Pinoy; you could have killed us both!"

The guests remained frozen in silence. Angel casually walked across the room, dislodged his weapon from the standard, and said, "To speak from the silence of your soul, in the name of those who have died that you might live, that is art." He crossed the room and exited up the stairs to his bedroom.

Ben threw some cold water on Allen's face, and the poet awoke abruptly, shouting: "Moloch! Moloch! They're all possessed by Moloch!"

Helping his friend to his feet, Jack said, "Come on, Allen, we're getting the fuck out of here."

As they both made their way to the alley door, Kerouac turned back toward Stuart, who'd observed the entire altercation from the porch, and shouted, "We'll be in the car!"

I turned to Stuart and said, "We'd best call it a night."

"That Filipino friend of yours is the biggest closet queen I've ever seen in my life," said Stuart.

"I'd say more like a decorated veteran with the absolute skill and right *to speak* as he will and *lead his life* as he wishes."

"I thought you had the makings of a real Beat, but you're not even close."

"Not all of us are beat, not yet anyway."

"Oh, but that's where you're wrong, Jake, we're all beat. You, me, and our whole damn generation, we're all nothing more than a lost, disinherited caravan of drugged up carnies and beat down outcasts of the American dream."

"And you're the big time organization man for this gang of mentally disturbed, literary malcontents. All of you determined to undermine 300 years of American storytelling with your bullshit, fragmented visions that come straight from your pre-packaged cowardly hearts and the darkness of your lower intestines. Wake up and pull your heads from out of your fucking, discontented assholes!"

"Fuck you!"

"Right back at you…Stuart Perkoff."

Perkoff stumbled back and away from me and headed toward the alley door.

"Fuck you! Fuck every inch of your fucking up-tight, straight, hardworking conservative asses!" he howled before exiting.

The party pretty much broke up after that.

I made sure I said my goodbyes to Leonor. I got her phone number and assured her that we'd get together soon.

It was a little after 2 when I poured myself a cup of coffee and went to sober up on the porch. Unfortunately, even the early morning calm of the canal couldn't relieve me of the pain that was running down my leg from the shrapnel in my right thigh. I'd forgotten to refill my prescription for painkillers and quickly realized I was up for one hell of a sleepless night. Things weren't looking all that great for my train trip to Oakland that I had to take in less than seven hours.

Around 2:30, Angel came downstairs and peeped through the porch doors. "How about some push hands at the soul's midnight from the Lookout Point?"

I thought for a moment. "Not a bad idea," I replied.

We quickly exited to the alley, jumped in the Packard, and headed for the Hollywood hills.

Chapter IV

Push Hands at the Soul's Midnight

Before heading to Griffith Park, I asked Angel to stop by the all night pharmacy on Venice Boulevard. Ralph, the night manager, always had my next prescription of Meperidine ready anytime I needed it. With the help of some water from his cooler, I popped a pill and figured it might kick in by the time we reached the park.

With Angel at the wheel, I rolled down the car window and took in the refreshing morning breeze blowing in from the east. There was a hint of citrus in the air, a fragrant reminder of the few remaining orange groves in the area. For a moment, I closed my eyes and tried to imagine what this boulevard must have looked like when it was a mere single lane road before it became Abbot Kinny's prized thoroughfare of towering electrical poles and quaint two-lane trolley tracks. For years, it had served as L.A.'s only direct access to Venice Beach and Kinny's wonderland of amusements and waterway abodes.

We were already halfway to the hills when I realized that Angel and I hadn't uttered a word to each other.

Turning onto Beverly, Angel drove into the all-night Gilmore Serve Yourself Filling Station, touted as the "Largest Gas Station in the World." It featured eight islands of three tiered gas pumps and, in the daylight hours, was attended by young women wearing service attire on roller skates. Angel, knowing that my painkillers hadn't taken effect yet, went to the pump and filled the tank. When he returned to the car, he just sat there staring blankly at the steering wheel.

There was obviously something on his mind, and I had a damn good idea what it was.

"You think that Allen fellow could be right?"

"About what," I asked, as if I didn't know.

"About being a fool to think I could ever marry a woman and have children."

"That jerk knows nothing of your inner strength," I said.

"You know, I've not paid for sex since we came from the Islands to the mainland," he said with a sense of pride.

"Maybe it's time you asked Hilo to set you up on a date."

"You think?" he asked, turning on the ignition in a sudden burst of enthusiasm.

"It's all within the power of the Tao, my man."
"Always has been, always will be."

Angel floored the gas pedal and we peeled out of the self-service station.

We'd often driven to Griffith Park at night to practice our Tai Chi Quan. Sometimes vets do best when they work off their anger in the dark. Daylight and its workaday offerings, that end in a paycheck, aren't enough to wipe the sights and sounds of slaughter from the hearts and minds of the warriors who have put their lives on the line in the name of their own. The wind in the trees and our elevated position above the nightlights of the city offered the ideal atmosphere for exercising our martial art skills. Of course, my abilities remained nothing compared to Angel's. He introduced me to the Wang Family long form when we first met up on a merchant ship in the Philippines. It had taken me two years at sea to learn the entire exercise and another year to even come close to an infantile understanding of my ability to control the internal flow of my meridians (Chi). I finally learned, to some degree, in the partnered discipline of Tuishou (push hands), how to transform this energy into the lethal tactical power (Ki) to overcome the harmony and balance of an opponent. After a year of practicing push hands, I found myself in a bar fight in Hong Kong and realized that I was capable of using the leverage of a drunk, who was twice my size, against himself. Still, it was only at the end of the war when I fully realized the value of Tai Chi. I returned home wounded and was recuperating in Letterman Hospital when Angel, having decided to settle stateside, visited me every weekend to work on our Tai Chi. He helped me gain the strength to move from my wheelchair to standing on my own.

The pain in my right leg had subsided by the time we ascended the snaking Western Canyon Road. We parked and on foot followed the moonlit path to a spot just above Griffith Observatory.

With the city's bright paralleled arteries of electricity below us, we began our ancient martial practice. This was an exercise composed in the form of a symbolic story that progresses through the threefold stages of life. This journey from youth, to maturity, to old age is revealed by way of the martial art's 13-part development of inner and outer alinement and its 108 chronological dance positions. Mirroring each other's every move, we finished in perfect unison. The entire exercise took us about half an hour, and then we proceeded to our push hands session.

I could feel a great deal of tension coming from Angel enabling me to throw him off balance several times over. However, by our seventh engagement of locking hands, his mastery of the form allowed him to regain his outer balance and inner harmony. In doing so, he remained the winner in all further push hand tactics. We finished some 20 minutes later.

As we walked back to the car, both in a sweat, we congratulated each other on our choice to drive to the hills. Snaking our way back down into the fading lights of the city, the first inklings of dawn drifting over the Glendale hills, we headed home content, sobered up, and knowing full well that we'd done, once again, the right thing in turning hate to love by reestablishing a healthy and mindful relationship with body, mind, and spirit.

By four in the morning, we were on Venice Boulevard and almost home. I told Angel that our session had inspired me to finish my translation of Wang Wei's most famous poem from the Tang Dynasty.

"Yes, it is most important that you finish it. As I have said, it is a poem about Tai Chi Quan and how you always 'return to the mountain' refreshed with new life and a greater understanding of death itself."

In our years at sea, Angel not only introduced me to a martial art but to the characters and ideograms of the Chinese language. Through long hours of memorization and practicing the basic strokes used in the creation of these images, I'd become relatively proficient at both reading and writing the language. Speaking it was another thing. I could understand when someone spoke to me but when it came to actually speaking it, myself, I had problems because of the tonal variations. I just can't hear them. Despite the fact that I couldn't speak Chinese, my efforts at translation had become a truly unique introduction to their poetry. At the moment, I was just about to finish my interpretation of a poem that had been written some 1,200 years ago.

When we arrived home, knowing I would be leaving in a few hours, I said goodbye to Angel. After assuring me that he and Hilo would take care of the mess from the party, he went upstairs to hit the sack. Despite the hour, figuring I'd catch some sleep on the train, I went immediately to my desk overlooking the canal. Taking out the ancient poem, I translated the last line that had come to me during our exercise.

In an audible whisper, I read the poem aloud:

An Exercise within an Enclosure of
Wisdom and Beauty
(A Monster Returns to Deer Park)

(Once you return to…)
Embrace the earth and
Fill the empty mountain
With your divine light…
…Search as you may for
Your people…
You will hear only the voices
Of your inner self – So far off –
…As to return you
To the limber branches of
The deep forest of your youth…
(This accomplished, Old One…)
You will return once more
To shine
A dark green moss
That climbs as high as heaven

Though I'd started the translation of this poem several months before my present situation had developed, it had only been in this last week that I realized the similarity between the poet's return to his Deer Park and my possible return to what Longdown looked upon as the "limited space of an infinite definition." So, what was the deal? In search of daylight, did I have to journey back to the darkness of death? My Tai Chi session with Angel had compelled me to finish the poem, but what was the poem telling me? Yes, I'd returned from my generation's war, but to what? Who was I really, and to what had I returned?

I set my alarm clock for 6:30 and hoped I'd catch a couple of hours sleep before my journey north to Oakland for my sister's birthday.

Chapter V

America's Treasured Obstacles to Passion

I woke abruptly when the alarm went off then jumped into the shower and shaved. After toweling off, I donned my brand new Navy wide pinstriped suit with matching silk tie. Putting on my snazzy light blue fedora, with its prominent c-shaped crown, I looked in the mirror. I was the perfect image of a successful Vegas gambler. The folks will be intrigued and proud at the same time, I said to myself.

Grabbing my suitcase, I rushed downstairs to call a cab. Hilo, Healani, and one of the bar girls he introduced me to the night before were at our dinner table finishing off their breakfast. Some guys have all the luck; only with Hilo, I'd come to the conclusion that it wasn't a question of mere luck, more like an inexhaustible quick bat all the way to the bottom of the ninth.

Hilo was about to take both of them home in the Packard; he offered to drop me off at the train station. With only 45 minutes to catch the 8:15 Coast Daylight, I suggested we'd best hurry up.

We reached Union Station with plenty of time to spare. I said my goodbyes to both of his (current) reigning courtesans and complimented him on how much I enjoyed his band the night before.

"Who can resist the songs of love," he said.

Smiling a knowing smile, I had no argument with that and turned to catch my train.

"Aloha to your Mom and family," he shouted.

"I'll do just that," I shouted back over my shoulder.

Mom was born in the Islands; she was a mix of Polynesian and Portuguese. When she first met Hilo, after

Pop died, she whispered in my ear, "Wahine o ka ke Kanaka" (lady's man), winked at him and said, "If I were only 30 years younger." Having heard what she said, the Polynesian charmer could only retort, "There is always something to learn from a lovely lady." Mom blushed and kept her distance from Hilo for the rest of the evening.

The Southern Pacific Railroad touted the Coast Daylight as the "Most Beautiful Train in the World." This streamlined, red, orange and black steam-driven locomotive pretty much hugged the California coastline from Los Angeles to the 3rd and Townsand Street Depot in Frisco.

I snuggled into one of the plush, foam rubber window seats to enjoy a panoramic view familiar as the back of my hand. Before I knew it, I was fast asleep.

Several hours later, I was awakened by the soft and pleasant voice of the Daylight's public address system: "As you look to your left, you'll catch a glimpse of one of most dynamic and beautiful spots along the western coastline. Big Sur, California is known for its towering wind sculpted cliffs and as a mecca for many California artists of renown; the most famous is the poet, Robinson Jeffers." The signature clouds of ocean mist, so uniquely nature's gift to Sur, were retreating seaward from their morning embrace of the shore's gigantic escarpments. Turning away from my view of the shoreline, I closed my eyes and thought back to the summer of '39.

There were two Jack London books I'd taken with me when I went to sea: *The Sea Wolf* and *Martin Eden*. Three years in, I added Robinson Jeffers *Roan Stallion, Tamar and Other Poems*; it was given to me by my sister to include in my "library-at-sea." I read London's novels several times over. Jeffers' shorter poems I set to memory. I was somewhere in passage on the Indian Ocean when I promised myself that I would visit Jeffers at his famed granite Tor House at Big Sur. Less than a year-and-a-half after my return to California, and my discharge from merchant service, I did just that.

I remember walking down the Old Coast Road as I hitchhiked south from Oakland to Mission Point. From there, I followed a newly paved street that led toward the sea. One of the locals gladly gave me directions to Tor House. Before I knew it, I'd reached the low stone wall that surrounded Jeffers' garden, house, and tower that faced seaward. I entered through the unlocked gate. After a few knocks at the wooden door of the stone cottage, I was greeted by a plump, handsome, and stern faced woman in her early 50s. I introduced myself as a fellow Californian, from Oakland, with a passion to meet Mr. Jeffers. I mentioned that I'd read and memorized several of his poems in my many years at sea. She told me she was Robin's wife, Una. She opened the door and graciously asked me in.

The interior of Tor house was as impressively romantic as its exterior. The exterior was a picturesque cottage, a primitive looking construction of masterfully mortared sea worn granite stones. This uneven assemblage, carved by centuries of ebb and flow, had been stolen from the beach below by a crafty and unimaginably ambitious stonemason. The house's elongated raked roof, quaintly leveled off to allow for a second floor, gave the craggy knoll topped stone lodging, overlooking the wild Pacific, the impression of a sorcerer's abode in a fairy tale or a strange and threatening hangout for pirates in a novel by Stevenson.

Within the high raftered space were oak paneled walls. The floors of polished mahogany, dusty and worn, gave me the feeling I had entered upon another time when words were magical and heroes real. My eyes were immediately drawn to the large window overlooking the sea at the far end of the living room.

"Go on, have a look; it's one of the best views in all of California," said Una. "Mind the piano, young man, the house was built around it."

"No problem," I answered, as I made my way carefully around the Steinway grand that stood between me and the magnificent view of the sea and Pebble Beach to the north.

"Did you drive down from Oakland?"

"No, I hitchhiked."

"Well then, you must be starved," she concluded in a motherly fashion. "Robin and I have already had our breakfast, but how about some coffee and whole wheat bread, fresh from the oven, with melted butter."

"That would be great," I said.

"How do you take your coffee…?"

"Black, no sugar," I said, finding it impossible to take my eyes away from the view of the seascape below. I wondered what it must have been like to have lived on such an isolated spot, for well over 20 years, and, now, to have streets and other houses creeping south from Carmel like some poisonous viper of civilization, elements of modernity that both Jeffers and his wife had legendarily escaped upon moving here.

After some time, Una reentered the wooden paneled living room and asked me to follow her past the staircase into the dining room that revealed the house's construction of naked stone with two windows facing the sea. There was a beautiful old spinning wheel next to the windows, and just off to their right was a huge ash-crusted hearth.

"Here you are, Mr. Salazar. Bon appetite!"

"Thank you," I said. Taking a seat at the oblong oak dining table, I bit into the wonderfully aromatic piece of fresh baked bread.

"Robin's still upstairs writing. He should be down any time now. He always writes in the morning, you know." She paused and, with a wise and curiously feral smile, asked, "When do you write, Mr. Salazar?" Here, before my very eyes, was the female guardian of Tor House and protector of California's greatest of poets.

"Oh…I…I don't write. I mean, I've tried to a few times…but…"

"Most of the young people who show up at our door are poets or writers of some sort, apprehensive novices who can't help but bombard Robin with all sorts of dubious concerns as to the worth of their work. They're usually jam packed with questions as to the risks of taking up such a thankless profession in our thought-provoking yet unpoetic world of industry, greed, and war."

"I'm not a poet, but if I were to ever write something it would be a novel."

"And your favorite novelist, may I ask?"

"Without a doubt, Jack London," I said, downing a huge gulp of pure black joe.

"Oh….yes, adorable, handsome Jack London, King of the Bohemians! He was a frequent visitor to Sur, a bit before our time. Jack had a suicide pact with a friend of ours, George Sterling. Poor, sad, old George kept his end of the bargain. As for Jack, it seems he consumed some bad mushrooms one evening. If you ask me, it was his workers, building his Valley of the Moon lodge, who did him in." Placing her right hand under her chin, she said, "They had it up to here with old Jack's socialist notions."

"I've read most of his novels, but I can't say I know all that much about his personal life."

"Trust me," she continued, suddenly lost to a strange and intractable air of melancholy, "there are far more prolonged, intimate, and loving forms of suicide."

At that moment, we heard Jeffers descending the stairs.

"Here's the great man now," she proclaimed, an evident strain of irony to her voice.

I looked in the direction of the stairs and there he was. Tall and slender, he was dressed in a redwood tweed jacket, brown khaki slacks, and a large collared white cotton shirt, open at the neck. I'd seen portraits of him, in his youth, dressed in exactly the same fashion. But here, in the flesh, some 20 years later, there appeared to be something missing. The savage and noble features of his high cheek boned and hawk-nosed face, having succumbed to the pressures of success and ongoing demands of intercourse with civilization, gave him the vanquished look of an elder Cherokee chieftain's portrait I'd seen at the de Young museum in Frisco.

"Well now. What have we here?" he asked, reaching out his hand to greet me. We shook hands across the dining table.

"His name is Jake Salazar. He's hitchhiked down from Oakland. He's not a poet and has absolutely nothing for you to read."

"Then he must be one of yours, a musician."

"These days, I don't play anything but poker," I chimed in, hoping to impress.

"And this game of chance is the extent of your instrumentality?" asked Jeffers.

"No, when I was younger, I was one hell of a baseball pitcher. If you'll excuse my French."

"And your best pitch?" queried Jeffers.

"Fast ball. Swear on a Bible, I threw it close to 90 miles an hour."

"Sounds like the young man could have turned professional," concluded Una, turning to her husband.

"As a matter of fact, I tried out for the Oakland Oaks, this spring, but didn't make the cut. After six years at sea, I'm not the pitcher I used to be."

"Nothing left, then, but to become a professional poker player," said Jeffers.

"Honest to God, I'm good enough to think about it."

"Truth is," admitted Jeffers, "I'm gambling on the start of a new poem. Why don't you join me in my morning walk. We can weigh the pros and cons of both."

"Sounds great," I said, abruptly standing and almost falling backward off the bench of the dining table. All three of us laughed. The momentary imbalance forced me to remember something. "Oh, I almost forgot." I unzipped my knapsack and retrieved a red, chipped, and bloodstained brick. "It's from the Frisco quake of '06. My father thought it might be an appropriate addition to your wall of antiquities in Hawk Tower. He pulled it out of the rubble when he freed a beloved neighbor who sadly did not survive." I tentatively handed Jeffers the macabre object. "Pop is from Peru. He's half Inca and Spanish. He's a bit of a primitive with a rather bizarre point of view when it comes to human sacrifice."

"A most appropriate and noble addition to *our* Hawk Tower," said Una.

"A sincere and virtuous example of California past," agreed Jeffers. "Come along, Jake, we'll walk directly to the tower."

As I followed Jeffers to the front door, Una whispered under her breath, "Man, proud man, dressed in a brief authority!"

I didn't recognize the quote, but the contempt on Jeffers' face was unmistakable.

As we walked across the garden toward Hawk Tower, Jeffers expressed that, in his college days, he, too, had been an athlete, running track and swimming. Furthermore, he explained how a regiment of physical activity had remained with him his entire life. He insisted that having the physical strength to build Hawk Tower led him to discover his own unique style of poetry. It also helped his relationship with his wife. I informed him that his poetry was one of the three books I'd taken with me to sea. Having memorized several of his shorter poems, I confessed how strange it had been to read his poetry half way around the world from California, only to realize that so much of the philosophy I was encountering in the Far East, specifically the fundamentals of Tai Chi Quan, was undeniably similar to what I thought Jeffers was getting at in his poetry. To my mind, there existed a unique use of the Chinese concept of yin (female downward movement) and yang (male upward movement) in his unparalleled dramatic poetry set amidst the wild and thunderous shores of Big Sur.

Jeffers was in full agreement with my analysis of his work and said that he had recently written a short poem entitled "Shiva," his one poem, he felt, that best portrayed the predacious image of a female hawk descending upon her prey. He quoted, "There is a hawk that is picking the birds out of our sky. She killed the pigeon of peace and security. She has taken honesty and confidence from nations and men. She is hunting the lonely heron of liberty."

Upon entering Hawk Tower, Jeffers placed Pop's surviving brick, from California's most deadly earthquake, on the bottom floor of the four-story stone tower. He promised me that, at the first chance possible, he'd mix up some cement and find a fitting place for it among the celebrated artifacts from around the world that lined the interior walls of the unique structure. We immediately ascended, by way of his second floor study, to the third floor battlements of the tower that overlooked the ocean. With the roaring sea below us, we continued our conversation.

"Are you married, Jake?"

"No, but I'm planning on it. A girl I've known since high school."

He asked me which of his poems I considered my favorite. I told him that it wasn't one of the poems I'd memorized at sea but one from the recent edition of his *Selected Poetry*. The title was "Rock and Hawk." He asked me if I'd like to recite it. While I remember beginning the poem, Jeffers didn't allow me to finish it.

The smooth clickety clack of the streamlined Daylight brought me out of my daydream. I was, again, on my way to my sister's birthday party in Oakland. As I was watching the seascape fade back into the distance, I recited the poem to myself:

> Here is a symbol in which
> Many high tragic thoughts
> Watch their own eyes.
>
> This gray rock, standing tall
> On the headland, where the seawind
> Lets no tree grow,
>
> Earthquake-proved, and signatured
> By ages of storms: on its peak
> A falcon has perched.

I think, here is your emblem
To hang in the future sky;
Not the cross, not the hive,

But this; bright power, dark peace;
Fierce consciousness joined with final
Disinterestedness;

Life with calm death; the falcon's
Realist eyes and act
Married to the massive

Mysticism of stone,
Which failure cannot cast down
Nor success make proud...

But that day, back in '39, above the wild shore of Sur, I hadn't gotten beyond the first stanza of the poem before Jeffers interrupted me. "Because of my infidelity, my wife attempted suicide last year." His sad honesty rendered me speechless.

"There are limits, Jake, to our ability to look into another's eyes and see our own tragedy. In that poem I envisioned how this wild, ferocious coast of California deserved to be challenged by untamed men and women, alike. Only primal equals were capable of surviving its terrifying beauty. In such a foreboding world, what does it mean when a beloved retreats from her own savage desires to avenge her lover's passion in an act of suicide?"

He turned from my gaze and looked far out to sea. How little I knew of wounds then.

When we returned to the house, Una asked me to stay for dinner and spend the night in the guest room.

Considering the dangers of hitchhiking along the coast at night, I gladly accepted the offer.

She made a delicious vegetable stew. Jeffers had invited a guest by the name of Pierson, the stonemason who helped him build Tor House and taught him the craft that would enable him to build Hawk Tower completely on his own. The stonemason brought a local newspaper with him. After dinner, the four of us discussed the situation in Europe. It had only been a week since Hitler invaded Poland.

Pierson, a man in his 70s, couldn't believe that the United States was about to enter another world war. Una, of course, feared for the life of her twin sons.

"If a war breaks out in Europe, I'll be one of the first to enlist," I blurted out.

Jeffers, who hardly uttered a word all night, looked at me with that same piercing and prophetic stare he'd given me on the tower that afternoon and said, "'The cold passion for truth hunts in no pack.' The dogs of war, their tails aflame, that shall emerge from the coming conflagration, will scatter a foxfire left and right, but the alpha wolf will not fall to the old savage ways of sacrifice nor allow their senses to be duped by the daylight greed of progress."

"...But prove a force of nature, 'which failure cannot cast down nor success make proud,'" I answered.

Jeffers smiled, stood up, and silently walked up the stairs to his bedroom on the second floor.

I woke the next morning ready for my journey north. Una had made me some scrambled eggs with toast and coffee. When I said my goodbyes to her, she kissed me on the forehead and said, "Go with God, my boy." She told me that Jeffers had started his new poem and knew I would understand his wish not to be disturbed.

I often wondered if the poem he began that morning was *The Double Axe*. Had his will to begin the poem been influenced by my visit, especially since I expressed such a willingness to go to war? Certainly, I had returned from the war with that soul of a zombie Jeffers had so masterfully envisioned. The innocent who had so willingly left for war had survived it, but only by forming an inescapable allegiance to that vengeful spirit of the walking dead.

The train reached Frisco a half hour early. It was 6 p.m. I called Mom to let her know that I'd arrived, caught the shuttlebus to the Ferry Building, and crossed the bay to the Clay Street Ferry Terminal in Oakland.

Mom said that Frank Bell was driving over to pick me up. Now, Frank's story was a long and complicated one. He was a hardworking six-foot-two Texan, with a drinking problem, who had survived the Depression by driving long-haul diesels throughout the southwest and California. Because of a childhood ear injury, Frank had a deferment and spent the war driving supplies in and out of the Alameda shipyards. One night, he wound up at a dance in Oakland that my sister Millie attended with a girl friend. Despite his size, Frank was quite the dancer. My sister was so taken by his grace and gentlemanly manner that, after several following dates, they became pretty much an item. And the rest, as they say, is history. In this case, a very screwed-up and rocky history, but lots of lousy things happen during wartime. They married in late '44, about the same time MacArthur had made up his greedy mind to send my worthless ass up against the Japs on Cebu. Scuttlebutt had it he wanted to regain access to the revenue from the coffee plantations that he owned there before the war. Strangely enough, I had never met Frank. I'd only heard about how, within a year's time, the arguments between him and my sister had gotten so bad that she had to file for divorce even though she was pregnant. She listed the cause as cruel and inhuman treatment. After Millie and Frank divorced, he decided to leave California and find work in New Mexico. For whatever the reason, perhaps guilt, he diligently sent her monthly checks for child support. About six months ago, having damn near killed himself in a trucking accident in the southwest, Millie had a change of heart and asked Frank to return to Oakland. A couple of months back, they remarried at City Hall. From that point on, Frank routinely begged my sister's forgiveness and promised her he would always do the right thing by my namesake, four-year-old Charlie. Ever since high school, when Cookie Lavaggeto nicknamed me Jake, my birth name, Charlie, all but vanished. Until the birth of my nephew, Charlie Bell.

I hadn't been waiting for more than five minutes, outside the Clay Street Ferry Building, when driving up in a brand new, cherry red '49 Ford Custom Convertible was my infamous brother-in-law, Frank Bell.

Frank pulled over to the curb, kept the motor running, and proudly exited his purring, sleek, state of the art automobile. Walking around its streamlined, pontoon bodywork that confirmed Ford to be the first of the Big Three to emerge with a truly unprecedented postwar modern design, he extended his hand to me with a genuine smile. His ingratiating beam was, unfortunately, blemished by a pronounced Mensur-like scar that ran from the bottom edge of his left eye to the middle of his cheek. As I got the story from my sister, the scar was not so much the result of dueling swords but the unmistakable impact of a two-by-four in a Tijuana cantina brawl circa '35. He was neatly dressed in a gray cotton suit and broad painted tie. His expensive and immaculately polished woven Oxfords were as righteous an extravagance as any I'd seen on an honest, hardworking family man.

"Well, damned if we don't meet at last, Jake," he said.

We shared a strong masculine handshake between us. "That's some piece of automobile you've got there," I added, nodding in the direction of his new convertible.

"Ain't she though," he said, as he grabbed my suitcase and easily placed it, with one hand, in the back seat of the car. "You can't imagine how hard it was to convince your sister to buy a convertible."

"Yeah, I heard about the difficulties you've had convincing my sister."

Ignoring my slight, he opened the shotgun door to his precious possession and gestured, like some over courteous doorman looking for a tip, for me to enter.

We'd driven a couple of blocks north in silence when Frank broke the ice.

"Your mom figured it might be best we shared a few words before we showed up to face the rest of the family."

"I'd have to agree with that."

"I already made my apologies to Millie and the rest of your family. But it's to you, seeing how you were away at war, that I really owe…"

"You ever kill a man, Frank?"

The question startled him but not so much that he didn't have the good sense to slow down, pull over, and park. Keeping one hand on the steering wheel, he turned to me with the stare of a player holding some decent cards in a high-stakes game. "I damn near beat a man to death in a Tulsa dive one night. If it hadn't been for some old cowboy, with the strength and guts to pull me off him, I probably wouldn't be here right now."

"Well, with the Japs I killed in the Pacific, things weren't all that personal, but I did get the job done. When you're a decent, rational man like me, killing another human being isn't all that easy. Sad to say, it can become bloody routine," I said, staring out the front window of the Ford. Then, I looked him square in the eyes and said, "But I swear, Frank, you ever lay a hand on my sister again, I'll put a bayonet through your gut as fast as you can yell, 'Bonsai.'"

"It was the booze, Jake," he said. "I'm off the hard stuff these days. I only have a
beer now and then. I swear to Jesus, I'll never raise a hand to Millie again."

"And why am I supposed to believe that?"

"Is it so hard to believe me when I tell you that I'm sick and tired of losing and I want more than anything to be a winner?"

"Yeah, I know what you mean. A bad pitch can cost you."

"I never killed a man, thank god, and I can't even imagine the hell you went through. I do know what it feels like to survive a four truck pileup on Route 66," he said, beginning to laugh. "It was booze sent me into that accident and the will to get off it that got me on my feet again."

"So I heard."

"Went through a year of damn painful therapy. They told me I'd never walk again. But I knew I would. I was determined to come back to your sister and my son, get a decent job, and make up for all the wrong I'd done them. Millie and I are good together. Now with the kid, nobody, not even you, is going to tell me my life isn't close to perfect these days."

"I hear Millie helped you get a job with a construction company," I said in a friendly manner. I was hoping to signal that I'd accepted his apology.

"Yeah, over the last few months, I've been hauling supplies to their building sites. They like my work and one of their backhoe operators just reitired. I'm going to put in a bid for his job." He took a deep and nervous breath and said, "I tell you, Jake, I'm up to proving to them and your sister that I've got the gumption and brains to bring home the bacon."

"You want to become a heavy equipment operator?"

"Sure as hell do," he said, turning on the ignition. "They make damn good money. And the way I hear it, where most might pass the written test to become a crane operator, there's few got the guts to climb the ladder to the operator's cab."

"I bet Millie believes you've got the guts."

"Truth is, I'm out to prove that I'm the rock she can build her life on."

"Just keep in mind, it's a bird of prey that's perched on that rock," I said, ironically thinking back to Jeffers' heroic poem and tragic marriage.

"I reckon you're right, considering the pecking order in any marriage," he admitted, laughing, while checking his rearview mirror and pulling into traffic.

I imagined Frank Bell to be a lot of things, but, after hearing his story, I knew he was no coward. If he didn't have the wit and intelligence to keep up with my sister, I was convinced he had the brains and strength to provide her and Charlie with a decent home and future.

Once we passed UC, I felt myself getting nervous. I hadn't been home in over a year. I knew Mom and Millie weren't all that happy about my seeming indifference toward family matters, over this time, considering how they'd been so attentive towards me when I was convalescing from my wounds at Letterman, Oak Knoll, and, eventually, my childhood bedroom. Especially Millie. Charlie was growing into boyhood and she wasn't a bit satisfied with my periodic phone calls and letters. Still, I think they both understood that it was taking some time for me to settle into living in L.A. What they didn't understand was my returning to my means of support that had served me so well before the war. To Mom and Millie, gambling was no way to make a living. It was only after this past successful year, of winning at high stakes games in Reno and Vegas, that I felt confident enough to return home and cash in on some bragging rights, and provide them with some proof that I wasn't in any danger of throwing my life away at a hazard of the die. They knew me to be as capable a poker player as Pop, and I even brought along my bank book as proof that I was saving a good percentage of my winnings each month. My determined thriftiness would go a long way in reminding Mom of the money Pop won playing late night, early morning poker games on the Matson Line cruise ships where he worked as a maître d'. She stashed that two grand in the Bank of America for close to 20 years. Then, using Pop's winnings plus the bank interest, they made a down payment on our new home in Oakland. It was a far cry from living in the tenderloin district off Market Street in Frisco.

We were within a couple of blocks of the house when I asked myself which of my siblings would have the most insight about how a sample of Pop's calligraphy could have been discovered at the scene of a murder. Tommy, my wildly curious younger brother, would definitely want to get involved and my older brother, Jimmy, would think I was crazy. My best bet was Millie, she'd be the most objective and helpful in solving the mystery.

We were moments away from Mom's when I thought about my unfortunate encounter with the Beats the night before. The nightmare hadn't even come to mind on the entire trip north. While I'd always imagined myself involved in a major literary movement, it obviously wasn't in Perkoff's gang of malcontents. Frank had just turned onto Rose Street and pulled into Mom's driveway when a thought came to mind. If I could actually find out why Pop's handwriting ended up on that note, I could take Cobb and Longdown up on their offer, then, eventually, try my hand at writing some decent detective fiction. Everything was starting to fall into place. Jeffers had it right, it was the 'lone wolves,' like myself, not the pack, that would survive to deliver the post-war literary goods.

We were getting out of the car when Mom, Tommy, and his fiancé, Theresa, emerged from the huge two-story wooden house. Mom was short, plump, and lovable as ever. She wiped her hands on her apron, held my face, and kissed me. There were tears in her eyes as she told me how wonderful it was to have me home. My handsome younger brother shook my hand and, giving me a manly pat on the back, turned to reintroduce me to his fianceé. Theresa was his lovely Italian American bride-to-be who'd been blessed with the most enchanting smile and infectious laugh. I embraced her and kissed her on the cheek.

As Frank grabbed my suitcase from the back seat, he followed as we all walked into the house. There, standing in the living room, was Millie with four-year-old Charlie neatly dressed in his sailor suit outfit.

"Say hello to your Uncle Jake."

"Hello, Uncle Jake," he said, extending his hand to me.

"You're a big boy now," I replied, shaking his hand.

"Today is my mommy's birthday; did you bring her a present?"

"I sure did, but I'll leave that surprise for later." Walking over to my suitcase, I opened it, took out a signed baseball, and handed it to Charlie. "It's signed by all the main lineup of the Hollywood Stars, including their manager."

"Wow!" He gasped and turned to his Uncle Tommy. "The Stars are in first place!"

"Yeah, but not for long," protested my brother, a lifelong Oaks fan.

"You'll have to get used to it, Theresa," warned Mom. "This home is nothing but a house of games, wagers, and bets."

"Just like mine," she said, laughing that wonderful laugh.

I walked over to my sister, Millie, and gave her a long, loving embrace.

"Welcome home, gambler," she whispered in my ear.

After informing me that we were having my favorite dinner (her incomparable wine and garlic marinated pork, vinha d'alhos), Mom suggested that I take my suitcase upstairs to my room and settle in. Frank insisted that he carry my bag and zipped ahead of me like some obedient bellhop in a posh Frisco hotel.

By the time I reached the top of the stairs, he'd already entered the room, placed my suitcase beside the bed, and was standing next to the open door. Between the cabbie and bellboy routine, it was obvious that I was entering my old familial digs under the auspices of Frank Bell's contrite gestures of friendship.

"I guess it ain't changed much," he said.

"No, not much at all," I answered, looking around the bedroom that my mother and sister had turned into a spotless corner of the earth in preservation of my youth.

"I just want to say that it's great to have met you at last. God willing, next time you visit Millie and me, we'll have our own place."

"God willing," I said.

He closed the door and left me to the silence of the room where I dreamed my youthful dreams. I would leave this magical place for the harsh reality of life at sea and survival in war. But here I was again, amidst the memorabilia that I'd gathered between my 11th and 16th year. The junior high and high school banners on the walls, baseball and football trophies on the shelves, and autographed photos of many of the Oakland Oaks stars from the '20s and early '30s on the bureau. All as I'd left them when I escaped Longdown and my old man. I looked across the room and saw, on the window sill, my old glove and the ball I threw the day of my perfect game. That day, I struck out Cookie three times.

I put my hat on one of the posts of my bed and walked to the bookshelf. There, on the bottom shelf, piled from left to right in the order of my gradual maturing interests in worldly things, were my Boy's life, The Modern Boy, and Saturday Evening Post magazines.

I walked to the window and picked up my old glove and baseball that had been sitting on the ledge for years. I put on my glove and pounded the old ball into it, several times over. After a moment, I went through the eight grips that I once believed were going to take me all the way to the Big Show. I hoped to be the first in the history of the game to master all possible pitches, throwing them faster and better than anyone before me. I had imagined myself gifted enough to change the game of baseball into a pitcher's game.

Through the bedroom window, I looked down on to the backyard garden. The apricot tree that had been there long before we moved into the house was old and gnarled. I could see that it was still bearing fruit, the memory of its fragrance was something I'd carried with me through the worst of times. I thought of my last talk with Pop before I shipped out for the Pacific. We were sitting together under that tree; it was at the height of its bloom just before the fruit appeared. On that beautiful late spring California night in '42, there was part of me, deep within, that didn't want to leave for fear that I wouldn't come back. "Your mother, your sister, and your brothers, they're the saints of this house," said this little man with the round brown Inca face. "But you and I, we've seen the dark one's world for what it is. Considering the games I've taught you and your years at sea, you are entering the worst of the devil's world well prepared. Still, you must never forget the saints. From them, we have both learned to draw a line between ourselves and evil. Our Lord will be with you, my son. You'll survive this war a better man."

There was a knock at the door. "It's Tommy," he said, entering the room. "I know you're only here tonight and tomorrow, so, would you like me to drive you over to Pop's and Jane's graves, since we have over an hour before dinner?"

I didn't hesitate. "Sure, give me a minute to change."

We walked downstairs and told Mom where we were going. There were tears in her eyes when she said, "It's a good thing to visit the graves of those who loved you so much."

On the drive over to the graveyard, Tommy started up about how he was sure that the Oaks were going to give the Stars a run for their money. Knowing that the conversation was only going to lead to Tommy chastising me for becoming a Stars fan, I decided to get off the subject.

"You know, I had a brief conversation with Billy and Cookie when they were in town playing the Stars last week."

"No kidding," he said.

"Billy asked about you. He wondered if you were still playing and said you were the best shortstop he'd ever worked a double play with in winter ball."

"Billy was nice to have said that."

"And that's coming from a guy who's never been known to be all that nice."

Tommy laughed and said, "I remember one afternoon when some guy had been heckling Martin from the stands all through the game. It must have been the top of the 7th; Billy called time, walked from second base to the fence that separated him from the stands, and invited this jackass to meet him after the game."

"And did the guy stick around?"

"Hell no. He snuck out in the stretch. No matter what he thought of Billy as a second baseman, he wasn't fool enough to stick around and get the crap beat out of him."

"With Billy's mom rooting her son on," I said, laughing.

The summer hours of the graveyard went till 8 p.m. We drove through the gate around 7:45. Even in the twilight, Tommy knew exactly where to find the graves.

We got out of Tommy's '41 Ford coup and walked up the hill to Pop's grave. Mom had given us some flowers to place there. Sadly, this was the first time I visited my father's or Jane's gravesite. Pop had passed away when I was still in the Philippines. I guess with all that I was going through, I never got up the courage to face the reality that he was gone forever. Jane's grave was another question altogether.

In the twilight, with the sound of crickets in the air and the slightest warm breeze drifting up the hill, Tommy and I said an Our Father and Hail Mary in unison. After a long pause, I recalled Pop's last words to me before I went off to war and I couldn't help but smile. Yes, I had survived, hopefully a better man.

Tommy handed me the bouquet of flowers that Mom wanted me to place at Jane Ferrera's grave. "I'll meet you in the car," he said, knowing that I'd like some time alone. He headed down to the gravel road at the bottom of the hill.

I knew exactly where to find the Ferrera's family plot. I'd been present at Jane's father's funeral in '39. Walking to my left, I descended the hill and eventually found her grave.

Jane was the girl I was going to marry when I returned from sea in '37. She was the girl I met in high school and the love of my life, who I mentioned to Jeffers that day overlooking Big Sur. She died of pneumonia in '45, right after I'd been wounded in Cebu. Millie and Mom didn't tell me of her passing until I was recovering at Letterman.

I kneeled down at her grave and crossed myself. Remembering the tunes that we danced to at our Senior Prom, I thought about how we had longed to make love, but never did. How frustrated she was when I told her I was going to sea; how cruel I'd been not to have married her in those few years that separated my return and the start of the war. I recalled us seeing *Wuthering Heights* together and how she cried when Cathy died. Then, I thought about our last goodbyes and our last kiss. How beautiful she was with her raven hair and green eyes. I placed the flowers on her grave and wept.

By the time Tommy and I got back home, my older brother Jimmy had arrived. He informed us that my sister-in-law, Sofia, couldn't make it. Their girls were down with summer colds and she didn't want to chance a sitter. She sent her love to all of us.

Shaking hands with Jimmy was always humbling. He had the firm, calloused grip of an honest craftsman that came nothing short of shaming my soft-palmed shake of a cardsharp. Even my hardened trigger-finger had lost its edge.

"What's up, Jake?" he asked, with that wise, indifferent smile that always spoke volumes to me.

"What else but the house limit and the sky, Jimmy."

He laughed and hugged me the same way he did after I pitched my perfect game and the day I returned home from the war.

Mom's dinner that night was really something special. In addition to her perfectly marinated vinha d'alhos, there was Linguica sausage and a pot of sweet, bacon-laced baked beans.

The talk around the table dealt with catching up on each other's lives. What was news to me was that Jimmy and Tommy were about to start a business together. After Tommy had returned from a stint in the Navy, Jimmy encouraged him to take up carpentry. Presently, they both worked for a cabinetmaker in Alameda. Having saved some money over the last few years, they were about to open a wooden windowframe shop. I wished them both the best in their new endeavor. Of course, I wasn't about to utter a word about the possibilities of my new job offer with the LAPD. That information I was saving for Millie at a private moment.

The meal ended with the opening of a second bottle of port. Moments later, we all went off in different directions returning with our birthday presents for my sister. Somebody turned off the lights and Mom entered with the three-layered, white-frosted birthday cake she had baked for Millie. It was topped by six candles, representing five years each, forming a circle around a single candle. We sang "Happy Birthday" and Millie blew out the candles. Little Charlie rushed to be the first to present his gift. He had made her a birthday card and bought a comb at the five and dime. Jimmy gave her a beautiful yellow and blue shawl that Sofia had knitted. Tommy and Theresa bought her Sinatra's latest 78, and Frank had gotten them two tickets for the Ice Capades. Mom bought her some new garden tools and I gave her a first edition of John O'Hara's *Rage to Live.*

The title, of course, got a laugh. If there was ever a woman with a rage to live, it was Millie. She put her arms around me and gave me a big kiss on the cheek. I got the feeling that mine was the best present of all.

After dinner, Jimmy said it would be best if he got back to Sofia and the girls. I wished him luck on his business venture, and he whispered in my ear, "Talk it up with Tommy, OK. He's still a little apprehensive, with his marriage coming up and all."

"Let me think about that," I said. Frankly, I wasn't anxious to influence a business deal 400 miles from my current address, even if it did involve my brothers.

After we got Charlie to bed and I promised to take him to his "first movie ever" the next afternoon, we all went into the kitchen and washed the dishes. After that,

Theresa said her goodbyes because she was going to an early Mass in the morning with her mother. Tommy walked her home, which was only a couple of blocks away. As soon as he got back, Millie brewed some Maxwell House, and the four of us sat down for some rounds of casino. If I was the poker player of the family, Millie was the whiz at casino. Her building and calling combinations were nothing short of daggers through the heart of any opponent. Even with Tommy (no slouch at any game of cards) and I partnering up against Millie and Frank, who I saw couldn't count cards if his life depended on it, the two of us were down three games before we knew it. To avoid any further embarrassment, Tommy yawned and said he was going to hit the sack and catch the end of the Oaks game on the radio. Frank retired to the living room where Mom was listening to music. As for myself, I thought I'd take a moment in the backyard.

"I need to take in a little of that delicious fragrance of apricots," I said, casting a glance at Millie.

"Just like old times, Jake," she said.

"You got it."

I hadn't been outside five minutes when Millie joined me on the red brick path that encircled the apricot tree. Ever since we were children, the garden had always been the place where my sister and I shared our secrets and gave each other intelligent and loving advice.

"So what ever happened with that psychology prof over at the Cal?" I asked.

"Philip?"

"Don't tell me there was more than one."

"Philip isn't the father of my child."

"Of that I'm sure."

"And besides, the money I'm making at Penny's combined with the money Frank's making in construction, well, we're earning ten times more than what Philip and I could have ever made."

"That's my little sister, always ahead of the game and counting the cards."

"Frank and I are going to make a go of it."

"Yeah, I had a good talk with Frank. I think the three of you are going to be just fine."

"I'm so proud of him. He even sold that palomino his cousin always kept for him over at Redwood Canyon. He got a good price for it."

"Mom said that horse meant a lot to him."

"He never raised a hand to it, I can tell you that much."

"I had a few choice words for Frank on that shortcoming."

"You don't have to worry about him hurting me anymore. He's off the booze. I tell you, he's a changed man. But, it's always good to know you're there when I need you."

"I'll always be there for you, Millie."

"And I'm always here for you." Millie took a pause and I heard her audible sigh. "Still hustling your behind between Hollywood and Vegas?"

"If you want to know the truth, I'm thinking of changing careers."

"Really?"

"I'm actually thinking of becoming a cop."

"You've got to be kidding me!" She laughed.

The whole family knew about my part-time job with Cobb; all I had to explain to Millie was what happened last Sunday. I gave her a few details about the murder, the possibility of the involvement of a Fifth Column of Nazis, and named the Chief of Homicide. I explained that

Longdown and Cobb had offered me the job as liaison between the Stars and LAPD in the investigation.

"Not the Rotarian from hell!" she laughed.

"Just my luck, right!"

I left the piece de resistance, concerning the crime scene, till last. When I mentioned the calligraphy on the strip of paper bag being Pop's, Millie argued, "That's impossible! Are you absolutely sure it was his?"

"As sure as daylight's not candlelight," I said. "You know, as well as I do, that Pop had been writing in his own distinctive style of calligraphy ever since he was an alter boy in Peru."

"Pop was strange and damn conservative, but he was no Nazi!"

"I agree. Somehow, the murderer had to have gotten hold of this oblong strip of paper bag where Pop wrote 'Begin with this one.'"

"What could that possibly mean, Jake?"

"Well, at the murder scene, it seemed to imply that this was only the beginning of a series of murders. But I have no idea what it meant to Pop when he wrote it. I was hoping you could shine some light on that."

"Obviously, we can only know that once we know why, and to whom, he'd written the note."

Millie was deeply troubled and confused. I ended our intense conversation with the caveat that she was not to share this information with the rest of the family. She agreed.

That night, in the familiar darkness of my adolescence, as I was falling asleep clutching my old baseball, I kept going over the eight major grips for throwing a ball: two seamer, four seamer, slider, cutter, curve ball, change-up, sinker, knuckle ball. As I drifted off, I thought about the strange coincidence of the 108 stitches on a baseball and the 108 positions in Tai Chi Quan. Angel always argued that this was no coincidence but evidence of the eternal relationship of man's internal soul and God's external cosmos, reflections of the same cycles of life and death.

I had a feeling, whether I found myself gambling my life away or entering upon the dangers of law enforcement, these cosmic insights would eventually be applied to some practical understanding of the world around me. Frankly, I was beginning to lean toward the latter. Unfortunately, this momentary preference wasn't about to amount to a hill of beans unless I came up with some clue as to how in hell my father's calligraphy found itself next to a corpse in a Hollywood bungalow owned by the inventor of the irresistible Cobb salad.

The next morning, I went downstairs and was greeted by Mom in her kitchen. She had cooked up some morcella blood sausage paddies. She offered them to me topped with two over-easy fried eggs. Here was a Portuguese breakfast that I'd honestly missed. I dug right into it.

Tommy and Millie were at church. Frank and Charlie were in the garden playing catch with a softball. I asked Mom what time we'd be leaving for the movies. She said it would be after Charlie's nap in the late afternoon.

"That's perfect; I was thinking of taking the ferry over to Frisco this morning."

"And what could you possibly be up to in The City?" she asked, with one of those all- wise gypsy stares of hers.

"I thought I might visit some of the guys still laid up in Letterman."

"Now that would be very honorable of you."

"When Tommy gets back from Mass, I'll ask him if he can drive me over to the…"

Falling into her native Hawaiian pigeon English, as she often did when she was angry, she asked, "You are sure it's not you want to sniff around O'Farrell Street for a Sunday quicky?"

"Come on, Mom."

"You picked up some bad habits going to sea so young."

"Yeah," I confessed, knowing the cat was out of the bag. "I guess I'm lucky it only remained a habit."

"You remember the madam, Mary Cross?"

"Sure, she ran a real spic-and-span parlor house over on Larkin. You used to wash and iron her sheets."

"And got a pretty penny for it," she recalled, taking a deep breath. "She passed away six months ago."

"Sorry to hear that."

"Last time I talked with her, she said the cops are really cracking down, now that the war's over."

"No more tenderloin cuts for the beat cops on *Taylor Street*," I said, laughing up my sleeve.

"Some fine example you are, promising Charlie that you're taking him to the motion picture show and you wind up getting arrested by some vice cop moonlighting on a Sunday."

"Oh, by the way, Hilo sends his love."

"Now, there's a man you wouldn't find in a whorehouse."

"All right Mom, I'll haul in the anchor," I promised, finishing off her unbelievably tasty morcella.

As I walked up the stairs, I couldn't help but think about the great woman who just happened to be my mother. She could see through anybody and was sharp enough to cut through a lie as thick as a porterhouse steak. She'd gone through a lot with my old man's womanizing. All those high-end poker games, at the Fairmont Hotel atop Nob Hill, with Pop dressing to the nines and sporting the pseudonym of Lanzon Chavin. On a great night, he brought home some damn good extra cash for our family, but when those big time games lasted well into the next morning, Mom knew what he was up to. She would chainlock all the doors and go to bed. Pop got the idea all right. Nothing worse than a satiated dick on a cold, damp Oakland morning in winter. I often wondered why she put up with him. But then, all of us had to admit there was something unforgettably mysterious and irresistibly charming about this half-breed master of cards, who was our father. For me, there was always the question of why he insisted on changing his name when he went to play cards for money. It was only years later, on shore leave in the Peruvian port of Chimbote, that I got the full dope on Pop's poker appellation, Lanzon Chavin. An old salt, with the same flat round face as his, told me the story of the legendary city, high in the Andes, that the natives of the Ancash region called Chavin de Huantar. These locals believed this site (still untouched by archeologists) was the very spot where all the civilizations of South America began. It even predated Machu Picchu. It was on this spot where all the high priests from the surrounding tribes brought their decoratively carved conch trumpets. They gathered around a central stela they called their Lanzon and jammed to the heavens in the name of the beautiful and natural things that surrounded them. Pop, no doubt, heard of this mythical place and decided to pick-up on some of its magical powers by playing poker under the spell of its name.

Pop's youthful fascination with Chavin de Huantar also accounted for his prized conch shell that still sits on an end table in Mom's livingroom. He carried this sacred instrument – Strombus Pututus – with him from his boyhood in Lima to his adventures as a card hustling maître 'd on the Matson Lines. Between the Islands and the Mainland, he met Mom. He even brought this heirloom, carved in images of Inca kings, with him when they married and settled in Frisco.

Since his death, despite any of her misgivings about her relationship with my old man, every morning and night, Mom has prayed to the crucifix above her bed for Pop's soul. She continues to do so in the belief that he is suffering in purgatory for all his misdeeds. Frankly, I can't imagine anything less on both their parts.

I stayed in my room, all morning into early afternoon, reading from my old copies of Boy's Life.

Around 2, I went downstairs and listened, along with Tommy, to the first few innings of the Oaks doubleheader with the Padres. The rookie, Jensen, hit a two-run homer in the top of the third, putting Oakland on the board. Tommy reminded me that Jensen and Martin, two of the best young players in the PCL, were the reasons why the Oaks were going to catch the Stars before the season was out.

It was a little before 3 when Charlie came down from his nap and asked if I was going to take him to the movies.

"Sure, what type of movie do you want to see?" I asked.

"A cowboy movie."

"Well then, a cowboy movie it is."

"There's a gangster movie with Barry Sullivan playing at the Gateway on San Pablo," suggested Tommy.

"What about the United Artist?"

Tommy checked the *Tribune*. We were in luck. The UA was featuring John Wayne in *Stagecoach* and a sneak preview of a brand new western he was starring in.

"You know, I think I got a good idea of just what that new western might be," I said.

"What is it, Uncle Jake?"

"I'm going to let *that* be a surprise. Come on, let's go. My treat."

Millie and Frank were house hunting, so it would only be the three of us. We hopped into Tommy's Ford and drove over to the United Artist on Shattuck. This was the perfect giant palace of a movie theatre for a kid like Charlie to experience his first film.

Stagecoach was ten years old and in black and white. *She Wore a Yellow Ribbon* (the film I thought would be the preview) was in Technicolor and had Wayne playing a role 20 years older than the one he played in *Stagecoach*.

I was trying unsuccessfully to remember my first film. I did my best to imagine what was going on in my nephew's mind. I could see that he was spellbound and cast into that moving, living dream that no other century had offered humanity. As soon as the giant screen encounter had concluded, Charlie was so thrilled that he asked to see the whole thing all over again. One hell of an art form, the movies.

On the drive home, Charlie couldn't stop singing the theme song from *She Wore a Yellow Ribbon*. "Ta tum, ta tum, she wore a yellow ribbon, she wore it for her lover who was in the Calvary."

That night, Mom served up the leftovers from the vinha d'alhos, always better the second time around. This sumptuous repast was preceded by one of Mom's own creations, a soup she called azordra. Roughly translated as "ambrosia from the Azores," it's a hot broth of garlic, coriander leaves, mint leaves, olive oil, topped with a poached egg.

After dinner, we all washed and dried the dishes. Charlie thanked me, with hugs and kisses, for taking him to the movies, and Millie took him upstairs to tuck him in. Frank excused himself and said he was going to listen to the nightly news on the radio. Mom, Tommy, and I walked out to the screened in back-porch to chat for the first time since I arrived.

By the time Millie came downstairs to join us, we were deep into a conversation about Pop's last year of life. He had passed away in the winter of '43, while I was still fighting in the Pacific. Ever since '45, when I came home, I couldn't recall us ever getting together to discuss his heavy drinking and how it contributed to the diabetes that finally killed him. We had a lot to talk about. From his insistence that "We ONLY speak English in our house, no Spanish or Portuguese, because we're Americans!" to his strange and bizarre ritual of blowing his conch shell each year, in the early morning hours of the spring equinox – Pop was quite a guy. Yes, he was!

We were all enjoying our nostalgic look at Pop's life until Tommy mentioned how sad he'd been that I wasn't present when Pop passed away.

"What could I do, Tommy? I was off serving my country, just like you did a few months after Pop died."

"You know, just like both of you, Pop served his country, too," Millie said.

"That's right, I remember you writing to me that he was an air raid warden."

"He was so proud to walk around the neighborhood making sure everybody kept their lights out at night," added Millie.

"But he did more than that," said Tommy.

"Like what?" I asked.

"Like stumbling onto a Nazi spy!" Tommy blurted out.

"That's right. That shoemaker, Hoffmann!" said Millie, her eyes lighting up like a thousand-watt klieg light in the cold dark of a wine cellar.

"What exactly happened?" I asked Tommy.

"Pop was always suspicious of this guy, Hoffmann. Not just because he was German, but, more so, because he was a latecomer to the neighborhood. So, on one of his nightly rounds, Pop took a short cut through the shoemaker's backyard, and as he's walking toward the street in his driveway, he hears a clicking sound coming from Hoffmann's house. He thinks he recognizes it and puts his ear to the side of the house. Pop learned Morse Code during his years at sea. Sure enough, Hoffmann's tapping out a message to some Jap sub off the coast."

"Always taking risks, your father," complained Mom, knitting in the corner of the porch.

"So Pop reported this guy?"

"Came right home and called the FBI."

"But they didn't get to Hoffmann's place in time. The Nazi must have seen Pop snooping around his driveway. By the following afternoon, he'd already flown the coop," said Millie.

"I don't remember a shoemaker named Hoffmann," I said. "I remember Losey's shoe repair over on San Pablo…"

Tommy thought for a moment. "This Hoffmann showed up sometime in '42. He set up shop in the basement of his house over on 56th Street."

"He was a good shoemaker," said Mom.

"Yeah, but more than a simple shoemaker, Mom," insisted Tommy. "I always figured there was something going on with this guy like he was working below his skill level. I mean, every time I walked into his shop he was reading something."

"What kind of something?"

"Manuals. Engineering manuals, to be specific; some of them were in German."

"You think this Hoffmann…," interrupted Millie, looking in my direction.

I shot her a look with the intensity of a ray-gun that could have bored through her head.

"And, not only that," continued Tommy, "it was like he was organized to the point of disinterest."

"What do you mean by that?" I asked.

"He'd have you write down the instructions for what you wanted repaired on these oblong strips torn from the brown paper of a grocery bag."

"Or, which pair of shoes you needed to be done first," added Millie. She wore the triumphant smile of her favorite girl detective, Nancy Drew.

"Exactly," agreed Tommy.

There it was, clear as day, the connection between Pop's calligraphy and this Fifth Column of murderous Nazis.

"Tell Frank, if he's finished listening to the news, I'd like him to join us on the porch," I said to my little sister.

"Will do, Captain Jake," she said, saluting me before she went inside.

"What's up, Jake?" asked Tommy.

I didn't answer and remained silent, staring out onto Mom's garden like some pensive general about to make a significant statement the night before the beginning of a grand campaign.

Once Millie and Frank came outside, I told everyone about Cobb and Longdown's offer for me to act as liaison between the Stars and the LAPD. I described the murder, the threat from the Fifth Column of Nazis, and the bizarre presence of Pop's calligraphy at the scene of the crime. I explained how I questioned taking the job, but now after learning the connection between Hoffmann and Pop's calligraphy, I'd decided to take it. "None of you can breathe a word of this to anyone," I warned. They all fervently swore they wouldn't tell a soul.

Mom, Tommy, and Millie were overjoyed that I'd decided to turn my life around and grab onto the possibility of a legitimate career. Furthermore, Millie was thrilled with her clever deduction about the way Pop's calligraphy ended up at the murder scene. "As I see it, Hoffmann, despite being a Nazi, was a craftsman. He must have appreciated the artisanship of Pop's handwriting and wasn't going to just toss it away. No, he kept it because he saw it as a thing of beauty. Then, when he realized that this elegant handwriting belonged to the same man who was the air raid warden walking in his driveway that night, catching him redhanded sending a message to his comrades, he held on to it. He was determined to use it against his sworn enemy when the time presented itself."

Even Frank threw in his two cents of well wishing. "Damn, Jake, sounds like we're on the same track, bound for glory and travelin' to the same destination."

"How's that?"

"If it's time I give up my beautiful palomino, it's time you give up your poker."

"Can't help but agree with you there, Frank."

"I bought my palomino from a Comanche. You know what his name was?"

"The Comanche?" I asked.

"No, the horse. Taibo Tatsinupi."

"What does it mean?"

"Star Soldier. The Comanche who sold him to me said, 'Let women follow the moon and men the sun, but those at sea or atop a horse follow the stars.'"

The next morning, when I said my final goodbyes, Charlie was still singing *She Wore a Yellow Ribbon* and wondering when I was going to visit again to take him to the movies. Tommy assured Charlie that, in my absence, he'd take him to the movies every weekend. With Frank ready at the wheel to drive me to the Clay Street Ferry Pier, Millie pulled me aside for a last word.

"You remember Eephus Pitch?" she said.

"How the hell could I forget the man who coached me to my perfect game. The man who changed his first name from Ethan to match the pitch he was famous for in the Negro League. Is he still playing chess at the Oxford Street entrance to Eucalyptus Grove over at Cal?"

"Every day from eight to six, 25 cents for beginners, 50 for intermediates, and a buck for those who think they know their ass from a scholar's mate." She took a pause and said, "It just crossed my mind that Eephus lived right across the street from Herr Hoffmann."

"That's right, I remember he lived on 56th Street."

"I thought I'd run over to Cal and ask Mr. Pitch if he remembers anything about this infamous German shoemaker of ours."

"Hell of a good idea."

We kissed and embraced. Mom gave me a final hug, then Frank drove me to the Clay Street Pier. Heading south on the Daylight, I knew damn well what I had to do when I got home.

The minute I arrived at Carrol Canal, I called Cobb and told him I was accepting the job.

Chapter VI

Murder in a Winning Season

By 10 a.m., Tuesday, Angel left for work and Hilo went to rehearse with a band member across town. About an hour later, Longdown and Richie Goodman arrived at the bungalow to administer and witness my oath of deputation. That done, the Colonel presented me with an LAPD-issued Smith and Wesson .38 snub-nosed Special with shoulder holster. Having used their Victory Model .38 on my Military Police shore patrols in Hawaii, I felt like I was shaking hands with an old friend who lost about six ounces of weight and four inches off its barrel. Longdown presented me with a badge and reminded me that this honorable accoutrement was no joke, only to be flashed at proper moments. Lastly, I signed the license to carry a firearm and was given my permit.

These formalities concluded, they both had smiles on their faces. "Cobb thought he'd throw in something to sweeten the pot," said Longdown, opening the backdoor of the bungalow. He and Richie led me outside into the alley. Richie mischieviously whispered to me to close my eyes. Taking me by the arm, he guided me several steps and then told me to open them. There, parked in the alleyway, sat a sparkling, just like new, sky-blue 1940 Plymouth convertible coup.

"Cobb bought it off a down-on-his-luck Chi-town hood he met at the Troc one night during the war. It's been in his ten-car garage ever since," said Longdown. "He figured you could make some damn good use of this little beauty."

"Certainly a notch above a refurbished prowl car," I said, lifting my eyebrows in Richie's direction.

"All right, halfback, you don't have to rub it in," laughed Richie

With that, Longdown changed the subject and told Richie to wait in the squad car; he wanted a word with me alone.

When Richie handed me the keys to the Plymouth, I promised, "We're going to find time to get together."

"Absolutely, we've got a lot of catching up to do."

"For sure."

"Welcome to the Force, Jake," said Richie. We shook hands.

Inside, we sat at my desk. Longdown reached into his breast pocket and handed me a piece of folded paper with the names of two individuals, their addresses, and the questions I was to ask them. First person was Howard Story's roommate, Sidney Upton. He had previously been questioned by a couple of detectives in Longdown's homicide division about the possibility that Story's death had something to do with the homosexual community in L.A. The officers who questioned him were not privy to the actual evidence at the murder scene. They were following through on the line of investigation, suggested by Longdown, that this was just another gay homicide in town. Their report came back stating that Upton was genuinely shaken up by Story's death. Seems they traveled here together from their mid-west hometown, both hoping to make it in Hollywood. Upton vehemently denied that he and Story were still lovers, insisting they were just the best of friends. Before coming to West Coast, they survived the intimidation and abuse of small minds in their small town; they were determined to leave together. Since he wasn't a suspect in the murder of his friend, the Colonel's questions for him, this second time around, were directed toward

Upton's knowledge of Story's activities outside of his sexual predisposition.

The second person of interest was Caesar Reich, a famous cinematographer from the silent era, who recommended Story to Cobb for the job over at Gilmore. Reich, who was in his early eighties and pretty much a daily fixture at the Brown Derby on Vine, had been known as a Nazi sympathizer in the '30s. He even went so far as to join the German American Bund for a short time. Reich's connection with Story was, most likely, coincidental. However, if there was any chance that he did possess knowledge of this Fifth Column, such information would prove vital in tracking down the murderer and solving the mystery behind the Column, itself.

At this point, I figured I'd best come clean with Longdown and tell him what I'd discovered about the calligraphic note left by the murderer. I began by asking him if he remembered how upset I'd gotten at the sight of the brown paper note. "Sure," he said, "but I figured you were just overwhelmed by the sight of murder a block away from the ballgame." I confessed that it wasn't the dead man that shocked me but the note that was written in the unmistakable hand of my father's calligraphy. At the time, I was certainly not capable of explaining why it was there, and I knew my best bet would be to hold off until my visit to Oakland. Perhaps someone in my family could shed some light on how my father's note could have possibly shown up at a murder scene. If I could get an answer to this enigma I would accept the job he and Cobb had offered me.

"That only makes sense," said Longdown, relighting his half smoked cigar.

I informed Longdown of Pop's midnight eavesdropping on Hoffmann, the German shoemaker. He was obviously a Nazi spy with orders to transmit information to Japanese submarines off the California coast. Despite my father contacting the FBI, Hoffmann was able to evade capture before they could apprehend him.

I explained that Hoffmann had a peculiar trait of demanding that his customers write any specific repair requests on oblong strips cut from brown paper bags. As it would happen, Pop brought in three pairs of shoes to be repaired. He had written 'Begin with this one' and stuffed his request inside the pair he needed within a day or so.

"Bingo," said Longdown enthusiastically. "Good work Jake; your old man would be proud."

"Thanks, Chief," I said, realizing these were the first words of respect I'd given him since our reunion.

"If this Hoffmann character is still in the States, we just might be able to link him to Caesar Reich. There's an FBI agent coming in from Washington within the next week or so. I'll make sure you two get together. He may be able to give us some information on Hoffmann."

"The Feds don't seem all that anxious to solve Howard Story's murder."

Longdown took a gigantic puff on his stogie. "Considering the possible source of the kid's murder, they no doubt see this investigation as a more drawn out situation."

The Colonel left me that morning with a firm handshake and "congratulations" on my decision to join the Force. Hell, before I knew it I'd be joining the Rotarians.

That afternoon, I called Cobb and thanked him for the Plymouth.

"Less than 10,000 miles on her," he said. "Have you taken her for a spin yet?"

"Not yet, but I've got these interviews that the Colonel gave me."

"Yeah, old Caesar Reich. There's a rare bird if ever there was one. He could have been one of the greatest cinematographers of the silent screen."

"So what happened?"

"He had a royal falling out with Adolph Zukor. Reich was one of the few conservative Hollywood Krauts who had a tough time getting along with the Jewish hierarchy in town."

"Obviously the reason he turned into a Nazi by the '30s."

"I suppose," responded Cobb.

"I understand he introduced you to Howard Story."

"Howard was Caesar's latest *protégée*. One afternoon, I saw them having lunch together at the Derby, and Reich introduced us. When the job came up over at Gilmore, I thought of him. You couldn't imagine a nicer kid." He paused. "Keep in mind," he continued, "the only reason you're re-questioning Upton is to get more dope on any old members of the Bund that Reich may have been in recent contact with. Story may have mentioned it to Upton."

I decided to change the subject. "So, what do you want me to do about my duties over at Gilmore?"

"Like I said, I've turned a couple of regular security into plain clothes men to circulate the park. But, you and your crew can still show up for a game whenever you want. Come to think of it, while you're chasing Nazis, I think it'd be a good idea if Angel took the lead on security at Gilmore, just in case anything serious comes up."

"That's a great idea. Angel's one hell of a good man."

"I take it you guys met up in the war."

"Fact is, we were merchant seaman together from '33 to late '36. As fate would have it, we ran into each other in the Philippines in '44. Angel was with a guerrilla unit on Mindanao. They fought side by side with us rooting out the Jap holdouts."

"I understand he's a bit of a genius with a knife."

"Oh, he's that all right."

"If you feel he can be trusted to keep his mouth shut, you'd best let him in on the situation. You never know, this damn Fifth Column of Nazis could show up at a game one night."

"How's it going with Haney and the boys?"

"We split a doubleheader with the Seals yesterday, and the Oaks are still hot on our tails."

"With Martin and Jensen in the lineup, they're bound to give you a run for the money."

"Once an Oaks fan, always an Oaks fan."

"No no, Boss," I insisted. "I'm 100 per cent with the Stars."

"One way or another, Jake, it's good to have a man of your character aboard, Oaks fan or otherwise."

"Good to be aboard, Boss."

"Watch yourself with Reich; he may appear to be nothing more than an old queen with a story of yesteryear, but the truth is, he's one of the slyest old foxes in town."

I laughed. "I'll keep that in mind when I interview Reich."

"Please do."

Before he hung up, Cobb reminded me that Haney and the team were not to be privy to the situation.

"Understood," I said.

He clicked off.

That night at dinner, with the caveat that they were not to tell a soul about what I was letting them in on, I informed Angel and Hilo of the circumstances that had developed in the last week: the murder, the existence of a

Fifth Column of Nazis in L.A., and my sudden induction into the LAPD. Although they both congratulated me on finally getting a grip on a career, Hilo expressed disappointment that I would no longer be gambling in Vegas affording him the pleasure of being with his favorite showgirls.

"Hey, look," I said. "It's not like I'm giving up poker. I'll eventually get some time off for a holiday and a good game of stud in Vegas."

For Angel, on the other hand, my venturing into law enforcement spelled excitement and a shot at the other portion of the globe he couldn't get his hands on during our time in the Pacific. When I told him that Cobb suggested he play top dog at Gilmore Field when I wasn't around, you'd think I had presented him with the Medal of Honor.

With the Twinks en route to Sacramento, for a seven game series with the Solons, there was no reason to head for the ballpark or catch the game on the radio. I suggested we all hop into the Plymouth Cobb gave me and take it for its inaugural cruising of the Sunset Strip.

"I was wondering who parked that convertible in our alley," said Hilo.

"A little added bonus for joining the Force."

With that, we all exited to the alley, put the top down on the Plymouth, and headed north for the Strip.

What a difference between our old Packard's shot suspension system and the smooth floating feeling of this Plymouth convertible. We picked up a six-pack of beer on La Cienega, turned the radio on to KLAC to hear Brother Harold Adamson "Laying down the hits," and drifted like some breeze-driven cloud toward the neon heart of Hollywood. On our way to the Strip, we recalled how the three of us became friends. I was in the hospital in Hawaii when Angel met Hilo playing a dive one night on Hotel

Street. He introduced us, and together they visited me everyday. At one point, Hilo and I convinced Angel to accompany us to the States. Once stateside, they continued to help me convalesce in the Bay Area. We talked about our choice of moving south from Oakland to L.A. and then pooling our funds to move to the Carroll Canal. Now, cruising in my Plymouth, in celebration of my newfound career, we marked yet another stage of our shared friendship.

After finishing off the six-pack and cruising the Strip, a couple of times over, we headed home singing along with the dramatic orchestration of Vaughn Monroe's *Ghost Riders in the Sky* coming off the radio. The intensity of the song brought to mind my brother-in-law Frank's palomino. I couldn't help but share the story of his beautiful stallion, Star Soldier, and how Frank had equated his selling of this treasured horse to my relinquishing of an addiction to gambling. Both of us were now on the straight and narrow.

Back home, Angel and I decided to practice our Tai Chi Quan and push-hands, canal-side, before hitting the sack. Because of his early morning rehearsal with a pickup band, Hilo headed upstairs for a good night's sleep. He momentarily stopped at the top of the stairs for a final word.

"So, how does it feel, Jake?" he asked.

"How's that?" I asked.

"How does it feel for a man who always believed he was above it all to find himself just a pawn like the rest of us?"

I'd never known Hilo to be so sarcastic, but I suppose my recent choice of a career brought something out of him that he held back all these years. I answered him as best I could.

"Ask me in a couple of months."

"Let me know and I'll write a song about it."

"I'll do that."

As Angel and I exited the double doors to the canal walkway, he asked, "Do you remember what I told you the true translation of Sun Tzu's *Art of War* was?"

"No what?"

"Sun Tzu's masterpiece *Bingfa* truly translates, "*The Way of the...*," he took a moment to phonetically replace his f sound for the proper p sound, "...Pa..wn. *The Way of the Pawn*."

After we finished our exercises, Angel went upstairs to bed. I stayed downstairs at my desk, nurturing a scotch and soda, contemplating the moonlit canal. After a moment, I reached into my desk drawer and pulled out my old brown and wrinkled hardball that I'd stealthfully lifted from my bedroom.

I moved reverently through the eight sacred grips. The fingers of my right hand feeling their way around the 108 stitches as my body had felt its way through the 108 positions of Tai Chi Quan. East meets West. I sipped at my scotch, stared out onto the canal, and put the ball back into the drawer. Hilo was right. No matter how much I imagined I was in control of my inner self and outer destiny, in truth, I was no longer the king of the hill or the dark knight of the poker table. By becoming a cop, I was no longer a amateur athlete or journeyman gambler but a mere pawn in the bigger game of life.

Lost to moonbeams twinkling on the canal, there came to mind a quote I'd recently translated from Lao Tzu:

"When I let go of what I am,
I become what I might be."

The next day, I drove to the address that Longdown had given me as the residence of Sidney Upton. It was a quaint duplex, nestled in a cul-de-sac off El Cerrito Place, a few minutes walk from Grauman's Chinese Theater on Hollywood Boulevard.

I rang the bell twice, waited, then knocked hard several times over. Nothing. I was about to cup my hands and have a look through the slight opening in the draperies when I heard the screen door of the adjacent portion of the duplex squeak open. I turned to catch sight of a pretty, overweight woman, in her 60s, with enormous sagging breasts and wearing enough makeup to keep Max Factor in business for a millennium. She called to mind a woman, about her same age, I ran into in a coffee shop on La Brea when I first arrived in Hollywood. Dressed in a tattered, beaded getup from the 20s, this dim witted old dame suddenly stood up, muttered something about having to call her agent, and ran over to the wall phone in the coffee shop. Apparently, she imagined hearing her representative say, "get over here right away before they give the part to Gloria Swanson." Suddenly, she darted out of the coffee shop, into the evening traffic, like some ghostly spark of a dream turned nightmare.

"You a cop?" grumbled the sister of lost dreams in a distinctive Brooklyn accent, a cigarette dangling from her sad, ruby red, crestfallen mouth.

Realizing that here was the first outright public recognition of my new status in life, I decided to savor the moment and play it to the hilt, "Yeah, I'm a cop, sugar."

"What da ya know from sweetness?"

I flashed my badge and said, "What do you know from cops?"

Having, no doubt, tolerated enough bad dialogue for a lifetime, she decided to move along to the reason she'd entered the scene in the first place. "If you're looking for Sidney, you just missed him."

"Have any idea of when he'll be back?"

"Oh, he's not coming back."

"How's that?"

"You have any idea how close he and Howard were?"

"Some."

"Poor kid was shattered by his friend's murder. Mind you, I'm not talking about their light in the slippers sexual thing. Hell, I've known enough of those so-called 'gentlemen' during my time in this town. No, I'm talking about how these two were real honest to God friends from childhood. Set out together from their hometown with nothing more than a pocket full of dreams."

"Like a lot of disappointed people in this burg, I suppose."

"You suppose right, copper," she said, staring through my sarcasm with all the menacing force of a .38 magnum pointed at my head.

"So where is he off to?"

"Left for Union Station about a half hour ago bound for New York City. I even gave him the address of a nephew of mine in Brooklyn."

"Thanks a lot, sweetheart," I said in a rather apologetic manner.

"Sweetheart, now that's better, much better."

I jumped in the Plymouth and headed toward downtown L.A. and Union Station. My only hope was that I would get there before the train pulled out of town.

As I turned off Los Angeles Street onto Marchessault, I noticed that what I'd read in the newspaper was true. The City had torn down the last remaining block of Old Chinatown that faced Plaza Square. Fook Wo

Lung's Curio Company and its adjacent Dragon's Den Restaurant and F. Sui One's Food Supply were gone forever. If I were to indulge my historical interest in L.A. architecture, I'd probably be saddened by the demolition of the first two story building in town, the Vicente Lugo adobe house, on the same block. But not being a historian or a tour guide, it was the Dragon's Den that stood out in my mind. Back in December of '47, I had bought a carton of century eggs there for a shared birthday feast. Since the end of the war, despite the fact that our birthdays were separated by a day, Angel and I always celebrated on the same day. Needless to say, what to most might have been an incidental purchase, proved for me a significant and memorable event. But that's another story for another time.

I found a space in the parking lot of the Union Station complex and hurried into the terminal. Rushing past the Art Deco information booth, I walked directly into the Grand Waiting Room. It was crowded with travelers leisurely awaiting their departures. Looking back momentarily at the information booth, I thought I might try to page Upton. I decided against it and started to walk down the center isle that separated the plush walnut lounging sofas on either side of the gigantic room. Though I didn't have a picture of Upton, I did have some idea of what his manner and stature might be. I was about to turn around and start back toward the terminal's entrance when I caught sight of a young man dressed in all white from his open cotton shirt to his high wasted pants and buffed shoes. He was returning from checking the departure board. Extremely effeminate, he was about as inconspicuous as a man in ballet tights lining up for rivets on a construction site. He sat down in the middle of one of the longer sofa chairs, checked his watch, crossed his legs, and went back to the movie magazine he'd been reading.

I walked toward the young man, I thought to be Upton, and silently stood in front of him. When he put down his magazine and looked me in the eye, I showed him my badge.

"Oh, for Christ's sakes," he hissed like some cornered alley cat. "Not another cop!"

"Leaving town, Mr. Upton?"

"The other two cops told me I was not a suspect in the murder of…," he put his right hand over his mouth and closed his eyes.

I sat down next to him and reassured him that he was right. He was in no way a suspect in his friend's murder. I told him there were just a few specific questions I had for him.

"Let me ask you a question, Officer….?"

"Salazar."

"Why is it, Officer Salazar, that every time one of my kind is murdered, the guilty party is always assumed to be one of our own?"

"Truth is, Sidney, as far as the murder of your friend goes, the department doesn't believe it was sexually motivated."

"Then why on earth did those cops go on the way they did?"

"I'm not at liberty to go into any of the details, but we do have a few more questions for you."

He took a deep breath and held it in. Closing his eyes, he briefly touched his right index finger to his forehead, exhaled, and folded his hands together. After a moment, he reopened his eyes and said, "Fire away!"

"To our understanding, a man named Caesar Reich introduced Howard to Bob Cobb. It was Cobb who gave him the job over at Gilmore Field. Do you recall how your friend met Mr. Reich?"

"I remember it specifically. We both met that old queen at a party in Beverly Hills. Howard was much more tolerant of the 'old folks' as we referred to them. Frankly, Reich gave me the creeps."

"Did Howard ever mention to you what Reich was like?"

"He told me he was an avid poker player and...oh, yes, Reich raised greyhounds that he raced somewhere in Mexico."

"Agua Caliente."

"Yeah, that was it."

"But he never mentioned any of Reich's old friends, somebody with extreme political points of view?"

"No. I don't recall Howard ever mentioning anything like that."

"And this party where you both met Reich. Who invited you and Howard?"

"All I remember is that Howard got the invitation."

So that was that. I stood up and thanked Upton for his cooperation. I wished him luck in New York.

"How did you know I'm going to New York City?"

"Your neighbor," I said.

"Of course, Miss Silverman. She's the kindest lady that Howard and I ran into in this lousy town."

Again, I wished him luck. Walking away toward the terminal's exit, I heard him calling to me.

"Wait a minute, I remember now! It was Howard's psychiatrist who got us the invitation."

I turned and walked back to where he was sitting. I stood directly in front of him. "Howard was seeing a psychiatrist?"

"Yes, he had this crazy idea that if he got to know himself better, he just might be able to fall in love with girls. It's all a lot of bunk if you ask me. I've never lived under such a delusion."

"Good choice, Sidney."

"I think so," he said smiling and brushing a miniscule speck of dark lint off his immaculate white slacks.

"So what's the name of this psychiatrist?"

"Oh, dear, I can't remember. Von…something, she was German. She practiced out of her home somewhere in the Hollywood Hills."

"Anything else?"

"She wasn't a Freudian. She was that other thing…a…"

"Jungian," I said.

"Yeah, that's it. She was a Jungian, whatever that's supposed to mean," he said, rolling his eyes.

The public address announcer called out the track numbers for all departures east.

"Well that's my cue," he said, tucking his magazine under his arm and picking up his small suitcase.

This time I shook his hand. I thanked Upton and told him he'd been a great help.

"You find that bastard who killed my dear friend."

"Oh, we'll get him all right."

There was a pause. He looked around the station as if he could see through its walls and onto the streets of the city that he and Howard Story had tragically chosen to make their home.

"Well, here I go," he said. Then he sang out, as if to draw the attention of those seated around him, "New York, New York, it's a *wonderful* town!"

"So I hear. Have a safe trip, Sidney."

He turned and made his way toward the departure gates. His campy short steps and high elbowed foppish stride drew stares and chuckles from those who were snuggled into their iconic sofa chairs of the great train station.

Of course, Upton's cynicism, regarding the possibility of any homosexual changing the nature of his sexual desires, couldn't help but make me think of Angel's efforts to do exactly that. If I wasn't aware of Angel's inner strength, I suppose I'd be more willing to accept the opinion of this sensitive young man whose fey exterior had caused him to suffer the indignity of being called a "flaming faggot" throughout his life. Aside from his lisp, Angel was a sleek and graceful panther of a man and could pass for any damn gender you might attempt to label him. At any rate, just as he'd done with Ginsberg, any judgment of him that was in direct opposition as to how he saw himself was thrown back at the accuser tenfold. Of course, if we're to consider all the types involved in this conundrum of appearances, there was Ginsberg, himself. Who was not in the least effeminate.

Before I left the station, I checked a phonebook for that von something-or-other that Upton mentioned. Sure enough, there it was, Dr. Eartha von Geist, 7920 Hillside Avenue.

When I got home, I called Longdown and gave him the details of my interview with Upton. I started with the fact that he had left town for New York City.

"No problem. Upton's in no way a suspect," he said, talking over the noise in his office. "Who knows, maybe the flit will do better in the Big Apple. Most of them do."

"He gave me a lead," I said. "It seems Story was seeing a psychiatrist by the name of Eartha von Geist on

Hillside Avenue. She invited them to the party where they met Reich."

He asked me to spell it; I did and added the doctor's address.

"What about my interview with Reich?" I asked.

"Cobb's setting that up. He tells me the old man's in Tijuana racing dogs, but he should be back by next week."

"Anything on Hoffmann?" I asked.

"I can't find anything on him in the FBI files. Nothing that's available to us, anyhow. I'll check the files for this psychiatrist, von Geist. Send over a few of our guys to interview her."

"What about Coleman in forensics?"

"He found a footprint of a workman's boot outside the open window."

"So, the assassin wasn't a suit. Maybe a gardener with a psychopathic grudge against baseball," I joked.

Ignoring my joke and wanting to get back to work, Longdown said he'd let me know when the FBI agent arrived from Washington. He hung up.

That night after dinner, Hilo, Angel, and I sat down to listen to Jack Sherman's play by play from the new Edmonds Field in Sacramento. The Solon's old stadium had burned to the ground a year ago. Due to the good fortune of a sizable increase in the owner's insurance policy, a couple of weeks before the fire, the stadium had been successfully rebuilt prior to opening day of '49. There's California state politics for you. No damn good reason to play with fire, but when it comes to the use of it as a source of progress, maintenance, and power, a discreet connection with your local pyromaniac has never gone against the grain of the more enlightened of civilized human beings.

After the game, Hilo and Angel left for a late-night double date with a couple of bar girls that Hilo had set up for them. This was Angel's first date with a woman in several years. When they left I wished him luck.

"Where there's a will, there's a way," insisted Angel, checking his railroad watch at the end of its short chain.

"Don't let this guy's chi move beyond his own good common sense," I reminded Hilo.

"I'll do the best I can," he promised. They both exited out the back door.

I poured myself a scotch and walked out to the porch. The moon was as full as the night before, its beams as playful and enticing. Sitting down at our small round porch table, and looking out onto the canal, I began to think about what I had just experienced over the last few days since my return from Oakland. Reflecting on my encounter with Upton that afternoon, it brought to mind the poignant conversation I had with the mysterious Dr. Wong, a couple of blocks south of the Station at Eddy See's Dragon Den. Again, another story, another time. I was wistfully recalling some of the details of the now demolished establishment when I caught sight of Aleksy making his way home along the towpath that ran parallel to our porch. He was, no doubt, returning home from the all-night coffee shop, on Venice Boulevard, that he often frequented for late night reading after his wife had gone to bed. Having taken to heart more quotable passages than women he'd taken to bed, his midnight assignations with the printed word proved to be his only acts of unfaithfulness over a lifetime of fidelity to his charming wife, Emilia.

Lost in his thoughts, a Life magazine under his arm, I hailed him over with an offering of a glass of port, which I knew to be his favorite.

"Yes, of course, Jake; that would be the perfect nightcap," he said, opening the gate to our small unattended garden.

I rushed inside and returned with a wine glass and the bottle of port. I poured the old man a handsome serving. He lifted his glass and I did the same.

He said, "To a better world than we have ever known!"

"I'll drink to that."

"It is more proper to say drink to yesterday, but *toast* to tomorrow."

"All right, I'll *toast* to that," I said, casually lifting my glass of scotch a second time

He hurriedly paged through his Life magazine dated July 11th. Finding the article he was looking for, he turned the magazine around to face me and said, "We must pray our beloved republic never turns to such means of terror by which one leader succeeds another." He pushed the magazine across the table for me to read. The headline read: *An Old Assassin Dies by Gunfire; Troubled Korea loses its Tiger.* The article reported the recent assassination of 73-year- old Kim Koo, nicknamed "The Tiger," by a young military officer with conservative leanings. Koo, an elder South Korean statesman who had been an active assassin during the war, sending many Japanese commanders to early graves, had, for some time, sided with the North Korean Communists. Our recent withdrawal of troops from South Korea seemed to have stirred fears in Washington that Koo's assassination indicated growing tension between northern Communists and the southern democratic capitalists based in Seoul.

I finished the article and looked up at Aleksy. Not wishing to mention that a couple of our Presidents had been assassinated, I said, "That's all we need is a world war in Asia."

"You have read Rousseau?"

"The philosopher?"

"Yes."

After all my years at sea, I'd learned it wasn't a good policy to answer honestly about my likes and dislikes. You can determine a lot about people by keeping your trap shut about yourself. "No," I said, "I've never been all that much into philosophy or poetry."

"In his famous treatise on democracy, *The Social Contract*," he began, as if suddenly cast into the middle of a lecture, "when he attempts to define sovereignty within a nation that has no king, he describes the supreme authoritative figurehead that rules such a republic in these words: 'It is in order not to become the victim of an assassin that one consents to die when one becomes one.'"

It could have been the buzz from the second scotch, but I was speechless. Staring at the old librarian, Rousseau's sentence went through me like a bullet to the heart, evoking all sorts of images, one upon the other. There was that kid, a sharpshooting deer hunter from Oregon, who'd survived MacArthur's island-crawl north. He was an ace sniper with an intuition and eye that enabled him and his deadly sweetheart to magically snatch Japs from palm trees at 300 yards. Closer to home, there was that blood oozing from Howard Story's neck and mouth.

"That's the reason I don't read philosophy, too many fucking imponderable sentences."

My senior intellectual was waist deep in political BS and shoveling ideas far above my boots and pay scale. I poured myself a third scotch, minus the water, and decided to change the subject.

"So, did you enjoy my party?"

"The most explosive poetry reading I've ever attended."

"You're right about that."

We both laughed.

"And that friend of yours…"

"Smitty Teste?"

"Very astute politically," he said, "though I fear much to the right."

"That, Aleksy, is as sure as four aces."

"Although, Smitty and I did agree that Alger Hess is as guilty as sin."

"Yes, but did you agree as to who's the best hitter between DiMaggio and Williams?"

"No, no, no, on that we did not agree."

From here, like some smooth pebble thrown playfully across the nearby canal, our discursive conversation skipped from one moon bathed, alcohol induced topic to the next. We finally came to rest upon the subject of architecture. It didn't take long before Aleksy began to become sentimental about how much he missed the medieval sites of his beloved Prague. I was right back at him, like some red necked drunk at a bar, with my own prejudicial passion for L.A. architecture.

"Ever had a close look at Union Station?"

"The train station?"

"That's the place."

"I passed through it when we first arrived in Los Angeles and, yes, it is a fine example of Art Deco. But to compare it to the great works in Europe, I don't agree. Prague is a magical place, and its buildings tell stories."

I began by explaining to him how, despite its Art Deco features and serving as a practical and functional edifice for transportation, Union Station was a modern enclosure subtly arrayed in a symbolic geometry of

Western spiritual history. American travelers, from different cultural backgrounds and religious upbringings, need only open their eyes to realize that all their traditions, cultures, and beliefs are present in its façade's geometrics and styles. I explained, "Union Station represents the present, the future, and the past as all great architecture does. You want a story, take a closer look at Union Station."

"You should write this stuff down," said Aleksy.

"And *you* should have another look at Union Station," I said, slurring my words a bit.

By one in the morning, as we were shaking hands goodbye, Aleksy told me to give my best to Hilo and Angel and promised me that he and Emilia would definitely have another look Union Station.

As the old scholar drifted and stumbled into the hazy dark of the moonlight, I couldn't help but question why my boozy conversation with Kowaczyk had ended on the subject of architecture, specifically the edifice of Union Station. Then I realized that in the back of my inebriated mind was the sight of that demolished block of Old Chinatown earlier that afternoon.

The next morning, with no more than a couple of hours sleep, I came downstairs for some coffee. Hilo was already up and cooking bacon and eggs.

"Would you like some?"

"Definitely, I'm starving. So how did the double date with Angel go last night?" I asked.

Hilo put his finger to his lips and pointed in the direction of Angel's bedroom upstairs.

"That good!"

"The boy's got what it takes."

"Like I always said, a real charmer from the get-go."

As we were finishing our breakfast, we heard sounds of an argument coming from Angel's room. We stared at each other. "Perhaps not all that charming," I laughed. The argument got louder and then suddenly we heard nothing. Two or three minutes later, the Polynesian knockout that Hilo set Angel up with came storming out of his bedroom. I recognized her from the party. While attempting to straighten her dress and hold on to her purse, she was cursing a blue streak in what I took to be Tahitian.

"Amura, what on earth is wrong?" asked Hilo.

"You tell your friend if he wants to play a dog looking for seconds, it's not through the backdoor he comes."

She turned and started out in a huff.

"Hold on, we'll call you a cab," I yelled.

"No, I can use a walk, and a long one at that."

Like some island whirlwind tearing through the palms, the displeasured beauty was out the door and into the alley.

I raised my eyebrows, smiled, and said to Hilo, "That's what comes from living in a world of infinite possibilities."

"I'll have a talk with the boy," said Hilo.

"You do that, Casanova. Remind *the boy* that sex on a first date, with a woman, doesn't guarantee all those infinite possibilities he had in mind."

"You should talk," he said, coming back at me.

"What the hell do you mean by that?"

"We ran into Leonor last night. She asked about you. She was disappointed that you never called her."

"Yeah, I suppose I've just had too many things on my mind."

"So, you admit you are just another case of a man plagued by his access to infinite possibilities."

"And you're not, I suppose?"

"Without a doubt, I am. The more women I gather around me, the better it gets. But, then again, I'm not like Angel or you. I'm not looking for someone in particular."

That afternoon, I drove into Hollywood to see if I could get some information on Caesar Reich. My destination was 6715 Sunset Boulevard. I caught Fairfax north and took a right on Sunset. I parked two blocks west of the Crossroads of the World then walked around the corner to the Hollywood Reporter.

The Hollywood Reporter had been the brainchild of a wiseguy from the East Coast named Billy Wilkerson. Back east, he ran nickelodeons, distributed silent films, and shared half interest with New York City's notorious mayor, Jimmy Walker, in His Honor's speakeasies. In the late 20s, he came west with the dream of starting a film studio. When that went belly-up, and he couldn't even get a mailroom job at any of the minors in town, he started a daily newspaper covering all the ins and outs of the "picture business." Since its inception in 1930, Billy Wilkerson has been the voice of the Hollywood Reporter. A towering kingpin and gatekeeper to Hollywood success, Wilkerson had even become the looming critical question mark above the heads of ruthless moguls, like Louie B. Meyer, sitting on their precarious thrones. The sovereignty of his personalized, Runyonesque judgments guarded the film industry's gates of celebrity like the muscle at the door of a gangland whorehouse.

A couple of years back, this spiffy, dandified, perfectly coifed provocateur openly attacked, what he believed to be, communist infiltration of the industry's trade unions. Billy argued that Stalin's surreptitious control of below the line union strikes was made possible by the endemic leftist politics in town and influential members of the Communist Party working in key positions in the studios. Together, they were undermining American capitalism's hometown for dreammakers. Billy's outrageous accusations were met by the average, middle of the road, red-blooded citizens of the Hollywood community as a plausibly correct and relatively justified political revelation. Others in town, on the left, mostly screenwriters and directors of the latest generation, looked upon his "naming of names" as the beginning of a political witch hunt. They were quickly proven to be correct. It didn't take more than a couple of months for Washington to reconvene the House Un-American Activities Committee, a Congressional gathering that had been originally formed to investigate both fascist and communist undertakings in the States. Wilkerson had opened a can of man-eating worms bloodthirsty for the lives and careers of some of Hollywood's most creative citizens. There were those in Hollywood who sensed a strange irony to Wilkerson's attack on workers below the line. His *Tradeviews* column, going all the way back to the Reporter's very beginning, had always sided with the workers at the crew and cutting-room levels over the bigwigs upstairs at the executive level. So, why did Billy suddenly turn on Labor when he'd always been out for the Chiefs of the studios? The wiseguys in town, with "nose" enough to reason out the meaning of such redolent paradoxes, called to mind the possibility that Billy was going after the communists because he wanted to leave the studios open to mob control. There was a rosy rumor that in the mid '30s, Wilkerson had headed up a mob-backed syndicate to extort money from the studio heads. The syndicate promised to quell any union strikes that might spread from a certain Chicago projectionist's union all the way to Hollywood and its mainline work force. While, for several years, the money was paid by the studio heads to the mob, averting any strikes emanating out of Chicago, ultimately, the Feds intervened. They were able to track a check written out to the corrupt union boss, Willie Bioff, by an old friend of Billy's, Joe Schenck, chairman of 20th Century-Fox. Word on the street had it that Schenck was in on the extortion scheme and receiving cash on the back end of the deal. Unlike all the other studio bosses, paying off the wiseguys threatening to turn off the fool's blood in Chi-town, Schenck was not only in on the scheme, but, along with Wilkerson and a mutual mobster friend, Handsome Johnny Rosselli, a mastermind behind the so-called Hollywood Syndicate. When Bioff decided to up the ante on his end of the deal, Schenck, realizing that his original take on the back end was turning into peanuts, decided to fold, spill the beans, and take it on the chin from the Feds. The rest is history. Joe and Handsome Johnny took the rap for Billy, and Schenck's enlightening testimony, that revealed the mob's control of the projectionist union in Butcherville, earned him a year in the pen. Billy's connection with his racetrack going pal, J. Edger Hoover, got it reduced to four months. In '45, President Truman pardoned both Schenck and Rosselli. Any attempt at defining some rule of law here, or semblance of justice, begs an inadmissible truth: the use of coercion in creating the threat of a union strike (extortion) or putting an end to them (armed military force or studio bosses' private security) is an accepted reality of our freewheeling and progressive democracy. When it comes to strong arming workers below the line, patriotic capitalists like publisher Wilkerson, moviemaker Schenck, and politician Truman are not above muscling in on union bosses or using force against strikers for *their* own benefit. However, it would seem that capitalists – right and left - do have a proprietary preference in livery; call it *appearances*.

They prefer their muscle well dressed in authorized army green or menacing pinstripes and spats. Nothing so extreme and politically uniform as Fascistic thugs in brown shirts or Bolshevik mobsters in red caps and leather jackets.

All said and done, whether it was payback to Hoover for getting his wiseguy buddies and himself off the hook for the Chi Town based extortion racket or not, the smart money had it that Wilkerson went after the commies in the unions to boost the circulation of THR. The promotion of this cause celebre was a sure way of reigniting the ire of his old enemies, the studio chiefs like Louie B. Mayer and others. Any way you cut it, Wilkerson's actions would prove to be money in the bank.

I remember Mom had a phrase whenever one of Pop's Rotarians decided to take a few steps deeper into the muck of Oakland city politics (this was in Portuguese of course): "It's best he knows where the devil carries his tail." Then, she'd bite down on the fingers of her left hand positioned horizontally across her mouth. That gesture complete, she'd cross herself.

As far as I'm concerned, Billy Wilkerson's an all right guy. One afternoon, about a year or so ago, between batting practice and a game, Cobb caught my poker act in the Stars locker room. He recognized my talent and skill, so he decided to stake me to a high-end game at Toluca Lake. I won big that night and impressed Wilkerson (his money was a greater portion of the pot) to the point of him bankrolling this horse to its first high-roller game in Vegas.

It was a bright, sunny California day, and I was clad to the nines, just in case I would run into Billy. I entered Wilkerson's sartorially-stamped, single doored, Art Deco, Regency Modern establishment, dressed in a white linen, cotton twill suit and dark-blue button down shirt, set off by an apricot yellow tie. My presidentially folded pocket square matched the tie, and my Borsalino Panama was both functional and stylish. The Hollywood Reporter's editorial offices, and on-site print shop, occupied the second floor of what was formerly Sunset House, Wilkerson's defunct high-end men's haberdashery. The exclusive boulevard level men's store had folded in '36, but it's sleek, polished, black and white marbled façade, replete with oblong display windows, gold-trimmed roof, and inset concaved approach to its noteworthy doorway, retained the inerasable and fashionable footprints of its former tenants. Once inside the massive, high ceilinged, pillared, and chandeliered gallery that branched right and left into the once occupied salons for Hollywood's well-dressed cliental, it wasn't difficult to imagine prissy salesmen scurrying about eager to please their well-heeled customers in hope of those 20 per cent gratuities at the end of a well-tailored suit. Wilkerson's showroom level of the building had remained unoccupied since '45. Only within the last year did he decide to refurbish an alcove space, that had once served as a reading room for those who were awaiting their alterations, into a reference library. THR's library contained all their back issues, an ever-growing number of showbiz biographies, studio pictorial catalogues, and the major encyclopedic reference books, technical and creative, pertinent to the history of Hollywood. Now reborn in the pensive, scholarly silence of a library, the alcove still seemed to echo the once pampering hush and sighs of elegant livery, while the gruff commands and mechanical rackets of the Fourth Estate carried on above. Tell me that ain't heaven on earth.

Once through the narrow gate I took an immediate left and entered the library. Since my success at poker, Billy had given me a free subscription to THR and carte blanche to its grand library. Jenny, the Reporter's librarian, and I were on the best of terms. She quickly provided me with the appropriate volumes of the *Encyclopedia of Productions* and the *Who's Who in Hollywood*. I found references to Caesar Reich in all of them. I was in the middle of jotting down some specifics in my pocket-sized notebook when I felt someone's hand on my shoulder. It was Billy. I noticed a glint in his mischievously enterprising eyes, an undeniable accentuation to that familiar wicked smile below his perfectly trimmed pencil moustache. Looking over my shoulder to see what I was reading, he took a big drag from his 14 karat gold Tiffany cigarette holder.

"So, the Colonel's got you investigating the grand old Kraut of cinematography, has he?"

"I suppose that same little bird told you the story about the rounder who chose to go straight?"

"Best damn poker player to hit Vegas in years and what do you do? You fold, cash in your chips, and decide to say *yes* to becoming a cop."

"There are worse *yes men* in the world," I pleaded.

"You got that right, kid. Most asslickers in town don't have the guts to carry heat."

"Good players make the best choices at the right time," I said.

"And, God knows, you were never one to bluff from the rags, Jake."

"Like my old man used to say, 'the cost of the call is the key to the game.'"

Billy laughed, bent down, and whispered in my ear, "Now you know I'm zipped on this Fifth Column thing you're dealing with, but I'll tell you what. You keep the last of these Nazis in line and I'll keep tabs on the Commies infiltrating the biz."

"Sounds like one hell of a plan, Billy," I said, looking him straight in the eye.

Billy stood up and turned to exit. At that very moment, Bob Hunter walked into the library. We both stared at him.

"What the hell are you doing here, Bob?" asked Billy. "Little out of your territory, aren't you?"

"Came in to get some info on the Babe's silent movies," said Hunter.

"Watch out for this guy, Jake," warned Billy. "He'll get everything he can out of you then take you out in the bottom of the ninth short of your perfect game."

"Not true and you know it, Billy!"

"Bad joke. I apologize. He'll take you out in the *fifth*," said Billy, winking knowingly in my direction.

Edith Gwynn, Billy's ex wife, chief editor, and ace contributor of THR's *Rambling Reporter* column entered the library. With a look of scorn on her face, she said, "Get your bony ass upstairs and help me with this Tracy article of yours!" She exited the library with a cordial, "Gentlemen."

Billy turned to us with a look of helplessness. He took a big drag on the holder. "I divorced that bitch over ten years ago. Trouble is, she's one of the best damn editors in the business, and I've never had the gumption to fire her." He hurriedly walked out.

"I'm glad I ran into you, Jake," said Bob. "I've been meaning to ask you about that…"

"…murder across from Gilmore."

"The boys in the newsroom just don't swallow what Cobb's putting out."

"Don't even ask, Bob."

"Come on Jake, rumor has it you're not just working for Cobb but…"

"You love baseball, Bob?"

"It's as close to my heart as my mother's embrace," he said

"Then drop it."

"Why?"

"Because it's big enough to eat the game alive."

"You know I trust you, Jake."

I played several poker games with Bob, who was known as a compromiser.

"Hold on to your cards, Chopper. In a month or so we'll split this pot," I said.

"Promise?

"You have my word."

"All right, then you have mine. I'll tell the muckrakers in the newsroom there's nothing to know."

That afternoon, I left The Reporter with just enough information on Caesar Reich to engage him in a civil conversation before getting to the hard stuff, received a blessing on my choice of a new career from the father confessor of the dark side of all things Hollywood, and got a promise from the most honest sport's reporter in L.A.

I got a call that night from Millie. She had been successful in meeting up with Eephus Pitch at his regular spot on the UC campus. He told her he remembered the shoemaker Hoffmann, but if he was to go into detail he wanted to talk to me personally. We agreed that he was looking for some cash for the information. Millie was in no position to pay out such a demand, especially if she was expected to ask the right questions that would come close to the information I was looking for. It was evident that I would have to come up to Oakland myself. I told her I wasn't sure when I could make it up and added that I would hopefully have more information on the current whereabouts of this Hoffmann character in the next week or so. The visit would have to be put off for awhile. She agreed that when I did make it north we'd just keep the knowledge of the visit between us and not make it a family thing.

On another front, it looked like my roommates were getting their act together. Hilo was coming close to the money he needed to buy the Teardrop Gretsch guitar he'd been dreaming of for years. He also had the talk with Angel I had suggested. That dose of reality left Angel walking around the bungalow with his head bowed low. Since Hilo informed me that Angel promised to be more discreet in his relations with women, I didn't attempt to approach him on the subject.

In the next few days, I spoke with Cobb and Longdown over the phone. Nothing new had come up. There had been no threating letters and nothing suspicious had occurred on the road in Seattle.

Hilo, Angel, and I caught most of the away games in Sacramento over the radio; the Solons took four out of six. Hilo and I decided to attend the night game on July 19th when the Stars would return home to take on their arch rival, the L.A. Angels, at Gilmore Field. Angel took a rain check because he had a date with another bar girl he met at the party, so I decided to invite Richie Goodman to fill his third base side seat. It would be the perfect opportunity to catch up on things and reminisce over old times.

The noble and dignified locking of horns between the Hollywood Stars and the Los Angeles Angels was the hottest sport's ticket in town. The fierce rivalry between the teams went all the way back to the '20s when the Stars won the PCL pennant in '29 and '30. This was a real slap in the face to the Angels organization and their fans, because they were leasing their own Wrigley Field to the

Stars. However, from '32 on it was downhill for the Stars and their owner, Bill Lance. In '34, the Angels, the greatest team to ever put on spikes in the PCL, won the pennant. From that day on, the Stars attendance dropped and they quickly lost a greater portion of their fan base. In fact, it wasn't until Bob Cobb picked up the franchise, successfully completed the construction of Gilmore Field in time for opening day of the '39 season, and made a deal with the Dodgers to become their farm club, that real talent on the field and the draw of movie star owners in the stands began to pay off. Over the past ten years, the Stars had gradually grown into a team to be reckoned with. This season, with the Oaks and Solons biting at their heels, the big bats of Irv Noren, Frank Kelleher, and Jim Baxes had, so far, kept the Twinks in first place and given their loyal fans the hope that they had a damn good chance of bringing home their first PCL pennant in close to two decades.

Tuesday evening provided fans with one of those quintessential nights of baseball under the lights. There was a warm breeze from the west and a moon on the wane, allowing the heavens above to twinkle even brighter on the Stars below. That night of baseball gave Richie and me the opportunity to catch up on all the things that had transpired in our lives since we'd been friends in high school. He was happily married with two young boys and a dog. I remembered how much he loved animals when he was a kid. As for the war, he had followed Patton into Germany and damn near froze his balls off in the Battle of the Bulge. He came out of it without a scratch. Most of our conversation consisted of a proud and loving rehashing of our participation in high school football and baseball. When the Stars shortstop, Moe Franklin, hit a bullet down the third base line, miraculously caught by a kid named Randy Jackson, Richie recalled the spectacular catch at third by our classmate, Rudy Cortez. It saved my perfect game in '31. He told me that Rudy had been killed on D-Day. He was one of those crazy motherfuckers in the 82nd Airborne who shook Ike's hand that morning and then 'Geronimo-ed!' out over Normandy in a gallant effort to cut off supply lines to the Jerries from the west. Anyway you cut it, Rudy covered the Hot Corner from start to finish.

It was around the bottom of the fifth when I recognized Phil, one of the plainclothes men who'd been filling in for Angel and me. Cobb had informed me that none of these guys had any idea of the real issues involved. They had been told to be on the lookout for anyone suspicious, anyone who looked like they might be concealing a bomb or packing heat. I excused myself and walked over to talk with him. Phil told me that he and his crew hadn't picked up anything out of the ordinary in the last few weeks. I returned to my seat to enjoy the rest of the game. Oddly enough, I wasn't the only fan in the third base box who had invited a guest. Smitty had Aleksy at his side, they'd been going on all night about politics and the possibilities of the Major Leagues moving west.

The grand finale to the evening was Haney calling in Bachman to hold the game at two runs apiece in the top of the ninth. I noticed that the righthander was back to leaving his left index finger outside of his glove. It obviously healed up from that line drive off Martin's bat. But that wasn't all I noticed. When Bachman came into the game from the bullpen, a member of the grounds crew was clapping like crazy as he walked to the mound. Maybe it only made sense. The kid was still an outsider, why wouldn't he have befriended one of the guys working the field. Still, it was a little curious. So, when Norris just happened to pass my box, I asked if he recognized the groundskeeper who was showing such enthusiasm for Bachman. He pulled out his opera glasses, that he always carried with him, and focused on the guy I was pointing at.

"He's not a groundsman, he's an electrician."

"Mind if I borrow those?"

I adjusted the glasses to my eyes. I focused on a heavy set, bald man in his fifties with a large handlebar moustache.

"What's his name?" I asked.

"No...something. No...Novak! That's it, Novak. Anton Novak. He's Czech. I know because Mr. Cobb's always making a joke about asking 'the Czech to check the power source.'"

Bachman's fast ball was sliding away from righthanded batters that night. He'd struck out two batters in a row when Butch Moran, the Angel's first baseman and former Hollywood Star, muscled an inside curve sky-high down the left field line. The Stars fans held their breath hoping for the best. But damn! It remained fair for a home run. The Twinks lost this first game of, what the fans on both sides of the field like to call, the Heavenly Series, 3 to 2.

After the game, Richie and I said our goodbyes in the Gilmore parking lot. We agreed that whenever we had the chance we'd get together for another night game.

When I got home, I called Cobb at the Brown Derby. I asked him about the electrician, Anton Novak.

"Novak? No, no he's all right. Best damn head electrician I've had in years."

"When did he start working for you?" I asked

"Let me see, it was '46. Yeah, middle of the season in '46."

"Where did he come from?"

"Jake, the man had all the right credentials. He worked back east for GE before the war. Fact is, he came to the States in '35. Had a damn good idea of what Hitler was up to and got the hell out before the going got rough."

I mentioned his reaction to Bachman's coming into the game and asked if they knew each other. Cobb said that Novak had often befriended cups of coffee, especially pitchers. He was the kind of guy who always wanted to give the underdogs a ray of hope. Before Cobb hung up, he said, "In spite of the fact that you're wrong about Novak, I'm glad you're keeping your eyes open for anything out of the ordinary."

Hilo was downstairs practicing a new song on his ukulele. As I started up the stairs, he pointed to Angel's room and crossed his fingers. I responded in the same gesture. If only Angel's lovemaking with a woman was as easy for him as killing Japanese.

I got up early the next morning, showered, and then dressed in my summer best. I'd been preparing for this interview with Caesar Reich for close to two weeks. If he had anything to do with the death of Howard Story, I was determined to get it out of him. On the other hand, from everything I'd read about Reich and the impressions of him I'd gotten from others, he appeared to have been an extremely skilled and talented cameraman who refused to go along with the studio bosses and never had the chance to go on to become one of Hollywood's leading directors of the silent era. Considering my present situation, any man with the guts to say no to the powers that be, in this vicious city of yes men, deserved some degree of admiration.

Reich lived on the southern periphery of a quaint and modest upper-middle class community known as Spaulding Square. The central portion of these charming eight blocks of varied Period Revival styled houses and bungalows was one of the earliest real estate developments to offer reasonably priced housing for actors and technicians in the silent film industry. Many retired silent screen professionals had lived in this unique neighborhood for well over 30 years. Reich's abode was nestled about eight blocks south of the main track of Spaulding homes and, curiously enough, exactly four blocks north of Cobb's bungalow where Howard Story was murdered.

I parked on Clinton Street, walked west to North Genesee, and took an immediate right. Reich's residence was in the middle of the block on the eastern side of the street. I suppose I was expecting something dilapidated and ill-maintained, but the newly painted, white, stucco-clad façade of his Spanish Revival Styled home seemed to sparkle. In front of the house was a well-manicured lawn encircling an aged palm tree climbing skyward into the clear blue of an 80 degree L.A. afternoon. A perfect reproduction of the neocolonial design, its immaculate alabaster white walls and Persian red roof tiles stood before me as a fine and well preserved example of one of the many Revival Styled forms of architecture that radiated south from Spaulding Square. Albert Starr Spaulding's creations – revival forms of Craftsman, Colonial, Spanish, Tudor, and Italian Mediterranean – provided America's incipient film industry's immigrant work force with an idyllic suburbanized retreat situated between an emerging Hollywood film industry and a bustling L.A. downtown business area. Here was the Hollywood working man's Beverly Hills, the whimsical and commemorative shelters of those who lived to serve the powers that be above them.

As I turned onto the pathway to the house and walked toward its arched portico entryway, I couldn't help but notice the intricate Moorish patterned, wrought-iron, double swing gate halfway up the driveway. It was padlocked and was an extended portion of the main house. Had it merely been the geometric pattern of the iron gate that caught my eye I'd have thought nothing of it. But, wrought within the dominant curvature of the gate's Islamic design was written: Veni, Vidi, Vici, I came, I saw, I conquered. Caesar Reich had obviously decided to publicly display his admiration for the great man of antiquity for whom he was named. By the time I had passed through the arched entrance-way and its small tiled patio, I needed only to look up at the green, half-moon-shaped stained glass window above the house's main doorway to understand the resounding significance of the quote hammered into the iron gate. The Tiffany styled cresent encasement imaged four iconic characters of the Hollywood scene: a director sitting upon his folding chair, a cameraman standing behind his wondrous instrument, and a man and woman embracing in a kiss. A new art had arrived. It had conquered and enthralled its audience with moving images of love as everyday humanity knew them to be. Reich had been present at the beginning of filmmaking and realized the significance of this unprecedented art form. Julius Caesar, the mere mortal, had become Caesar Reich, the human component of a divine machine capable of providing the modern world with moving, true to life images. The once warrior politican had, at last, become an artist.

I removed my Ray-Bans, put them in the breast pocket of my coat, and rang the doorbell. Its chimes rang out a prolonged version of the first four notes of Beethoven's Fifth. I was about to push for a second chorus when the interior oak door, in back of the decorative iron one, opened. I was greeted by a handsome black man in his 60s. He was wearing a white waiter's suit with a white cloth napkin draped over his left forearm.

"I am Maurice," he said in a rather aristocratic Virginia accent. "And you are, sir?"

"Officer Jake Salazar. I have a one o'clock appointment with…"

"Yes, of course." He turned the latch and opened the outer iron door.

As I entered, he closed both doors and walked in front of me with the everyday indifference of a loyal servant.

"Follow me. Mr. Reich is expecting you."

From the outside, Reich's home, with its soaring twin quarter-circle windows and asymmetrical façade, gave the impression that it was a two-story structure. However, once inside, its 20-foot high ceiling allowed for a stretch of uninterrupted space offering comfort, elegance, and unquestionable taste to recede into three, one step, tiered levels. The third level, at the back of this enormous room, was some 40 feet from the front door. At this vanishing point, dark lacquered French doors opened to an expansive patio and pool. The room's polished mahogany overhead beams accentuated the bright, white walls with its vintage, Spanish Colonial wrought-iron chandeliers. The massive space allowed for a commanding view of Reich's unique array of exquisite antique furnishings, objet d'art, and an authentic collection of Native American textiles and Pre-Columbian Mexican art. Covering the walls, was a discriminating and refined selection of original sporting prints and oil paintings of beautiful horses and pedigree dogs. Most dramatic were the impressionistic oils of greyhounds racing at Aqua Caliente.

I was right behind Maurice as he walked through the French doors to the pool when the juxtaposition of two oil paintings stopped me in my tracks. The one to my right was familiar, and I remembered that Pop had a print of it, which Mom hated, in our living room. The one to my left was an original Kandinsky. What the hell was Cash Coolidge's ultimate kitsch rendering of bespectacled, anthropomorphic Saint Bernards around a poker table doing on the same wall as Russia's incomparable abstract-spiritualist!

Maurice re-entered the room.

"Are you with me, Officer Salazar?"

"Sorry," I said, continuing in the direction of the French doors. As I looked to my left, I was struck by the incredible vibrancy of the pastels in one of the oils depicting canine competition in Mexico. The colors were similar to those in the Kandinsky.

"Dogs are not hindered by riders on their backs. They are free to run, out of pure hunger, for that rabbit in front of them," said an old tenor voice to my right.

I turned to greet a very tall, stooped, and well-tanned elderly gentleman who I could only assume to be Caesar Reich. He was dressed casually in light blue Bermuda shorts and a bright yellow short-sleeved shirt.

"Mr. Reich, I presume." I walked over to him and shook his hand.

"Officer Salazar, can I get you a drink?"

"Well…I…ah…"

"Trust me; I promise not to tell if you don't."

"Sure…why not. I'll take a scotch and water."

"You heard the gentleman, Maurice. And I should think heavy on the scotch and light on the water."

"Sounds good to me," I said.

Maurice exited the patio and Reich smiled and gestured to his left. "Please," he said, and pointed to a patio chair at the umbrellaed table beside the pool.

I was half way to the patio chair when I noticed a young, trim, and muscular Latino male, in racing trunks, taking laps in the pool.

"I hope Rodrigo won't be a distraction to our conversation," said Reich.

"I don't see why he should."

From the information I had on Reich, I don't know why I was expecting him to have a German accent, maybe it was his last name and the Nazi sympathizer thing. Such a supposition was far from the truth. He sounded more like a well-to-do New Englander.

There was a coat rack next to the house on the patio. I took off my sports coat and straw fedora and hung them on the rack, then I grabbed my notebook and pencil from my coat pocket. I sat down at the table, opposite Reich, and situated myself comfortably under the shade of the umbrella. When Maurice arrived with my scotch, I found myself staring at Reich. Though I'd never seen a photo of him as a young or old man, he looked familiar.

"You're looking at me as if we've previously met, but you're not quite sure where."

"We have met, haven't we?"

"Do you recall a high stakes game at the Flamingo about six months back?"

Then it hit me – face, place, and game! I've always had a photographic memory for such details.

"I took a $3,000 pot right out from under you. It was one of the best damn pure bluffs of my life," I said, with a great deal of pride.

" Then what in hell was the *tell*, Officer Salazar?

"If I recall correctly, you'd been giving off fake tells all night. They paid off with you raking in big pots at the top of the game. But then you had a bad run of cards.

Card dead, but you stuck it out. And like the rest, who didn't fold, you were all in on the last hand."

"A damn full house," he confessed.

"I remember, now, exactly. You had two kings up by Fifth Street and a damn well possible third in the hole. But I wasn't all that sure you had that two of spades on the board or in the hole to make that pair for a full boat. So, when you hesitated on Sixth Street, after I'd gotten a second seven up, I knew you were counting on finding that two on the river. That meant it was a damn long shot you'd come up with that pair."

"Odds taken, I did just that."

"But you weren't ready for me to bluff my way to Seventh Street because you weren't so sure that those two sevens of mine weren't about to find brothers stoking coal in my hole or piloting my river."

"So, my hesitating on Sixth Street was a dead giveaway to my swallowing your bluff of holding four of a kind. That done, you knew damn well I wasn't about to match your over bet."

"Yeah, and that choice on your part was just the tip of the iceberg, as far a I could see it."

"How was that?" he asked.

"You pinned me as the enemy from the get-go. A new face at the table. Whatever it was, there was something on your mind and you were bringing it to your game."

"And you picked up on that."

"Like my old man used to say, 'they all go off-kilter before they go full tilt.'"

"Your mentor in poker, I take it."

"Never beat the man," I said.

"All said and done, the loss of that pot, by way of nothing less than a bluff, was my worst *bad beat* in years."

"It happens to the best of us."

Reich took a sip of his Bloody Mary and turned to observe the young man swimming in his pool.

"Officer Salazar, I owe you and Bob Cobb an apology. I'd have preferred giving you this interview a couple of weeks back, but unfortunately…"

"…or *fortunately*, you were whisked off to racing dogs in Agua Caliente," I said abruptly.

He stared at me in direct refutation of my sarcasm and said, "*Unfortunately*, the races and my departure were all prearranged. Truly, I was quiet shaken by the demise of Mr. Story."

"Howard Story was murdered, Mr. Reich."

"I'm aware of that. Howard was a lovely young man."

"As lovely as Rodrigo, there, taking his dutiful laps in your pool?"

"I understand what you're getting at, Officer Salazar. I can assure you, as an older *gentleman,* my relationships with young men are purely Platonic."

"I suppose I'll just have to take your word on that."

"I only hope that you have some idea of who may have killed that bright and talented young man."

"I understand that you were introduced to Mr. Story through a certain Dr. Eartha von Geist."

Reich looked at me in a surprised manner and said, "Yes, if I recall correctly, Eartha introduced me to Howard and his friend…ah…"

"Sidney Upton."

"Yes, Sidney Upton. I met both of them at a party given by George Cukor at his home in Beverly Hills."

"And you and Dr. von Geist, you'd been friends for…"

"…Since the early '30s," he said.

"Was she a member of the German American Bund, as well?" I asked.

Having raised the stakes, he looked at me as if he wasn't about to fold.

"And what exactly does this line of questioning have to do with the murder of Howard Story?"

"I can't go into detail, but it seems that Howard's murder has something to do with a group of Fifth Column Nazis currently working undercover in Los Angeles."

"My word!" he said. He looked shocked, but I couldn't tell if he was lying or not.

"So, again, was Dr. von Geist a member of the GAB?" I asked point blank.

"Hardly," he said. "Eartha was a Jungian psychiatrist, an intellectual, and a known communist sympathizer. She got out of Germany as soon as Hitler came to power."

"To my understanding, your failed relationship with Adolf Zukor ended your career as a cinematographer. Was that the reason you joined the GAB?"

"Unfortunately, I'd have to admit that it was. The fact is, for over 20 years my hatred for Zukor festered. By '36, I'd become extremely anti-Semitic. I foolishly joined the Bund. But by '39, I had renounced any alliances with the GAB and the Nazis."

"And why did you leave the GAB?"

"Because I realized what Hitler was up to. I knew, in my heart of hearts, that I didn't hate Jews, I hated Zukor!"

"And that wasn't because he was a Jew?"

"Far from it. It was Zukor's monopolization of film production, from the top, and his systematic destruction of the horizontal and creative core of filmmaking, below the line, that I rebelled against. And trust me, I wasn't alone in my opposition to his so-called 'vertical integration' of the movie industry."

"So, once Zukor cornered the means of production, distribution, and exhibition, the executive power to produce films became top dog."

"Prior to Zukor's willful executive takeover at Paramount in 1916, the film industry's primary link between the production and exhibition of movies was distribution. It functioned as the judicious kingpin between the public's taste and the creative innovations of a burgeoning art form. In short, distribution maintained the formidable and necessary separation of the three entities involved in filmmaking, and only this separation assured the creative sovereignty of this unquestionably unique and artistic industry of ours."

"Changed the whole damn deal overnight."

"And opened our business to racketeers," he said bitterly.

"Kind of like FDR's attempt to purge Congress of conservative Democrats to legislate the New Deal."

"Only Zukor was completely successful," he continued. "Neither was immune to arrogance, but Zukor had the hubris and balls to succeed at producing films at the level of a brand new *socialized* studio system. FDR failed to muscle the votes for all his liberal reforms."

"Some would swear your criticism sounds fascistic."

"Heavens no!" he exclaimed. "If I were still a fascist, or ever dreamed of becoming a communist, I'd do as Hitler did and Stalin's still doing. I'd control filmmaking at the level of exhibition. If I was a Nazi, I'd provide my people with films that reinforce their belief that they are a superior race. Or, on the other hand, that their admittedly totalitarian government is a guiding light to a future proletarian utopia."

Reich's opinions were quite insightful, so I decided to stay on subject. "So, what happened when you refused to go along with Zukor's New Deal for moviemaking?"

"Before Zukor's new system for producing films, directors and screenwriters were below the line. They didn't dictate the big boss's wish list to those they worked with but worked on the level with set designers, costumers, and lighting technicians. After Zukor's takeover, I decided to remain below the line and work as a cameraman. I refused to join his hierarchical BS."

"And never became a full-fledged sound cinematographer or director."

"I worked well into the 30s as a cameraman and assistant director," he said sadly with a forced smile.

"As I understand it, you've lived practically your entire life in Los Angeles." I liked the old man and was hoping he wasn't involved in Story's murder. Anyway, the friendlier I got, the more questions I could ask. All said and done, he just might slip up and provide me with some information he may have regarding this Fifth Column of Nazis.

"In 1869, when I was three, my dear mother died in Hamburg," he said, as if he had always begun the story of his life in such a manner. I got the feeling that it had been sometime since anyone had given him the opportunity to do so. "The following year, my father and I moved to England. He was the first generation of hydroelectric engineers who envisioned the clear water of mountain ranges as a power source for electricity. I received my education in England and studied two years at Oxford when my father decided to move to the United States in 1885."

"And you moved directly to L.A?"

"No. First, we moved to Wisconsin where my father worked as a chief engineer at the Fox River Power Plant in Appleton. It was the first hydroelectric plant in the world to actually convert the natural force of a river into the light giving power of electricity."

"And then you moved to L.A?"

"Yes, two years later. My father foresaw the coming need for hydroelectricity in the Los Angeles area."

"And perhaps even a future for his son. No movie-making without electricity."

"Absolutely correct, Officer Salazar. At first, of course, we used the natural light of the sun, but once we were inside a studio, it became a question of enough electricity to light the celluloid dreams of the movie-going public."

"And where did you live when you first came to L.A?"

"Where all Europeans lived when they first came to Los Angeles, the old Pico Hotel."

"Just south of L.A. Plaza?" I asked.

"The Pico Hotel, the Mercer Theater, Masonic Lodge 42, a bank, a grocery store, and a saloon were the essential mercantile components that provided the good citizens of Los Angeles with their first true business district, so aptly named Main Street."

There was no question in my mind that Caesar Reich was a most interesting and charming gentleman and lived up to his uniquely legendary Hollywood status. If I was to get anything more out of him, it was going to take a second interview and further information supplied to me by the FBI. I did, however, have one final question for him. I'd thought a lot about this question and had decided, in asking it, to add a certain status to our shoemaker Hoffmann that just might be right on the mark.

"Mister Reich, when you were in the GAB, did you know of any SS officers who made their way from Germany into the United States?"

"Schutzstaffel in the Bund? I suppose they were there, but they wouldn't have advertised it."

"This officer's name may have been Hoffmann."

"Hoffmann…"

From the top of my conversation with Reich, I noticed he had a slight tremor in both hands. When I mentioned the name Hoffmann, the index finger on his right hand began to twitch. When he realized I saw his nervous reaction, he clenched his fist and laughed.

"You know, Officer Salazar, Hoffmann is a very common German surname. One could conclude that at least a third of the German Americans in the Bund had some version of Hoffmann as their last name."

"I understand," I said. I stood up to indicate that the interview was at its end. "I'm hopeful that you'll make yourself available, Mr. Reich. I may have more questions for you. I might even have a picture of Hoffmann for you to have a look at."

"Of course. Personally, I've enjoyed our conversation very much."

"As have I, Mr. Reich." Stuffing my notebook and pencil into the pocket of my coat, I removed it from the coat rack, along with my straw Fedora, and turned to shake Reich's hand. He was already at the French doors.

"Here, I'll walk you out," said Reich.

Undisturbed, Rodrigo continued his laps as we walked through the double doors and exited the patio. We were about to step down to the second tier of the living room when I couldn't help but take a last look at the Kandinsky and the Coolidge.

Reich stopped, turned, and said, "Lovers of modern art are outraged by my side-by-side placement of the two paintings. Lovers of poker are just confused."

"You'd have to place me in the second category."

As we continued toward the front door I asked, "Have you always raced dogs?"

"Ever since the '20s. Though, in the last ten years, not as often as I used to," he admitted. "But I do have my own track, up north, in the Ventura Hills. That's where I train my Four Horsemen."

"Four Horsemen…?"

"That's what I call my four greyhounds," he said. He walked over to the grand piano. It was positioned next to the huge stone fireplace that made up the central portion of the interior of the house's asymmetrical façade. He reached into the middle of a mass of framed photographs on the piano and retrieved one from the multitude. He turned, walked a few steps, and handed me the gold framed photograph. "This is my father and me, a couple of years after we arrived at the Pico. It was taken right outside the hotel by Carlton Watkins. He was a very famous photographer."

I looked down at the old sepia-tinted photo. It pictured Reich as a young man. He was standing next to his father. They were both dressed in suits, surrounded by aproned working men. All were standing outside of the Pico Hotel. Despite profession or class, everyone was wearing bowlers.

"Do you play, Officer Salazar?" asked Reich, as he gestured to the piano.

"No, no I don't," I said, placing the photo at the edge of the piano.

Taking a seat, Reich began playing something classical. "Do you like Chopin?"

"More of a Teddy Wilson man, myself."

"I used to play for Howard. He loved Chopin."

"What about Rodrigo, is he a music lover?"

"No. He's a purely physical being. My sovereign fish."

"So it would appear."

He abruptly stopped playing and looked directly at me.

"I want you to know, Officer Salazar, that I cared a great deal for Howard. I only hope that you and the LAPD will do everything in your power to apprehend the individual responsible for that beautiful young man's murder."

"We'll do what we can, but we can only successfully track down Story's murderer with the help of individuals like yourself."

Once again, he began to play. This time, something modern and reflective, perhaps a composition that was all his own. It was as if his ability at improvisation functioned as a stimulus to his own thought and his ability to express his ideas.

"Mind you, it's not just the loss of that beautiful young man but the very fact of murder in Hollywood. I know I must sound rather naive to an officer of the law who experiences the cruel and savage underbelly of this city day in and day out, but to one such as myself who has seen this city grow stone by stone, outward from its simpleminded and well-ordered interests of Main Street, well, murder is an unnecessary and alien thing."

"Really," I said.

"When you look at the juxtaposition of those two paintings on the wall over there, what do you see?" he asked.

I turned to the Kandinsky and Coolidge behind me and answered, "The dogged reality of a poker game in opposition to the… geometric abstraction of infinite things."

"Exactly. The murderous concrete vs the sublime abstract," he mused as he improvised. "The Coolidge represents the simple and discrete countablity of poker chips at the end of a ruthless game. In the Kandinsky, on the other hand, the task of measurement is transformed into the complex yet reasonable angles and objects that constitute a society of diverse things of equal importance. The sacred tools of geometry have enabled the artist to make the uncountable countable in his rendering of the eternal. Only here, among the squares, rectangles, and circles, does virtue become measureable, in an everlasting maintenance of spiritual continuity and peaceful concord. Imagine, Officer Salazar, a language existing amidst the silent nothingness of things, spoken as it is, when one's power to see becomes the same as the power of the object to be seen."

"You're quite the philosopher, Mr. Reich," I said.

"My beloved Hollywood was the first city, upon the face of the earth, to be fully invested in the magically electrical pursuit of the industrial creation of moviemaking. It was not built on murder, but something far more subtle. And, in its purest form, the furthest thing from extortion, theft, coercion, and murder."

Considering our conversation, I had an idea of what he was getting at. And, the next words out of his mouth confirmed my suspicions.

"When a man looks upon himself as a thoroughbred, what he fears most is being scratched from the race, the embarrassment or disgrace that might threaten one's character and career. Do you see it there, Officer

Salazar, in the Kandinsky: the silent and secretive love of reason and objectivity that pays eternal homage to the sovereignty of order?"

I left Caesar Reich's home with an open invitation to visit his greyhound track in the Ventura Hills. He also promised that he'd call Dr. von Geist and encourage her to take an interview with me despite the fact that she'd already spoken to a couple of Longdown's detectives assigned to the investigation of Story's murder.

When I got home, I called the Colonel and filled him in on my meeting with Reich.

"I think he's lying about not knowing Hoffmann," I said.

"Probably is. The sooner the FBI gives us more information on Hoffmann, the more pressure we can put on Reich."

"Reich seems to have survived an on-the-quiet culture of 'something for something.' It appears to have left him with his own personal fear of character assassination," I added.

"The magical spell of obligations in this town can become one hell of a burden. An old- timer like him has both thrived and suffered under them."

"How so?"

"As above, so below."

"What the hell does that mean?"

There was a long silence between us.

"You just have to be patient," he said, changing the subject. "Don't worry, we're going to catch up with these fascist bastards and root them out, every damn one of them. By the way, you'll be meeting up with that FBI agent next Friday, the 29th."

"Good. Reich invited me up for a visit to his dog track in the Ventura Hills. I'll hold off until I get more info from this FBI agent."

"Let me see…," he said.

I could hear him shuffling around some papers.

"Yes. The FBI agent's name is Jenkins Hill."

Unbelievable; I knew the guy! But I wasn't about to let on. Keeping my cards close to the vest, here was one more divine coincidence lighting the path to this pawn's own Deer Park.

That night, Angel upstairs with his new girlfriend, and Hilo downstairs practicing, I stepped out onto the porch and sipped at my scotch, canalside. As I reflected on the past couple of weeks, I had to admit I'd pretty much settled into my own little "square yard of space," a willing pawn determined to remain fixed and forward looking.

For now, I was looking forward to reuniting with one of my fellow survivors from the days of my recuperation at Letterman. One of the guys, like myself, that the public insists on calling heroes. But, in the darkness of night and our nightmares, it's the dead, the real heroes, who come to taunt us with the truth of why we survived. In fact, the very reason for which we were born - to remember the horrible way in which they died.

Chapter VII

<u>He Lives!</u>

It was the family Hill's proud legacy of selfless service to an elite community of US Intelligence agents and counterespionage tradecraft that inspired Paul Hill to name his only son Jenkins. His father had been the youngest Pinkerton to guard Lincoln during the Civil War. Paul continued the family's tradition of government service by playing a major role in the US Secret Service efforts to bring down German spy rings in WWI. Frankly, I didn't even understand what 'Jenks' was getting at whenever he laughed about the joke behind his name until we shared a butt one night on the porch of our Area A mess hall at Letterman General. Once I understood that the hill our Founding Fathers built our capitol on was originally named Jenkins Hill, I got the joke. We were both recuperating from the wounds we'd received during the war. I needed a wheelchair because I was completely messed up on my entire right side. Jenks, who was serving undercover with the OSS in Spain, had been tortured by Nazi agents and left for dead in a Lisbon cellar, but not before they shot him twice in both hands at close range with a ten-round 9mm Parabellum Luger.

When I'm talking about sharing a butt, I was the one doing all the sharing. While I wasn't happy to be temporarily immobile, Jenks was in worse shape. He couldn't do a damn thing with his hands. He'd been flown out to the West Coast to see a hand specialist at Letterman. It was an understatement to say he stood out like some eastern Big Time Officer biding his time among the cornplaster commandoes, like myself, who'd taken a few for Uncle Sam in the Pacific. Beyond the clever conceit of

Jenks' name (over all of our heads), the joke around the ward went something like this: "Just how stupid are these Intelligence guys to get shot twice in the same place?" or "Did you hear the one about the Foreign Intelligence Officer who was shot through both hands and lost his ability to pry his head out of his own OSS-hole?" Jenks was more than willing to take the ribbing, knowing full well that we all needed a laugh here and there to overcome the pain of losing all those GIs who'd held their guts in long enough to get back home but weren't lucky enough to walk out of Letterman alive.

As I drove over to meet Jenks that afternoon, I was wondering if he'd given up the straights. On the advice of a doctor at Letterman, I stopped smoking right after I recouped and got back to civilian life. And, that wasn't easy with all the pain. The pills were never strong enough to keep life on the sunny side.

Since my interview with Reich, nothing new had come up on Story's murder, and Hoffman was still nowhere to be found. The only real dark cloud on the horizon was the fact that the Stars had split their eight game series with the Angels and, now on the road in Portland, had already lost the first two out of seven. I was hopeful they could take all of the remaining five though such a hope was totally unrealistic. Furthermore, the Oaks bats had heated up in the last week and they were within a half a game of tying the Twinks for first. And the Solons were just a game behind the Oaks.

Whether it was solving the murder or clinching the season, there was no sure thing in sight.

I couldn't help but assume I'd be meeting Jenks in some Bay City dive filled with rummy misfits and good-for-nothing cons. There, seated in some grimy booth, he'd whisper to me the truth behind this Fifth Column of Nazis.

But that was far from the high stepping accommodations that the Office of the FBI provided for their one and only Jenkins Hill.

Unlike Union Station, that had surrendered to its own myriad styles of geometrical and architectural historicism and failed to truly exemplify a fully liberated example of L.A. Art Deco, the Sunset Tower Hotel, at 8358 Sunset Boulevard, triumphed. Within its floor-to-ceiling opaque windows, Hollywood carried on its business from boardroom to bedroom. Since '31, all of screenland's whispered rumors of yesterday's failures and tomorrow's bankable successes have echoed throughout this lavish hotel's glamorous celebrations, deals, and infidelities.

I parked around the corner, in the Tower's basement garage on DeLongpre Avenue, and walked up toward Sunset. I was about to turn left to the entrance of the hotel when I decided to cross the boulevard and bask in the sun that was just coming over the inset portion of the Tower's penthouse. That's where I was headed. I was going all the way up to that penultimate frieze where the Art Deco reliefs mysteriously transformed into nothing more than vegetation and the mindless desire to encircle, conquer, and bury its lesser forms of living things below.

As I walked back across Sunset, I recalled reading an article in THR stating that Howard Hughes occupied the penthouse of the Sunset Tower. I couldn't help but wonder what the hell Jenkins Hill was doing occupying the top floor suite of such an illustrious address.

Inside the hotel lobby, there weren't many people. I went to the desk and had the clerk ring up to Jenks' room. "Mr. Hill, Mr. Salazar is here to see you." Jenks told him to let me up. The desk clerk turned to the bellboy and said, "Stanley, take Mr. Salazar up to Mr. Hughes' penthouse."

When the elevator doors opened, Stanley pointed to the dark oak doors directly across from us. "It's those central double doors, sir," he said.

I walked across the plush red carpet of the impressive foyer and rang the bell. In no time at all, one of the doors opened. There, standing before me, was the reigning member of the Hill family. One of the few entrusted to protect our country's sovereignty by way of spycraft and murderous doublecross. Jenks looked exactly as I remembered him: tall and slender with a handsome, high cheek boned face. With his perfect aquiline nose and red hair, you'd swear he was the illegitimate son of Thomas Jefferson. He was dressed casually, but immaculately, in a blue short sleeved sport shirt and white slacks.

"I'll be damned, Jake, it is you! Come on in!" I entered the penthouse apartment; he closed and locked the door behind me. We shook hands and embraced. I took off my fedora and followed him in.

"When I saw your name as my contact I couldn't believe my eyes. I was hoping it was you."

"When I heard Jenkins Hill, I didn't have to hope. I mean, who the hell else could it be," I laughed.

Jenks turned toward me and lifted both arms to a 90 degree angle with his palms facing in my direction, and said, "What do you think, Jake. Just like new, right?"

"What do you take for the pain?"

"Three packs a day and bourbon straight as needed," he said. He walked over to the mahogany leather padded bar. "I got one palm that looks like a map of China and the other like a map of Central America."

"You FBI boys have always been known to cover a lot of territory."

He laughed. "I'm not FBI, never was. Though, in this particular case, I'm acting as a go-between for the CIA under the umbrella of the FBI."

"Yeah, I read about Truman's National Security Act in the papers. I suppose most of you OSS boys ended up in the Central Intelligence Agency."

"Something like that. What about your right leg, how are you coping?"

"I can get around all right. As for the pain, I take pills and…ah…"

"Scotch and water!"

"You remembered."

I looked around the enormous expanse of Hughes' penthouse living room with its two- toned walls of off-white, above, and dark lavender, below, that made the already huge space look even bigger. Several potted palms, a white sectional sofa fronted by a large ornate teak coffee table, and a long rectangular dining table with plush saddle brown leather chairs were perfectly positioned to point in the direction of a drafting table and adjoining desk. On the desk, were several rolled up blueprints and a scale model of Hughes' H-4 Hercules strategic airlift flying boat – a.k.a. the Spruce Goose.

"Some layout, huh," said Jenks, while pouring my scotch and water.

"So how did you pull off these digs?"

"It seems Hughes owes Hoover a few favors."

"I bet," I said, as I walked toward the glass doors that led to the terrace.

"Go on, take a look at the view; it's something all right."

I opened the glass sliding doors and walked to the edge of the terrace. Looking southeast, the commanding and authoritative presence of L.A.'s City Hall, an ever present watchtower and stronghold of law and order, dominated the lowly downtown area. Recalling the day Richie and the Colonel came over to the house when I swore my allegiance as an officer of the law, I remembered the quote from Cicero etched in stone at the entrance of City Hall: "He who violates his oath profanes the divinity of faith itself." I was up to my neck in this thing but, so far, nothing was over my head. My oath was still intact and my conscience clear and forthcoming. A mild breeze was blowing up from the south onto the first slopes of Hollywood Hills. From the heights of Hughes' penthouse, the mere 15 stories of the Sunset Tower seemed to proudly stand in equal stature to City Hall's 32-floored, sword to the sky.

Lost in my musings, I failed to see that Jenks was suddenly behind me. He tapped me on the shoulder and handed me the scotch and water.

"To the real heroes," he said, lifting his glass.

"Hands on the vertical, feet on the horizontal, to the 37th!" I said, lifting mine.

There was a pause as we both looked out over the city.

"Some view," he said.

"Some city," I added. After a moment, I decided to cut the small talk and turned to Jenks. "So, what do you have on this Fifth Column situation?"

"Let's sit down, Jake," he said. He motioned to the marble patio table with two ornate chairs. As I sat down, Jenks walked around the table and picked up a dark leather attaché from the other chair. Placing it on the table, he sat down and said, "In the last few months, I've walked halfway around the world with this thing handcuffed to my wrist. As a matter of fact, I just got back from Mexico City this morning."

Unbuckling the attache, he asked, "You remember the sigh of relief that went through all of us at Letterman when we heard the news that Hitler finally had the guts to bite down on that cyanide capsule and do the world a favor by blowing his fucking brains out?"

"Hell yeah. I remember that kid from Texas. He'd been up and about for a couple of weeks when he came running into the ward with a stack of newspapers yelling out, 'the bastard's killed himself!'"

"You remember Hitler's last will and political testament?"

"Not completely."

"Though he alluded to the fact that he was about kill himself, the general tone of Hitler's statement was the same as his final radio address in January of '45. He said that the German people must continue to fight against the two factors of western bourgeois civilization that he, Mussolini, and Franco had always looked upon as the prime enemies of their Fascistic regimes: 'International Jewry and their helpers.'"

"Helpers?"

"It's general knowledge that the Nazis killed 6,000,000 Jews in their concentration camps. But, in those same camps, they also murdered over 200,000 Freemasons," he said, as he took a manila folder out of his attaché.

"Their helpers," I said. While I remained silent and pokerfaced, Jenk's information brought to mind my bizarre interview with Reich and my conversation with Longdown that abruptly ended in an air of mystery.

"In the last few years, the Bureau has dealt with rumors of Fifth Column Nazi activity throughout the States, but most have come to nought or just end up being some balloon-brained ex-member of the Bund jerking off in a basement full of Nazi memorabilia."

"But you're saying this Fifth Column situation in Hollywood is for real."

"Especially with Jews heading up most of the major film studios in town and the Masons functioning, as they do in all of our prospering cities, as the confidential link between the managerial and working classes."

"So guys like you and me are out to protect what Hitler was trying to destroy."

"Not *was*, Jake…*is*!"

He pulled out a black and white photo from the manila folder and pushed it across to my side of the table.

"Our nation's well-ordered capitalist foundation may be flourishing in Hollywood, but the devil himself, who's out to destroy us, is still alive and well and living in Paraguay."

I looked down at the photo. Minus the toothbrush moustache, it was Hitler all right. He was shaking hands with a military officer dressed in the uniform of, what appeared to be, Franco's elite guard. He and three of Franco's high ranking majordomos were surrounded by several robed Catholic monks.

"That was taken by a Spanish agent with a telephoto lens in May of '45. He'd been in place for over a year working as a gardener at the Samos monastery in Spain."

I was shocked. I just sat there looking at the image for quite some time. Finally I said, "So the bastard didn't kill himself."

"Exactly. Once the Soviets were in possession of his so-called remains, they were never fully identified as his. The corpse that the Russians found in the Fuhrerbunker was one of Hitler's doubles.

"So how in hell did he get out of Germany?"

"We discovered a system of subway connections and hidden tunnels that led directly from the Fuhrerbunker to Tempelhof Airport. On April 21st, the day after Hitler's final public address, there was a mass exodus of Nazis out of Tempelhof. Hitler was with them."

"And he flew to neutral Spain," I concluded.

"On a Focke-Wulf Condor 200. Fucking transport with a range of 2,000 miles."

"But I take it he didn't stay in Spain."

For the next 20 minutes, Jenks filled me in on what the CIA concluded to have been Hitler's plausible route to South America once he boarded a German U-boat at the port of Vigo, Spain. Crossing the Atlantic, with a stopover for some R&R in the Canary Islands (a well-known supply and maintenance port for U-boats), he successfully, despite his bad health, made it to the coast of Argentina. From there, making his way through a ratline of safe-houses in Argentina and Uruguay, he reached a remote, well-fortified, and isolated compound near Salto Suizo in southeast Paraguay. It was a well-known fact that there were a great deal of Nazi sympathizers in these three Latin American countries. However, what John Q. Public wasn't aware of was the degree to which the Nazis had been responsible for attempting to politically undermine the governments of these nations while contributing to the modernizations of their infrastructures by way of civil engineering projects. These elements of infrastructural improvements were accompanied by the procurement of preexisting real estate, in many cases locales previously owned by the Catholic Church. This was in order to secure safe-houses should the leading Nazis need to escape to South America upon the Third Reich's fall to the Allied forces. In fact, the Nazis constructed their state of the art civic works with the intention that these marvels of modern engineering could eventually form a power, transport, and communication grid for the possible establishment of a Fourth Reich that would gather momentum from the large and loyal German population in South America. It seemed that, in consideration of the latter, the Nazi's construction of the hydroelectric dam and power plant, at Rincon del Bonete, Uruguay, was a special case in point. Though the Uruguayan government okayed the project in '37, by the early '40s, they'd had enough of Germany's infiltration of their republic. With information supplied by US Intelligence that the Nazis were attempting to distill heavy water that might contribute to the Axis Powers production of an atomic bomb, they kicked the Nazi engineers out of their country and replaced them with an engineering firm from Chicago. According to Jenks, despite the fact that we had stopped the Germans from creating heavy water, with the building of this power plant, the damage was already done. Over the years of the Nazis' influence on South and Central American nation's politics and infrastructures, they'd successfully built an impressive arsenal of giant broadcasting transmitters running north and south. Since the early '30s, these tranmitters helped with their spreading of propaganda and their efforts to unify the German population in many of these nation states. Now, with the completion of this hydroelectric plant at Rincon Del Bonete, the obvious increase in voltage availability gave these broadcasting transmitters a much longer and stronger range of radio transmission.

"Think about it, Jake, Hitler could make a speech in a radio station in Asuncion, Paraguay and about three skywave hops of 2,000 miles each, he could…"

"Wait a minute," I said, "why the hell can't you guys just send in a team of Rangers and take out this old fascist bastard in this compound of his?"

"Too risky. There are large populations of Germans in practically every one of the major South American countries. A good portion of them are Fifth Columnists well aware of Hitler's presence in Paraguay. Trust me, we can't just go in and take him out. Given the iron grip that these Nazi sympathizers have on several of these nation's military elite and precarious economies, FDR's Good Neighbor Policy could find itself facing fascist coup d'etats in several of these countries over night."

"So let me get this straight, you're saying that Hitler could be thinking of…"

"…sending a final radio message right into the lap of your average Hollywood Stars baseball fan," he said, finishing my sentence.

"And this is what this Fifth Column thing is all about?"

"Given his state of health, Hitler knows damn well that his days are numbered. So, why not go out on the same wicked note he came in on. What better farewell than to address his Fifth Column diehards, north and south, with the encouragement to live on and form the Fourth Reich that will ultimately destroy the international Judaic-Masonic conspiracy. To add insult to injury, Hitler's final address to his faithful followers would take place at the very heart of the Hollywood machine. His tyrannical voice in a ballpark would result in nothing less than the ultimate blasphemy against the great American game itself."

"And Howard Story's murder, do you think he was executed as a means of instilling fear in Cobb and others on the inside?"

"Frankly no. I think Mr. Story knew something about this Fifth Column thing and was about to spill the beans to Cobb."

"I'd have to agree," I added. "I interviewed a certain Caesar Reich about his relationship with Story, and I'm sure he lied to me."

"The Bureau's familiar with Mr. Reich."

"Another thing, when I asked Reich if he knew a member of the Bund named Hoffmann I could tell he was nervous," I said.

"Oh yes, the shoemaker," he said with a smile.

"So you know this guy?"

Jenks reached into his attaché; he pulled out several more pages from FBI and CIA dossiers. Along with these papers was a photo of seven SS officers that would prove to be the most important evidence he shared with me that afternoon.

"Here's where we put two and two together, Jake. This was taken in the late '20s. Hoffmann, whose real name is Holderlin, is the third from the right. There are no other photos of him that we're aware of. All we know is that he was a German operative in the States in the late '30s and possibly a member of the Bund."

"So, I had it right when I figured him to be a member of the SS."

"An early and key member at that. He's a university graduate in electrical engineering and, strangely enough, toured Germany as a child actor with his family."

"Sounds like a deadly combination."

"A theatrical chameleon with the brain of a Tesla."

"So you figure he's key to the rigging of the sound system over at Gilmore."

"Certainly capable of it," he admitted.

"You know, there's a middle-aged European working as Cobb's head electrician," I said.

"Anton Novak. No. We checked him out. He's clean."

"You're sure Novak isn't Hoffmann coming in under the radar?"

"And why are you so convinced Novak isn't legit?"

"I was at a night game at Gilmore. Haney brought in a kid with the name of Bachman. Novak went nuts, like he was rooting for some Austrian cup of coffee from the fatherland."

"Does Bachman spell his name with one n or two?"

"One."

" That means he's Jewish. If Novak's a Nazi, I can't see him rooting for a Jew."

"True."

"Probably just a Czech immigrant in love with baseball," he concluded.

"Yeah, that's the way Cobb sees it."

"Look, Jake, the problem with Hoffmann is we're not even all that sure what his name was when he was a member of the American Bund."

"So, Reich could be reacting to a totally different individual by the name of Hoffmann."

"Could be. The fact is, after '39, the spy known as SS officer Holderlin dropped out of sight. It was only after your father's run-in with the shoemaker, in Oakland, that we were able to identify him as Hoffmann."

"And why exactly was that?"

"According to Holderlin's dossier, it seems he picked up the trade of shoe repair when he learned to repair the actors' shoes in his father's troupe."

"Regular jack-of-all trades."

"No shit."

"So, if Hoffmann's not working from the inside, at Gilmore Field, where do you figure he's going to show?"

"We're not quite sure. He could be preparing a mobile unit in the Santa Monica Mountains, as we speak.

Some sizable relay transmitter, built into a truck and trailer, capable of picking up a radio signal, from the south, and shooting it right back in the same direction at a stronger frequency. An RF that will compromise the public address system at Gilmore," he speculated, with some degree of certainty.

"So, is it really worth keeping an eye on Gilmore if this…"

"Absolutely. The point is, anything can happen anywhere. But there's one thing for sure, these Nazis aren't going to make their move until the Stars have reached the climax of their season. Hitler's going to speak to the biggest crowd possible." A look came over his face that I was sure had little to do with what we were talking about.

"What's wrong, Jenks?"

"Christ!" he exclaimed and stood up. "Damned if I didn't pick up a bit of Montezuma's Revenge when I was in Mexico City. I'll be right back."

As Jenks hurriedly made his way toward the john, the doorbell rang. He yelled out to me, "Probably one of Hughes' starlets living in the apartments below us. Say you're a business friend of Hughes and he'll be back next week. Make it short and, for Christ's Sake, don't get all that friendly!"

"No problem." I walked to the front door and opened it.

Holy mackerel! What an able Grable this dame was, stacked to the rafters, a real dream puss. She couldn't have been more than 17. No doubt, the most irresistible little package of platinum blonde in Hughes' Sunset Stable on the Sunset Strip. And yet, even with a body destined for the voluptuous wing in the Smithsonian, there was still a sparkle of innocence in those deep, alluring blue eyes. She reminded me of the proverbial girl next door. Unfortunately, when I was a kid, "the girl nextdoor" lived in a brothel off Market Street.

"Hi," she said, batting those neighborly blues, as if she was about to borrow a cup of sugar.

"Hi yourself."

"Is Howard here?"

"No. He'll be away for the next week or so. I'm a business friend."

"So am I," she said, reaching out her hand. "I'm Holly Cocklock from Surecock, Missouri. And you are…?"

Oh, what the hell, I thought. I shook her hand and said, "Jake Salazar from Oakland, California."

"Well, the hometown's a joke, but my last name's for real. Howard thinks I should change it," she giggled. I have to say, she had the cutest little laugh this side of Des Moines.

"In a town like this, it may not be a bad idea," I said.

"Say, I'm going to a Beverly Hills party tonight. How'd you like to come along?"

"Sounds great. What's the address?"

"You got a card? I can give you a ring."

"Sure," I said. As I reached into the pocket of my sports coat for my card, Jenks suddenly appeared out of nowhere.

"Thank you, my dear, but the gentleman and I are in the middle of a very important business meeting," Jenks said, politely.

"But…," she squeaked.

He slammed the door in her face and locked it shut.

"What the hell do you think you're doing, Jake!" Jinks whispered.

"Did you happen to get a good look at that bombshell?"

"I told you to get rid of her. What's your problem!"

"Sorry, Jenks," I said, as I followed him into the interior of the penthouse.

"You're not a gambler anymore, Jake; you're working for the FBI. And not for long, if you keep this crap up!

"Right you are."

"You can't trust anybody, Jake, not anybody."

"I understand."

When I left the Sunset Tower, Jenks assured me that when he got to Washington, he'd send an old and trusted SIS courier west with all of the dossiers and photographs that he had shared with me that afternoon. As well, as soon as possible, he would return with other FBI and CIA agents to help the LAPD with the Fifth Column penetration. All in all, aside from my blunder with the knockout blonde, the afternoon had been a nice reunion with an old friend.

I decided not to immediately contact Longdown about my meeting with Jenks. I drove over to the newsstand on Melrose and Fairfax. It was the one that Smitty frequented for his *New York Times*. I bought a *Herald-Express* and thought I'd take a few moments to read Bob Hunter's column. I wanted to see what he had to say about the Stars away games with Portland. I walked down the street and into a coffee shop on Melrose. Before I got to the sports section, I noticed that the front page was filled with the trial results of the blacklisted screenwriters Wilkerson had drawn into the public spotlight. It was enough to dampen my enthusiasm for reading Hunter's column. Apparently, once in front of the committee, most of the blacklist refused to give names of those they knew with Communist Party ties. For this infraction of the law, the Representatives and Senators held them in contempt and took them to trial. Several of them were now receiving jail time.

Even the quaint afternoon solitude of the dirty spoon wasn't enough to encourage me to read the sports section. I closed the paper, took a sip of coffee, sat back in my chair, and stared out the window at the passing crowd on Melrose. Apparently, while our government's investigation of communists in America was plastered over all the front pages of every newspaper in the US, gumshoes, like me, were secretively chasing down fascistic threats, totally unknown to the general public, dangerously close to taking center stage at Gilmore Field.

Here were the fanatics, left and right, desperately working out Smitty's next nightmare. Looking down on the headlines, I couldn't help but call to mind an argument that often transpired between Mom and Pop. Mom was a strick Catholic, attending Mass every Sunday. The problem was to get Pop to do the same. Sure, he'd manage go to church on holidays, and even high holy days, but on most Sundays he would pull out Occum's razor, insisting that there was no damn good reason for "doing with the *many* what can be done with the *few*." "Oh yes, those *authentic few* Big Wheels of yours!" Mom would snap. "What ever you make of it, my dear, it is my form of devotion." "A devotion that has led you to shake hands with the…" Pop would then end the argument with a proverb, short and sweet: "Better the devil you know, than the devil you don't."

Another glance at the headlines only confirmed in my mind that the idea of standing up against Hitler's assault on the powers that be in Hollywood was a hell of a lot more inviting than going to bat for what was coming at us from the ungodly, eggheaded left and the book burning, militant, knucklebrained right.   After a pause, I took another long look at the passing crowd outside the diner. I finally stood up, left a quarter tip, and started out of the coffee shop with the paper under my arm.   Once on the street, taking a cue from Pop's knowledge of the ways of the world, I had to ask myself why I was obliged to go along with Jenks and his burearcratic Feds and their insistence that this Fifth Column thing wasn't going to turn out the results of an inside job.   Hell, I'd seen too much collusion at the poker tables of Reno and Vegas not to conclude that the best of the criminal few were always working from the inside.

I drove home, poured myself a second scotch, and called Longdown.   I filled him in on all the information Jenkins Hill had shared with me.

Chapter VIII

Dr. Eartha von Geist's Mysterious Profession

With my driver-side windshield wipers on the blink, motoring up the Hollywood Hills to Dr. von Geist's home, in the middle of a torrential downpour, wasn't exactly a piece of cake. The fierce, pelting volley of the summer cloudburst on my convertible top reminded me of a monsoon in the Philippines when I was a driver for the brass. Not only was the top on the convertible jeep equipped with the same stayfast, three-ply canvas as my Plymouth, but it had the same damn problem with its windshield wipers. Be it the Philippines or Hollywood, a lemon's a lemon.

Through the passenger side of the windshield, I caught sight of a large wooden mailbox with Dr. von Geist's name, address, and office hours. I took a sharp right up the steeply graveled, tree lined driveway, and could soon make out a redwood house at the end of the ascent. Its oriel bay windows were cantilevered over the side of a sizable cliff. The commanding perch rested on an industrial concrete retaining wall and three enormously round, unhusked redwood stilts.

Amidst the downpour, the light from the psychiatrist's house seemed to hover like some whispered lullaby gently sung above the foresakened, rain soaked avenues of neurotic stardom. Here was Hollywood's undaunted and reassuring fortress of hope, its lyrical, beaconlike berceuse proclaiming to those below that they might, once again, experience that long forgotten innocent night's sleep.

I'd just crested the slope of the driveway and was about to park a distance from the house under some eucalyptus when a tall, grey-haired woman, with a gigantic black umbrella, crossed directly in front of me. I slammed on the brakes. She ran around the car and tapped on my driver-side window. I rolled it down to hear her. "You can park here, Officer Salazar," she shouted over the pouring rain. This handsome woman, in her 50s, who I presumed was the good doctor, had a distinct Austrian accent. "Please get under my umbrella before you catch your death of cold." I was glad for her offer. Although I'd worn my Burberrys trench and waterproof fedora, I'd forgotten my umbrella. I would have been drenched making a run for it. Rolling the window back up, I turned off the ignition, exited the car, and accompanied her down the limestone steps. I followed her through the sliding, aluminum-framed glass doors that led into the vestibule and living room of this precariously-placed modern abode.

Once inside, she closed the umbrella, tapped the rain off of it onto the thick reed woven doormat, and placed it into a tall empty Chinese ceramic vase. "Please, you can put your coat and hat on the coatrack behind you." She removed her yellow poncho rain slicker, tossed it onto the reed mat, and turned toward the living room with a smile that I was sure would have been a wink 20 years before. She was an extremely attractive woman who had obviously taken some effort to maintain her physique. Her stunningly youthful body was, perhaps, the result of a Nordic contrarian's natural approach to physical fitness. I imagined her on a daily run performed in direct defiance to those who dolefully descended the hills for a Sunset Boulevard massage parlor or the stuffiness of a gym.

I followed her slim, graceful silhouette as she led me into her spacious living room of aromatic redwood. To my left was a lacquered, red brick wall, to my right, floor to ceiling bay windows. A hint of champa incense in the air added to the impressive array of ritual masks mounted on the sanquine wall. Opposite these masks, pedestaled and placed along the curvature of the oriel glass windows, were three miniature Greek statues: Apollo, Venus, and an ancient fragment of an embossed nude young man and woman. Facing the three framed bay window, and its magnificent view of the city, were a vintage La Corbusier chaise lounge and a low riding, white upholstered swivel chair. To the far right, was a classic Bedermeier desk and chair. Directly below the primitive masks was the typical brown leather couch that, I assumed, was used for her psychoanalytic therapy sessions. A huge, well-worn, decorative Chinese rug of cerulean blue and white, covered a greater portion of the enormous room. At the far left corner of the brick wall was a filled-to-the-brim bookshelf and a bamboo and glass mobile bar.

Having taken in the entire room, I couldn't help but observe how the three objects of Western art seemed to constitute a proud and stoic tradition of rational thought standing in direct contrast to the savage complex of irrational deities peering forth from the other side of the room.

When she reached the middle of the Chinese rug, she turned and said, "Are you a drinking cop or a non-drinking cop, Officer Salazar?"

I was getting used to this and said, "A drinking cop, scotch and water, if you please."

"Wunderbar, a man who knows what he wants," she quipped. "In my profession, you would qualify as a most unique specimen."

"And if I changed my mind before you reached the bar?"

"Average," she said, with no hesitation.

"Beautiful place you have here."

"Yes. A little known, early experiment by an architect, now, quite famous."

"H.H. Harris, I'd say."

"Ah, you're not only a man who knows himself but architecture, as well."

"Along with art, it's a hobby of mine." I walked to the bay windows and attempted to see beyond the murky, wind-swept dance of the rain against the plate glass. Though still coming down cats and dogs, the feline-pawed pitter-pat of rain on the roof was far cozier than the dogged torrents of the downpour on the convertible top of my Plymouth.

"Here you are," she said, handing me the glass of scotch.

"You're not drinking?"

"Office hours." She flirtatiously batted her baby blues. As she looked at me, I could envision her having many memorable afternoon delights with some muscled superman who probably nailed her knees to her ears.

"As you can see, Officer Salazar, I have chosen to sparsely furnish my home."

"Less is more, right?"

"Especially, when your architect is gifted enough to maintain the natural surroundings upon which he's built his masterpiece."

"A balance between nature and progress is nothing short of damn good horse sense."

"Horse sense, a term I've often utilized in my psychiatric practice."

"Good to know."

"Take, for example, my precise arrangement of furniture," she said. "I always offer my patients a choice." She pointed to the brown leather couch. "The traditional Freudian view of the ceiling, the past," then pointing to the petite white sofa chair and the La Corbusier lounge recliner, facing the bay windows, "or the Jungian view of the world we live in, the future."

"And which seating arrangement did Howard Story choose?"

"Ah yes, our sad, beautiful Mr. Story," she lamented. "You know, I've already been questioned by your department as to what I knew of Howard's life, but when my old friend, Caesar Reich, called and encouraged me to take a further interview with you, I jumped at the chance. Anything I can do to bring the murderer of that wonderful young man to justice, I will do."

"So what was it, past or future?

"Sadly enough, it was the future."

"Yeah, I can understand preferring that point of view, myself," I said, looking in the direction of the windows and the rain.

"I noticed your limp," she said. "I take it you were wounded in the war, yes?"

"Yes."

"Well then, when you interview me, this morning, we shall both look to the future."

And with that, she walked to a spot between the black leather chaise longue and the white sofa chair and said, "I think it best that you sit here," pointing to the armchair, "where I would normally be. I will sit on La Corbusier's beautiful but uncomfortable lounge.

"It's your call, Dr. von Geist."

"Oh please, you must call me Eartha. Every day, it is Dr. von Geist this, Dr. von Geist that. No, when I'm to be interviewed, or is the word interrogated, I wish to be addressed by my Christian name."

As we stared out the window and attempted to see through the blinding flashes of lightning and the swirling downpour of rain, little did we know how prophetic this afternoon's storm would prove to be. Our fates, as imperceptible as the distant cityscape below us.

"I understand you were treating Howard Story in the belief that he could transform his sexual desires for men into an attraction for women."

"Yes," she said, relaxing into the contours of the chair. Folding her fingers together, she stared out the rain soaked windows.

"And I take it you believe such a change is possible," I said, hoping to get some insight into Angel's determination to change his propensity for male companionship.

"If I was a Freudian analyst, perhaps not. He believed that our entire psychological makeup is fully formed by age seven. On the other hand, Jung believed that our souls gradually take shape by the mature spiritual choices we make once we have successfully analyzed the forces of light and darkness that have influenced our lives."

"Jung was a believer in the endgame," I said.

"Absolutely," she confirmed, readjusting her gaze toward the bay windows and the rain. "Howard Story was just beginning to analyze his dreams and understand the shadowing archetypes that were preventing him from a loving relationship with a woman when he met his unfortunate end."

"And what about his relationship with Sidney Upton?"

"They'd been lovers as boys, but only because they were outcasts in their hometown. Once they came to Hollywood, they became true friends and were no longer lovers."

"And Howard's relationship with Reich…?"

"Purely platonic," she said, with all the determination of a security guard at Fort Knox.

"You're sure about that."

"Howard confessed as much, and there was certainly no good reason for him to lie."

"Yeah, Reich gave me the same story."

"I've known Caesar Reich close to 20 years. Over that time, he has had several relationships with young men in which he has put aside his own desires in order to mentor them."

"Sounds downright ideal," I said, with a cynical air. I continued with the question that I'd been edging toward from the top of the conversation. "Did Howard ever speak about his impressions of Reich's political views?"

She turned toward me and said, "Don't think I'm unaware of what you're getting at. In my conversation with Caesar, he told me that you may attempt to implicate us both in a theory that Howard was murdered by some Fifth Column of Nazis operating in L.A."

"It's no speculation, Eartha; it's a fact."

"Caesar always regretted his association with the GAB."

"And what about you? Ever find yourself raising a hearty 'Heil, Hitler!' in the name of the fatherland on American soil?"

"You're barking up the wrong tree, Officer Salazar. My father, bless his soul, was a doctor. I came from a very liberal and educated family in Vienna. As a student, with communist connections, I was lucky to get out of Germany with, how do you say, my own behind."

"So you had no association with the Nazi party?"

"Not exactly."

"Which means what?" I asked.

"My sister married a Standard Bearer of the SS."

"What was his name?"

"Why do you ask?"

"Just curious," I replied.

"SS-Oberfuhrer Frederick Wolfe."

After a pause, I said, "I gather that your liberal father wasn't all that happy about that."

"He was outraged," she said, with a rather curious smile on her face. "But what could he do? He had no choice but to tread very carefully."

"Coming from a family that stood in direct opposition to the Nazis' political policies, why would your sister do a thing like that?"

"Why does any young girl fall in love with the most beautiful specimen of manhood, in a uniform, that the world has ever seen? Are you familiar with the ancient phrase, 'Death and the Maiden?'"

"Read about it somewhere, but I can't say I know what it means."

She pointed to the embossed stone image of the naked youths on the pedestal next to the window. "That fragment from a Greek frieze represents the myth of Psyche and Eros, the tale of a beautiful young woman falling hopelessly in love with a monster who is capable of a most ruthless cupidity and slithers about the world in the name of love."

"And that's what your sister found herself up against when she hooked up with her SS officer?"

"Hitler and his Nazis established a ruthless reality in Germany for the women of our generation. While I escaped to Paris and America, my sister was raped by her husband-to-be. But still, she maintained her virgin's smile and lived to carry the fruit of that monstrous night for nine months in her body."

"So what happened to your sister and her child?"

"Once the Russians entered Berlin, all three committed suicide."

"And you never married?"

"I never married. No, my story was not that of 'Death and the Maiden.' My story was enduring the death of so many I loved and admired in concentration camps."

"I'm sorry."

Believing there no more information that I could gain from questioning her any further, I decided to end the interview. However, as I stood up from the sofa and turned to leave, I noticed a most curious framed photograph, the only photograph, on her desk. Three fishermen on a pier, with their poles held vertical at their sides, were holding the catch of the day in front of their faces. The fisherman in the middle was the tallest. He held the largest fish. On either side of him stood two young boys, of similar height, holding smaller fish.

"What a bizarre photograph," I said.

"Oh, yes, an old Jewish collegue of mine," she said. "Another victim of the Nazis' atrocities. He had a wonderful sense of humor. He married into a wealthy family of fishing merchants and often joked that he'd found himself over his head with the responsibilities of a distasteful enterprise. Notice the brief title of the photo, 'in der tiefe,' written there at the bottom. It means 'in the deep.'"

"And those are his two sons?"

"Yes, they were born within a year of each other. Their father encouraged them to be sportsmen of many turns."

"And did they survive the genocide?"

"Frankly, Officer Salazar, I don't know. Strangely enough, I've had a recurring dream, over the years, in which they show up at my doorstep, happy, carefree, and well-adjusted adults of our newly liberated world."

She walked me to the vestibule. As I was putting on my raincoat she said, "I noticed something in your expression when you were asking about the possibilities of Howard Story changing his sexual desires from men to women."

"Did you?"

"I have a hard time believing that you were thinking about yourself. Perhaps a friend?"

"Yes," I admitted, "we fought side by side in the Philippines. He's definitely homosexual, but his fondest desire is to marry and have children."

"Tell your friend he must rid himself of the dark shadows of a domineering mother and a cruel and distant father."

"I suppose I could try."

"Or perhaps you could suggest he have a talk with me," she said. She reached into the pocket of her blouse and handed me her card.

Taking the card I said, "That might prove a lot easier."

"In my profession, it is often argued that attempting to change one's sexual orientation is unrealistic. But, I don't agree. In my opinion, it's definitely possible through ongoing analysis of a deep seeded neurosis that has developed in childhood. On the other hand, if the transition from homosexual to heterosexual is unsuccessful, and one is attempting to exist in the wrong skin, the result can be borderline psychosis, a very tragic and unfortunate turn of events." She came to a sudden stop and looked at me as if she wasn't quite sure what she was going to say next. "What I'm trying to suggest is that being relatively unrealistic and being downright psychotic are two very different states of mind." Again, she stopped. She gave me that look that I'd seen countless times at Letterman when a vet went to express what it took to survive the horrors of war. "I mean, when it comes to psychosis, that's another *story* altogether, no pun intended. You see, I earned my doctorate in a sanitarium in Hamburg. It was there, I realized that those who had been declared insane became more so once they were institutionalized. By the time Hitler and his madmen came along, I was convinced that the most malignant form of insanity could only come about in an atmosphere in which an entire society has been encouraged to lose touch with reality. In the case of the German people, it was the instituition of fascism that led to their incurable form of mass psychosis."

"So, to your mind, the most treacherous form of insanity is a mass psychotic adherence to a cause."

"The human experience is a dangerous one. Like a daring tightrope walker, should one fall to a psychotic extreme, left or right, one loses his balance in relationship to true liberty."

"And what's that exactly?"

"The liberty to know oneself."

We shook hands and agreed that we'd both enjoyed each other's company that afternoon.

Walking outside, I realized that it had stopped raining. As I drove out of the hills, I couldn't help but reflect upon Angel's altercation with Ginsberg, the night of my party, and how Angel's uncalled for display of violence had, so eloquently, cut through the pretense of Ginsberg's bad poetry.

But what intrigued me the most, that afternoon, was von Geist's explanation of survival in a Germany that had split in two. Frankly, I didn't know what to make of it. Although, I couldn't help but wonder which way von Geist found herself leaning when she went to perform that highwire balancing act of hers. Was she really that smart cookie of a psychiatrist or just another looker with a university degree willing to do anything necessary to keep her balance when she went to cross that political abyss under the reign of the Natioanl Socialists. What was the real cost of that ticket out of hell, my bright, seductive Eartha?

And then there was that photograph. Why was my gut telling me it had a lot more to do with this Fifth Column riddle that I wasn't even close to figuring out?

Chapter IX

Race from Fear, Run from Hunger

Ten days separated my interviews with Caesar Reich and Dr. von Geist. Several developments in the case occurred over that time. First of all, the photos and files that Jenks shared with me at the Sunset Tower had arrived at Longdown's office. Secondly, unlike Cobb and Jenks, I refused to write off Novak as a suspect. I asked the forensic portrait artist in Longdown's department to age the photo of SS Holderlin and compare it with Novak's Gilmore Field employment photo. The results of his sketches were quite revealing. Though Novak's facial features were totally different, the shape of his head and his ears were an exact match. The sketch artist and I agreed that he could have had plastic surgery.

Now that I was given a desk at City Hall's Homicide Headquarters at 122 West 1st Street, I could easily walk into Longdown's office and bypass the obligatory phone call. When I showed him the sketches, he leaned back languorously into his office chair like some beached walrus on his favorite rock and said, "Could be pure coincidence." He changed the subject. "What about those reports I asked for?" I handed him the envelope with the written results of my questioning of Upton, Reich, and von Geist. "Good work, Jake," he said, taking the cigar out of his mouth and smiling. "Police work can become damn routine and pedestrian after a while."

"Understood," I said.

"You know, Cobb and I haven't exactly ignore your suspicions concerning Novak. As a matter of fact, we were together at a game the other night, and there just happened to be a rain delay. We both noticed Novak entering the maintanence doors in right field. So, when the rain stopped, Cobb asked Norris to walk out there and take a snapshot of his bootprint."

"And?"

"No match."

"All right, I'll throw in the towel on Novak."

"What about that invitation to visit Reich at his dog track?"

"He called me the other day, said he'd be up there between the 9th and the 14th. He suggested I visit on the weekend of the 13th."

"Why don't you surprise him; show up this afternoon."

"I'll do that," I agreed.

"You said you thought he was lying about that Nazi, Hoffmann."

"I know he was," I said.

"Catch him off guard. You just might go deeper into his lie," he suggested. "Remember, your FBI buddy, Hill, should be in town with his crew by the beginning of next week. The more we have for the Feds, the faster we'll all get to the heart of this thing."

I caught the Hollywood Freeway west then hit 101 North at the split. Just west of El Rico, I took a sharp north on 33 and headed toward Oak View. Reich's ranch was just a couple of miles south of Casitas Springs.

The road leading to the main entrance of the walled adobe complex was pillared by a grove of highly-scented eucalyptus. When I parked in the graveled circle, in front of the cast iron gate to the interior, I noticed two other vehicles nestled under the shade of the trees. One was obviously Reich's. It was an immaculately preserved classic 1927 LaSalle convertible coupe. And the other, I couldn't believe my eyes, was that familiar green maintenance truck from Gilmore Field. What the hell was it doing here?

I peered through the iron-gate and noticed a small, adobe, flat-roofed Spanish style structure about 30 yards beyond the entrance. On the other side of the quaint house was Reich's dog racing track. At the far edge of the track, I could make out three workmen pouring what appeared to be a concrete foundation. I was about to ring the gate's corded bell when I observed Reich emerging from the pale ochre, clay brick house. The old man didn't see me as he turned in the direction of the workmen. I rang the bell.

Reich and the laborers glanced in my direction. The old man abruptly turned and attempted to continue walking toward the workmen when he obviously realized there was no avoiding me standing there. He stopped, turned around, and walked toward me.

"Officer Salazar, I was expecting you tomorrow."

"Am I catching you at a bad time?"

"No, no, not at all," he said, in a feigned apologetic manner. "It's just that I've got some workmen here today. Tomorrow, I have all the time in the world to give you a grand tour of the kennels and a chance to see my dogs at a run."

"So what's the project?"

"It's a very ambitious one," he said, as he opened the gate and led me in the direction of the track. "For years now, I've had to deal with bad radio reception coming up from Tijuana. These men are building me a radio tower so I can pick up the broadcasts directly from Agua Caliente. I believe the stimulation from the sounds of actual races could do wonders when it comes to my four horsemen preparing to compete there."

As we neared the old adobe structure and the track beyond, I couldn't help but recognize the older workman who was directing the two younger workers in the laying of the concrete.

"Isn't that Anton Novak?" I asked, patting myself on the back for taking Longdown's advice and visiting Reich a day earlier.

"It is," he said. "Oh yes, I remember now, Bob Cobb told me that before you became an officer of the law, you worked security at Gilmore Field. So you would know Mr. Novak. An excellent electrician and well-experienced in working on radio towers in Europe before he came to America."

"I'll bet he was," I said.

We walked past Novak and his workers. He looked up and our eyes met. I think he recognized me but immediately put his head down.

"My beauties won't be running today," Reich explained. We walked toward a brick one- story structure, just beyond the adobe house to the left of the track, that I assumed was the kennel.

"So, why the sport of queens and not kings?" I asked, as we neared the kennel.

"Actually, before my little run in with Zukor, I raced horses. But, after my choice to remain a cameraman, the expense was quite literally over my head."

"Not interested in dying broke," I joked.

"Frankly, by the late '20s, it was far more realistic that I…'go to the dogs'… so to speak."

We entered the red brick kennel through its old wooden carriage-house doors; they were opened to the morning sunlight streaming in from the east. Obviously well-kept on a daily basis, its interior floors looked as if they had just been washed down. There were seven large, galvanized, steel poled, and wired stalls mounted against an oblong brick wall. At the moment, only one of them was occupied. Within the stall was a loving and attentive blue brindle greyhound dam and her needy pups. A limping, portly, red-faced man, with a grizzly white beard and wearing a beret, was reining in five leashed, frisky greyhounds of varying size color and breed.

"Officer Salazar," said Reich, "this is my trainer, Reilly Lovelady."

"Quite a handful you got there," I said.

"I prefer to call it a full hand," the old surly trainer said, in a distinctive Irish brogue.

"Reilly likes to call them his Royal Flush," added Reich.

Reilly transferred the leashes from his huge, pudgy right hand to his equally massive left and extended his right hand in my direction. "A fellow wounded patriot home from foreign wars, is it?"

"The Philippines,'45," I answered proudly, shaking his hand.

"Black and Tan sharpshooter, Easter Rebellion, 1916," he responded with a devilish smile.

"I gather with an Irish first name and an English last name, it wasn't all that easy to choose sides."

"Not when your Brit father's a son-of-a-bitch and your Irish mother's a Catholic saint," he exclaimed, pulling back on the leashes of his sighthounds eager for their morning walk.

"Sounds similar to my Portuguese Catholic upbringing," I said.

"Ahhh, but you had nothin' more than a bloody world war to go to, and not a blessed revolution!"

"Well, I did escape to sea for six years before Uncle Sam took a bite out of my ass."

"Good for you, young man, good for you!"

"What I call my four horsemen," said Reich, "Master Lovelady calls his four cardinal virtues."

"But I count five dogs like any Royal Flush," I said.

"Well now, you've hit upon my trade secret when it comes to the trainin' of these hungry coursers," Lovelady said, kneeling down to the middle dog and opening the catch on its leash. This one looked to be a mix of German Shepherd and greyhound. Unleashed, the dog ran barking onto the track, then, suddenly coming to a full stop, it turned and bounded back toward the four purebreds. Assuming an attitude of command, the German Shepherd continued to bark. Holding, even tighter, onto the barking, impassioned four, he said, "There's their leader – the Fuhrer of my leash!"

"An appellation I do not approve of," insisted Reich.

"It's their Fuhrer who leads 'em to the launch and brings 'em home to the kennel," repeated Lovelady. He wore the unrepentant smirk of that race of Celts who came just short of joining the Axis Powers during the war.

Old Reilly introduced me, one by one, to his canine horde of cardinal virtues trained in the sport of queens. The last two introductions included a slim bodied Saluki, named *Temperance,* and the silky coated Afghan, named *Fortitude*. Once *Prudence* and *Judgment* had tactfully run the race they'd been taught to execute, Lovelady had bless the former (*Temperance* and *Fortitude*) with a will and eye for nothing less than victory.

"Of course, it's *Temperance* and *Fortitude* that I've trained on the straightaway. Just as if they were thoroughbreds, I've blinded them to their senses. No longer dependent on their hunger for that rabbit in front of them, they fear defeat and hanker only for that kingly feeling of victory."

"Light travels in a straight line," I said.

"Sure as the track is a circle, in the straight-out stretch, it's a tracer bullet all the way," he blurted, as he was overcome by the forward thrust of his visually stunning, aerodynamic squad of hounds.

As Lovelady's greyhounds began their morning sojourn around the track, Reich suggested we retire to the small adobe house that, as he explained, was once one of the many Pony Express stations between Frisco and L.A.

Though I doubted the colorful former member of the Irish Republican Brotherhood had anything to do with what Reich and Novak had up their conspiratorial sleeves, I couldn't take my eyes off Reilly Lovelady and his ever obedient hounds.

The one room adobe house was far less furnished than Reich's home in Spaulding Square. The space was "decorated" with a wooden single bed, industrial desk and chair, tiny refrigerator, and sink. A long redwood coffee table was placed in front of the large picture window that looked out onto the dog track. The tiny room, accoutred with a W.C., was an interesting contrast to the massive and lavish interior of his Spanish style digs in West L.A.

Grabbing a bottle of scotch from his modest collection of spirits on the coffee table, he said, "That's scotch and water, heavy on the former, as I recall."

"I'd prefer to skip the refreshments and cut to the chase," I said, undermining any of Reich's attempts at cordiality.

"Oh," he said, with a hint of nervous anticipation.

"In our last conversation, you said you never met a certain member of the GAB by the name of Hoffmann," I said.

"Yes. I believe I said that the name Hoffmann is such a common German name that…"

I interrupted him. "...What about a certain Standard Bearer SS Officer, by the name of Holderlin, who happens to be right outside working on that foundation for your radio tower and living in the States under the name of Anton Novak!"

His expression of warmth transformed into an irreversible countenance of guilt. Damned if I hadn't read Novak right from the top of the game. Slowly, placing the bottle of scotch back down on the table, he walked to the window. With his back to me, he stared out at Novak.

"You're chin deep in this Fifth Column crap, but if you tell me everything you know, the Feds just might offer you a deal."

"I doubt that."

"At least by coming over to our side, you just might be able to live with yourself, considering what you obviously know about Howard Story's murder."

He turned to me and said, "I'll tell you everything I know, but not here."

"What the hell does this monster have on you?"

"Everything!"

"Where can we talk?"

Reich asked if I was familiar with the Arroyo Seco Branch Library on the corner of North Figueroa and Piedmont in Highland Park. I said I knew the place and he gave me his word that he'd meet me there at 8 p.m. I was confident he would show and quickly concluded that Reich had little to gain by informing Novak that the Feds were on to the fact of his true identity. No, if ever there was a man in search of redemption, it was Reich. I agreed to meet him outside the library. Why in hell there, I had no idea. Maybe he wanted to return some overdue library books before we cuffed him and locked him up.

When I got home, I immediately went to my desk and took out the notebook I used to develop ideas for my novel. As I jotted a few things down about my afternoon with Reich, I could hear Hilo composing upstairs in his room. Since we had moved to the canal, he'd been practicing and composing on an electric guitar he'd borrowed from a friend. But there was something different about the sound I was hearing. About five minutes into my writing, he opened his door and shouted down to me.

"Jake, my friend, it has arrived," he said. He was holding the iconic 1939 Electromatic, two-toned, sunburst Gretsch that he'd only dreamt of possessing all these years.

"New guitar, new songs," I said.

"You can bet your gambling ass on that, Jake Salazar."

"No more 'Honolulu Baby,'" I said.

"You are looking at the next Hawaiian Sinatra," he prophesized.

"Always room for an original, I say."

"So tonight, do we go to the game or listen on the radio?"

"I've got an important appointment tonight. I won't make the game one way or the other."

"I think Angel and I will stay home and listen on the radio."

"Angel may be needed over at Gilmore."

Hilo shrugged and turned to reenter his room. Then, he stopped and turned back to me. "Oh, I almost forgot, are you going to be home for the next couple of hours?"

"My appointment in Highland Park isn't until 8."

"Angel called and said he wants to talk with you."

"How's his love life doing?"

"Not bad, close to two weeks with the same girl."

I pressed him further. "But he wants to talk to *me*?"

"He says it's something about the war."

"Ok, I should be around till 7."

"Good," he said.

"The guitar sounds great; I'm looking forward to those new songs."

"So am I," he said. He walked back into his room closing the door behind him.

Putting my notebooks aside, I typed out the confession I would have Reich sign at the library.

It was a little after 5 when Angel got home from the docks. He asked if we could talk in his room. "Sure," I said.

Angel had the best bedroom in the house. While Hilo's and mine faced the alley, his faced the canal and had a balcony above our porch. I'd only been in Angel's room a few times since our remodeling. It had remained as I remembered it, a sacred space that paid homage to his family, his country, and the war. On his bureau were several framed photos of his mother and father. Alongside these were pictures of relatives in the Philippines and L.A., some living, some dead. A bullet-riddled national flag of the Philippines, that had once flown over our mobile headquarters, was encased in glass and hung on the wall as proudly as it had flown over our advance. Several photos of those we'd fought side by side with, against the Japanese, were placed around the flag. Closer to the balcony doors, that opened to the canal, and mounted on the wall in a circular pattern, was a frightening collection of eight deadly swords and knives. All these weapons from the Philippines were encased in glass. In the center of his wheel of weaponry, he had mounted his most cherished of knives, his Punyal. This mother of all knives was the double edged blade of Angel's native island of Mindanao.

In his youth, he learned to use it as a means to protect himself from the invading elements of Japanese business interests in the city of his birth, Davao. Angel had carried this specific Punyal, now the centerpiece of this awesome array of cutlery, on his person to be used in hand to hand combat throughout our campaign against our mutual enemy. Considering the importance of this specific knife and its impact on Angel's memories of the war, it only made sense that, below this hideous relic of combat, he had placed an exquisitely framed print of a painting by the famed Filipino painter and revolutionary Juan Luna. Entitled *The Spoliarium,* the painting depicts the corpses of slave gladiators being dragged out from the blood and sand of the Roman Colosseum. When it was painted in 1884, its straight forward, realistic rendering of an ancient event bravely reflected the socio-political realities of the Filipino peoples' struggle for liberation. *The Spoliarium* was to become symbolic of Spain's and the Catholic Church's suppression of the Filipino's longing for freedom and the eventual formation of their own Republic. This gruesome image of the strong wasting their lives, entertaining their captors by preying upon each other to survive, would remain within the hearts and minds of the men, women, and children of the Philippines for several generations of failed or compromised revolutions. The actual founding of a Republic would not take place until 1946.

I sat on the old rocking chair that Angel had picked up at a flea market, and he sat on the edge of his bed.

"So what's up?" I asked.

"I been thinking a lot these days."

"Yeah, well, maybe that's a problem in itself. Guys like you and me shouldn't go around thinking all that much," I said.

"I been thinking how easy it is for me to kill."

"Welcome aboard the good ship *Survivior.*"

"Yet, in all my killing, there is some good.

"What's that?"

"I have never killed a woman, and I would pray to Shiva that I never will."

"You killed men because you had to kill them. You killed because you had to save your loved ones and your country from the Japanese. End of story."

"Only sometimes, I think I kill so well because I hate myself for the way I love."

"Listen to me Angel, there's not a damn thing wrong with the way you love."

"I had a nightmare, Jake. A beautiful Japanese boy that I killed, he comes to me. I remember cutting through his throat as if it were a willow in the wind. This beautiful boy, that I would have wished to kiss and make love to, he says to me, 'Did you take my life because you hate yourself for loving as you do?'"

My brave friend – the destroyer of the lives of many men – broke into tears. As he sobbed, he pleaded to a higher power, "Lord Shiva, forgive me my sins. I will not fear to love a woman, and I will give her a child."

Despite Angel's desperate state of mind, the conversation ended on a positive note when I convinced him to take Dr. von Geist's card. He liked the idea but was concerned as to the expense. He was looking forward to putting a six-month down payment on a storefront space for his Tai Chi studio.

I tried to give Angel an idea of the price. "Somewhere between what a decent piece of ass might have cost in Singapore, back in '36, and the cost of a high-stepping call girl, working the Waldorf Astoria, today."

"I prefer Singapore '36."

"It was a good year at that, Mister."

"Many beautiful boys in Singapore '36."

"Money's no issue when you know he or she's a good way to get well quick…"

Together, we said in unison, as we had so many years ago at sea, "…but not for long!"

We both had a good laugh.

Before I left for the library, I convinced Hilo and Angel to attend the game that night. I reminded Angel that if anything suspicious caught his eye, security would fall in right behind him and he could take charge. Angel taking on some responsibility at Gilmore was a good idea. It would keep him on track.

I decided to leave early, around 6:30, to miss the traffic coming in and out of the city for the Friday night sporting events and entertainments. On the drive north to Highland Park, I wondered why in hell Reich had insisted that we meet at a library resting on the knoll of this uniquely peninsular shaped corner where North Figueroa crossed Piedmont Street. The interviews I had conducted with Upton and Jenks, including my first one with Reich, had serendipitously taken place in some of L.A.'s prime real estate. And now, I was on my way to one of the most enchanting architectural crossroads in L.A: the Arroyo Seco Library. This humble little library, overlooking the intersection of two great thoroughfares leading in and out of northeast L.A., was an exquisite reimagining of an Ionic columned Palladio-like temple. When viewed from the point at which the two streets cross, the library created its own horizon. I swear, you'd think you suddenly found yourself back in the Renaissance era. Until this evening, I'd never visited the Arroyo Seco library at nightfall.

It was about 7:15 when I parked to the left of the library on Piedmont Street. The reddish rays of the sun on the off-white cast-stone surface of the building was turning a crimson afterglow. For quite some time, I remained inside the car listening to Jack Sherman's pregame show. But once the twilight became all too beautiful to resist, I turned off the radio, exited the car, and walked directly to the rounded corner where the two streets met. I didn't turn around until I reached the farthest point of the promontory; there it was in all its classic glory, the perfect replication of antiquity, undeniable evidence of the ancients among us. All at once, I was taken aback by an unexpected silence that came over my surroundings. I turned east, in the direction of the incoming and outgoing traffic, but there wasn't a car in sight. It was a strange nocturnal and lonely silence that I'd experienced only once before, in the Philippines. I remember Angel describing this awesome quietude as the silent voice of the dead. It occurred when the guardian of souls, a thieving, mischievous, degenerate divinity, lured the living to the borderline of the underworld.

But why here, why now? Why, at this same instant, in which the darkening takes ownership of the light, should I again encounter this eerie, crepuscular, silent voice.

I must have been lost in reverie for some time when I heard a voice behind me.

"I thought I was the early bird."

I turned to find Reich standing before the steps of the library. He was immaculately dressed in a fine white suit accentuated by a powder blue dress shirt with a dark blue and white polka dot tie. He sported an eloquent gold tipped cane and a Stetson straw. Some livery, I thought, for a man about to spill his guts on the murderous Nazi's who obviously had him by his elder, sagging balls. As for me, I was wearing the same Levis, penny loafers, and army-issued T-shirt I'd worn that day at Gilmore.

"Come, Officer Salazar," the old man said. He placed a pillow on the steps. 'Let us sit upon the ground and speak of the death of kings.'"

"That bad is it?"

"Worse, the death of the American middle class," he said.

As I walked toward the library steps, I caught sight of Reich's La Salle parked to the right on North Figueroa. A mere change of clothes and the faithful Maurice had become chauffeur for the evening. Simultaneously, the round electrical bulbs atop pedestals, to my left and right, and pendant sconces on either side of the library's arched doorway lit up. The electrical lighting added to the mysterious atmosphere. The library's three-quarter rotunda, with its two Ionic pillars, seemed an appropriate twilight shelter for the old cinematographer's confession.

"So why here?" I asked. The library doors opened, its interior lights dimmed, and two attractive, giggling bobby soxers in their drop pleated skirts, books in hand, exited the library in the direction of North Figueroa.

"I'll explain later. First the confession," he said. We heard the lock on the large oak doors click shut.

"What does Novak have on you?" I asked, as I sat down on the steps beside him.

"Pictures of Rodrigo and me, poolside."

"Not exactly business as usual."

"No, this was closer to a violent act of extortion. He threatened to publish them in *Beauty Parade*."

"*Beauty Parade*?"

"Only the biggest scandal magazine in town."

"So, are you saying you knew nothing of Novak's involvement with the Fifth Column?"

"Absolutely nothing!"

"So what did he ask of you?"

"Something that seemed quite straightforward and innocent at the time."

"Like what?"

"He wouldn't publish the pictures if I allowed him to park that hideous green truck, from Gilmore Field, in my driveway."

"And that was the day Story was murdered."

"Had I known what he was up to, I'd have allowed him to destroy me."

The image of that green truck speeding toward Gilmore Field, the afternoon Cobb and I were walking across the parking lot to the murder scene, came to mind.

I pulled out the confession I had written earlier. It stated that he knew Novak to be Holderlin, a.k.a. Hoffmann, an active member of a Fifth Column of Nazis currently out to undermine the security and freedom of the American people.

"I find it hard to believe you didn't know what Novak was up to."

"Truly, I had no idea he was involved with a Fifth Column of Nazis. I was only thinking that it might have something to do with Gilmore Field. Perhaps he was working with others to rob the box office."

"Even after he killed Story?"

"After he killed Howard, I was frightened to death."

"And the rest of the Column, ever meet any of them?"

"If I did, I wasn't aware. Trust me, if I was familiar with any of the others, it might have given me some leverage on Novak."

"So he's the only thumb you're under?"

"As far as I can see, yes."

"And what about those workers who were helping him lay the foundation of your radio tower?"

"Couple of Mexican kids, as I recall. Though, he did say he'd be bringing in more skilled workers once he started constructing the tower itself."

"And just how did you get Novak to build your tower?"

"A little counter blackmail on my part. Once he killed Howard, he knew it was time I got something out of this dreadful deal."

I handed him the confession and a pen. "Sign this, and I'll pass it along to the Feds. I'll see what I can do for you."

Reich unfolded the confession, read it, placed it down on the smooth stone steps and signed it

"Done," he said, with a great sigh of relief. He handed the pen and paper back to me.

"And what about that trainer of yours?"

"Lovelady? No, he has nothing to do with this mess. Merely an old cantankerous Irishman in love with his leash."

I folded the confession and stuffed it and the pen into the back pocket of my Levis.

Once again came that same deep silence at dusk. Only this time, the voice wasn't calling to me, but to Reich. He appeared to look around in search of ghosts from his past.

"So I ask again, why here?"

"Indeed, beyond a confession of guilt, there exists the revelation of truth."

He stood up, walked a few steps towards the edge of the sidewalk, and turned to face me.

"Isn't the light marvelous here," he said.

"It is indeed."

"It's what cinematographers of the silent era termed the magic hour, the time when our primitive cameras could best capture the argent light of dawn or *this* hushed light of dusk."

"L'heure bleue," I said.

"Yes, that's what the French call it," he said. "But you see, once we were no longer shooting Sur le Vif…"

"…From life on the spot…," I said.

"…whether on a street corner or under the old sunlit glass-roofed studios, well, the whole racket transformed when we went inside and began to work with shadow and light; those setups demanded electrical power, and a hell of a lot of it. In those early years, the studios monopolized close to 50 per cent of the voltage in the greater L.A. area."

"So what the hell happend here, anyway?"

"Electrical power to the people happened here, Office Salazar."

Taking out his wallet, he opened it and handed it to me. Inside was a photo of Reich and his father, smiling into the camera, with a crowd behind them. The photo appeared to have been taken on this very spot. Father and son were older than in the photo on his piano; both were no longer wearing bowlers. Young Reich wore a backward-turned newsboy cap, the signature crown of Hollywood cameramen of that era, his father, a large brimmed Stetson worn by engineers.

I closed the wallet and handed it back to him. "Interesting photo."

"On March 30th, 1916," he said, taking in his surroundings in a reflective manner, "my father and I, along with a crowd of concerned citizenry and civic dignitaries, ceremoniously ushered in the start of a municipal electrical distribution system that, to this very hour, is on its way to becoming the largest city-owned electric utility in this great nation of ours."

"Wasn't that the same year Zukor locked down the studio system?"

"And there, Officer Salazar, is the great irony of the year of our Lord, 1916. At the very same moment that the subjective creativity of those below the line, in the studios, was decapitated by the executive powers, electricity – that up to then had been monopolized by the studios – was given to the outlying population of the greater Los Angeles area.

"You see that pole there, the one to the left of the promontory?"

"The tall one with no wires attached, looks like a giant cross?"

"It's the pole we set that day. That's no mere object used to hold up copper wires bringing affordable electricity to the suburbs of L.A. No, it stands as a symbol of the unity and oneness of the workingman and the powers of finance above them. Thirty linemen then and going on 400 now," he added with pride.

"So, despite Zukor, hope still sprang eternal from within the lower-middle-class breast."

He laughed and said, "All hope for a prosperous middle class remained intact among conservative types, such as myself, until FDR ushered in his New Deal in '33."

"You'd get one hell of an argument from the average workingman that it was FDR who saved his hopeless, hustling ass."

"But, you see, Officer Salazar, the average hardworking individual doesn't understand what really happened when Zukor took over the studio system. Before Hitler initiated his National Socialist planning in Germany or Lenin's Bolsheviks secured their communist rule in 1918, and long before FDR attempted to socialize our capitalist democracy, it was Zukor who cut the hearts out of the managing class and heads and hands off the creators below him."

"So, before Zukor's takeover, what unified management and workers?"

"It was the secret of 'something for something.'"

"What do you mean?"

"I can't say I know this for a fact," he said in earnest, "but, I often felt that prior to Zukor's "vertical integation," the relationship between the craftsmen and the executive powers was most unique. You might say, it was a form of partnership. We shared a customary decency of a brotherly concern for the quality of the movie productions we were mutually involved in. The studio heads knew their executive positions did not give them license to propagate a controlling profit motive in the films they chose to produce. Below the line, actors and *craftsman*, such as *myself*, would best heed the uselessness of cultivating an attitude of entitlement that might result in the flaunting of our sexual conquests or *preferences* publicly."

"As above, so below," I said.

"An almighty alliance between the capital to produce and the freedom and skill to create. And it is an imitation of this unity that forms the essential solidity of the American middle class. A middle class soon to be politically undermind by homegrown fascists and communists, just as it was in Europe."

For the next few minutes, we bantered back and forth about the possibility of the working class and managerial class maintaining a balanced relationship that would enable them to sing the same harmonious song. Ultimately, I argued that such a concord, even in the worst of times, was possible. Reich, in his ageless wisdom, did not agree.

"You're wrong, Officer Salazar. Our beloved nation will not survive splitting left and right – emotional vs. rational. Just as in the terror that followed Nazi racism and, to this day, drives the poisonous doctrines of the communist government in Russia, our dear America will not escape its epitaph in terror."

We eventually shook hands and I reassured him I'd do what I could for him with the FBI. As well, we agreed he would change nothing in his relationship with Novak and report to me if he became privy to any additional information.

Entering my car on Piedmont, the one towering streetlight directly above me lit up, the only one servicing the intersection.

On the drive home, I thought about Reich coming clean concerning his relationship with Holderlin. He had nothing to lose by telling the truth. The Feds would obviously be more lenient with him than any of the others involved, considering his key information in identifying Novak as Holderlin. When I came to a red light, it crossed my mind that there was a damn good possibility that Reich hadn't been as forthcoming when it came to his information concerning von Geist. That old man knew something about her that he refused to reveal. I had no idea what it was, but I swear I'd put all my chips on the number that would supply me with the answer as to what the hell that absurd photo was *really* all about.

Chapter X

Lights Out!

When I got home that night, I decided not to call Longdown about Reich admitting that Novack and Holderlin were one and the same. I don't know, maybe it was because they all refused to go along with my gambler's hunch in the first place. Besides, even with the knowledge of Novak's true identity, Longdown and the Feds weren't about to arrest him overnight, not without more information. Was he heading up the whole operation, or were there others controlling him? Anyway, Jenks and his FBI crew weren't due in from the East Coast until the weekend. That was the reason Longdown and Cobb had scheduled a Monday morning meeting (the 15th) with all of us at City Hall.

It was obvious that I was developing a sympathy for old man Reich, though I wasn't about to accept his dire prophecy concerning our nation's eventual epitaph in terror. One could only pray that things wouldn't go so far as to create an irreparable divide amid a religious adherence to fascism and the intellectual demands of socialism: a political abyss easily capable of driving an indomitable wedge between the managerial and working classes of America.

When Hilo and Angel got back from the game, I approached Angel privately and brought him up to speed on the situation. We agreed that we would attend the games this weekend, between the Stars and Portland, and stake out Novak. The more information I had for the investigation the better.

For Angel and me, those games possessed a strange and familiar quality. Sure as hell not as dangerous as hunting down Japs in the Philippines, just the same, we were covering each other's back. Over the next three days, the two of us were able to enjoy the games while, at the same time, observing Novak's movements, the men he was in charge of, and what key points in the stadium he controlled.

I put in a call to Millie that weekend. I told her it looked like I wasn't going to have to speak with Eephus. I informed her that we were getting closer to catching up with these Nazi bastards, but I wasn't at liberty to give her details. Millie was sure he'd be disappointed because he was anxious to see me again. I felt the same way and told her to assure Eephus that the next time I was in Oakland I'd pay him a visit, maybe even take a shot at playing my Caro Kann against his London. I asked how everyone in the family was doing, and she filled me in. Frank was boning up for his company's heavy equipment test and, "Oh, yes, little Charlie and Tommy got into an argument the other night when Charlie insisted that the Oaks weren't about to catch the Stars. It seems, he worships that ball with all the Stars autographs that you gave him." I insisted she tell Tommy that the kid had it right. "He knows damn well which side of the diamond the pennant race is *betted* on." I told her to give my love to all and a big kiss to Mom.

I wasn't lying about my feelings toward Eephus. Fact be known, he'd been the reason for my perfect game. The summer before my senior year, I worked with him practically every day. I can still remember the last time we got together on the University High ballfield. Word for word, Eephus's sermon on the *mound* went something close to this:

"Seein' how baseball's one of them few games where the defense is in possession of the ball, it gives a man pause when he goes to consider the offensive importance of the pitcher and his sovereign ability to pitch. Damn strange thing bein' the offense in a defensive position. The strike out is that magical thing that can happen even before the offensive batter gets the chance to do his thing. Right pitch, at the right speed, at the right time of the game ain't nothin' short of perfection. Hell, you strike 'em out ain't nobody gets on base. When anybody goes to talk about how it is the best defense is a good offense, they's talkin' 'bout baseball. And why? Because it's the pitcher controls both the pace of the game and the speed of the ball. And if he do it right to perfection, he's an artist, for sure. Hittin' ain't nothin' more than a science, but it's pitchin's a thing of beauty in itself. It's a language turned a form of poetry when you get the knack for even three of those eight different grips I taught ya. Just keep in mind, Jake, you is the voice of truth comin' from the mound, 'cause there you is defending the wilderness of the field. You is that critical form of attack that's nothin' short of an art. You is a movin' point of gravity up against the grace of a merciless and intelligent swing. The wrong pitch and it's out of the park. Or, even worse, an error in the field turns a double into a triple. And before you know it, right under your artistic nose, your catcher gone past a ball, and they done stole home on ya!"

Bob Hunter's Monday morning column – aware of his precarious position with L.A. Angel fans – seemed to edge gently towards the prophetic: "As I see it, there's still some question as to whether the Stars will clinch this thing before the beginning of September."

I arrived at the City Hall meeting that Monday and decided to cut through the crap of the previous suppositions. When I reintroduced the idea that Novak was Holderlin, there was an immediate negative reaction from Cobb and Longdown. However, when I pulled out Reich's signed confession, there was no question that Novak and Holderlin were one and the same. Furthermore, having lent an ear to my original suspicion, Jenks had looked further into Novak's recommendations out of Chicago. Sure enough, the president of Novak's electrician's union had been a member of the GAB in the '30s.

So there it was, our first true lead. Suddenly, it wasn't all that difficult for all of us to agree that, given his background and history, Novak was a formidable enemy. A man who would stop at nothing in order to air the voice of his Fuhrer amidst the silent and perfected diamond of America's national game.

Once I began to explain the details of this Fifth Column operation, as I'd gotten it from Reich, a lot of things became clearer about what had happened the day Howard Story was murdered. Not wanting to park too close to the scene of the crime, drawing attention to the Gilmore truck, Novak had blackmailed Reich into allowing him to park in his driveway.

Suddenly, it all made sense to Cobb.

"Sure, I remember that truck," he said. "We were crossing the parking lot, heading toward Beverly, and it was speeding in the direction of Gilmore."

"And you asked me to remind you to 'do something about that,' remember?"

"Right. Little did I know," he replied

"But the bootprint outside the window wasn't Novak's," said Longdown.

"Then it was somebody else who pulled the trigger," I added.

"And Reich claims never to have met any of the others in the Column?" asked Jenks.

"Never. His only concern was that he'd been threatened by Novak with a scandal that could have destroyed his respectable Hollywood retirement. It was only after Story was murdered that Reich realized just how deep he was into something he wanted nothing to do with."

"And you believe him?" questioned Longdown.

"I do. Look, the old man made a big mistake when he joined the Bund, but it might be best to consider that he did jump ship when he realized what Hitler was up to."

They all agreed that my surmise made good sense. More than likely, Novak had shown up one day, out of the blue, to become a thorn in Reich's side from his Nazi heyday. Furthermore, we agreed that instead of taking any action against him, it would be best if he remained an asset. If the law was to catch up with Reich, it would have to come after we tracked down Novak and his crew. I expressed the hope that nothing of the sort would be necessary.

For the next hour, we all speculated on how this new revelatory information might be handled. Jenks had already placed a couple of his agents, disguised as deer hunters, in Los Padres National Park. They were driving around looking for the mobile radio tower that he believed was going to increase the transmission signal to Gilmore Field. Now, with the information of Novak's indentity and his connection to Reich, Jenks would instruct his agents to stakeout Reich's ranch. Certain that the old man's tower wasn't the one we were looking for, Jenks was still concerned about those *other technicians* that Novak had mentioned to Reich who were going to construct it. They could very well prove to be part of the Fifth Column. At the same time, Jenks would put a tail on Novak and wiretap his phone.

The last order of business dealt with the time table of when Jenks thought this Fifth Column would most likely attempt their broadcast at Gilmore.

Cobb chimed in. "The team is away for the next few weeks. They'll be back in town to play the Angels, but I doubt that these Nazis are going to…"

"Attack Wrigley?" interjected Longdown. "I sure wouldn't put it past them to throw us a curve when it comes to the where, when, and how of their fanatical insanity."

"Yeah, but Novak doesn't work at Wrigley," I said.

"There *are* 10,000 more seats at Wrigley than at Gilmore," warned Cobb.

"Could be a goddamned bomb they're planting," Longdown argued. "And this theory of yours, agent Hill, about Hitler addressing the American masses could be false information to get us to look the other way."

"No," argued Jenks. "The way the FBI sees it, Hitler's out to kill two birds with one stone. First, to address his true believers throughout the world, and second, perhaps far more important, is the venue from which it'll take place. Hitler's speech, radioed to the world from Gilmore Field, will be a direct attack upon the power elite of Hollywood that, as far as the Fuhrer believes, is inseparable from the sovereign powers at the foundation of the United States, itself."

Jenks' insight was met with silence by all of us gathered around Longdown's desk.

As sure as Jenks was, about Hitler's purpose and target, he wasn't about to make a mistake and diminish the magnitude of Longdown's theory about a terrorist bombing at Wrigley. He insisted that Cobb contact the Angels security.

"Just inform them," suggested Jenks, "that you got wind of some troublemakers who might be creating some problems at Wrigley in the up and coming series. Let them know you want to send over a couple of your guys to familiarize themselves with their security system. Tell them your security people know what these agitators look like."

"Got it," said Cobb.

Jenks designated me the liaison between Gilmore and Wrigley. He said I should choose some of the best security guys to cover the series. Of course, Angel immediately came to mind.

For the next week or so, with the Stars away at Oakland, Angel and I acquainted ourselves with the security staff and layout of Wrigley Field.

When you're a cop, the difference between carrying a gun and using it pivots on that moment when the mere appearance of your lawfulness demands an immediate execution of the authorized deadly force entrusted to you. While I was a capable marksman with a rifle, I was one hell of a shooter with a pistol. In fact, Pop owned a .38 Smith & Wesson Military and, much to Mom's outrage, bought me a 1918 Colt Automatic .22 Longrifle pistol for my 11th birthday. Two years later, Mom was infuriated, again, when Longdown hauled me in for taking off with my uncle's car. "First, he's stealing a car, before you know it he'll be robbing banks!" I could hear her arguing with Pop from my room.

Between my 11th and 16th year, Pop took me to a pistol target range, several blocks from home, on San Pablo Avenue. Every other weekend, Pop and I would carry our black leather gun satchels (he said we looked like a couple of doctors making house calls) over to the practice range to cultivate my shootist skills. Thanks to this early training with a .22, by the time I was an MP handling a .38 in Hawaii, I was capable of shooting a huge meat cleaver out of the hand of a drunken non-com. Though I took a good portion of his thumb off in doing so, I was sharp enough to know it was best to aim at the hilt and not the blade. Hell, if I'd hit the blade the damn bullet might have ricocheted and gone through the dickhead's brain.

Truth of the matter, I hadn't picked up a firearm since I was wounded in Cebu. With the high probability that I would be forced to use my weapon, at any time in the future, I thought it best to find a target range somewhere in the L.A. proper. Longdown suggested the L.A. Police Academy, better known as the Los Angeles Police Revolver and Athletic Club, in Elysian Park. Leaning back in his swivel chair, he said, "And take the time to try their roast beef sandwich. It's the best in town."

I was just about out the door when I got a phone call from Jenks. He wanted to see me. I told him I was on my way to the Police Academy firing range and I'd come by the Sunset Tower after.

"Police Academy," he said. "That's where I am."

"You're kidding."

"Me and my crew are holed up here."

"So, what happened to the penthouse at the Sunset Tower?"

"What the hell you think happened? Hughes happened!"

We agreed to meet at the Athletic Club Café around 14:30. This gave me time to practice shooting. I hadn't been at the range more than 15 minutes when I got this really sharp pain up my right leg. Fucking weight of the gun reminded me that I was back to doing things I never thought I'd do again. But my aim was still there, solid, continuous, and deadly.

I arrived early at the surprisingly quaint and quiet café on the second floor of this stone complex, dedicated to the education of police officers, sat at a booth and ordered. The waitress was bringing me a black coffee when I caught sight of Jenks. I noticed he had his attaché with him and thought well of my decision not to order the roast beef sandwich that Longdown had recommended. This was, more than likely, a mere cup of coffee chat between the two of us.

"I hear they have a great roast beef sandwich," I said.

Jenks didn't fall for the cordiality routine and said, "Jake, I'm afraid I'm not going to have time for lunch, but there's something I want to go over with you."

He ordered a cup of coffee. After some small talk about Jenks' deer hunters reporting that no work was being done at Reich's ranch and, furthermore, that they'd found no sign of a mobile radio tower in Los Padres National Park, he finally got down to business.

Pulling a photograph out of his attaché, he handed it to me and said, "I understand you took this photo."

The photo was of a phonograph sitting at one end of Novak's desk.

"It was taken last weekend by my wingman, Angel, before I furnished you with the evidence that Novak was Holderlin," I said. "We were able to sneak into his office in the electrical power room and snap that photo. I can only conclude you got it from Longdown."

"Yes, along with your theory that Hitler's speech could end up a recording instead of being broadcast live. That's a load of crap, Jake." He was unable to hold back his anger.

"Come on Jenks, for all you know, Hitler could be on his deathbed with barely enough energy to put two sentences together. It only makes sense that he could have recorded his speech."

"That's not the way it's going to happen."

"Says who?"

"The psych warfare crew over at the Office of Policy Coordination at the Pentagon," he said.

"Psychology isn't everything when it comes to figuring out the next move of a wounded snake like Hitler."

"Jake, Hitler's going to make his speech live, and he's going to make it in English."

"English! I thought the Fuhrer doesn't speak English!"

"He's read it for years. He started speaking it when he lived in Liverpool for six months in the 20s."

"I once had a three-day layover in Liverpool. I don't know if I'd call Liverpudlian, English."

"Our electricians found a booster antenna over at Gilmore. Novak spliced it onto the main one and it's facing north."

"But you still haven't found that mobile unit in Los Padres."

"We'll find it," he said.

"If you say so."

"Besides, we've just received intelligence from Paraguay that Hitler's been in contact with a radio station in Asuncion."

"Probably wants to book some time to make a record."

"This is the last time I'm going to ask you to layoff the recording idea."

I gave him a look that I'd often used in the service. "Roger that."

We sat in silence, finishing our coffees, for the next few minutes. Then Jenks stood up, said he'd be in touch, and exited the little café.

I asked for a refill and ordered the roast beef sandwich. Longdown was right. A meal in itself and well worth the price. Needless to say, far more tasty and comforting than my conversation with Jenks.

The Oaks took five out of seven from the Stars in Oakland. I even got a phone call from Tommy arguing that the Stars days in first were numbered. In fact, by the third game into the Stars series against the Angels, the Oaks were within two games of a tie for first.

Despite our in-depth surveillance of Wrigley, between August 23 and 28, and the Stars taking four out of seven from the Angels, nothing out of the ordinary took place.

With the Stars in Frisco from August 30th to September 1st, Jenks and Longdown agreed that an obvious target date for Hitler's broadcast was, more than likely, on or after September 2nd when the Stars returned home.

On Thursday, September 1st, Angel's new girlfriend came over for dinner. She was a lovely, petite Japanese girl named Ai. She was from an educated samurai family in Japan and understood the values and virtues of a martial artist. As for Angel, despite any hatred he may have harbored toward the Japanese, I could discern none in his feelings for Ai.

After dinner, Hilo sang us one of his new love songs, dedicating it to Ai and Angel. Then, we all listened to the game over the radio. The Stars were up 7 runs on the Seals by the bottom of the sixth, when Angel and Ai left for a night on the town.

Hilo gave me a look.

"Has he shown her his wall of knives yet?" I asked.

"I'm pretty sure they've already climbed that wall," Hilo laughed.

Before hitting the sack, I walked out to the porch. No scotch, just me and my thoughts.

I was feeling a strange sense of anticipation, like the night before we hit the beach at Cebu; it was tinged with the fear that I wasn't going to live beyond the next day. My gut was telling me something was going to go down at tomorrow's night game when the Stars took on the Sacramento Solons.

For the last few weeks, the Feds had staked out Novak's every move. On the afternoon of the 2nd, I was called into Longdown's office; he informed me that Novak had called in sick. Jenks and his crew, having been given this information that morning, had driven north to stake out a newly built radio tower in the Ventura Hills. He was playing a hunch that Novak had taken the day off to join his Fifth Column at this relay transmission point that the Feds had been searching for all along.

"Are they sure Novak left Gilmore last night?"

"The Feds tailed him from his office to his apartment downtown."

"And they're sure it was him?"

"It was him all right. As far as we can tell, he still hasn't left his apartment. Who knows, maybe he's really sick. Regardless, Hill is checking out this tower."

"So, one way or the other, Jenks is figuring on catching Novak's crew red-handed."

"Latest intel from South America has Hitler driving south to that radio station in Asuncion last night."

"So, Hitler is going to make his address live."

"Look, all you and Angel can do tonight is what you do best. And don't forget, Cobb's plain clothes guys are in on the deal now. Not only that, the Feds have set up some radio-radar guys who can shut down any transmission coming from outside the park."

"No sweat, Colonel, Angel and I have got this."

An hour before we left for Gilmore, Angel and I performed our Tai Chi Quan together. For a moment, I'd have sworn we were back in the Philippines attempting to get our heads straight before an advance.

There was a element of nostalgia about the Solons starting pitcher that night. The name, Tony Freitas, tugged at my memory and heart strings. Back in '29, when I was fourteen, Pop, my brothers, and I loyally attended Oaks Park every weekend. There, we hoped to see the great Oaks outfielder, Buzz Artlett – known as the Babe Ruth of the minor leagues – hit yet another game winning homerun. That was also Tony Freitas' rookie year. Tonight, some 20 years later, he was to take the mound for the same team I'd seen him pitch for when I was a kid.

To my young mind, Freitas was David facing Goliath. Artlett was six-four, weighed 230, and, in that year of '29, hit 39 homers, with a batting average of .374 and 189 RBIs. The 21-year-old's movement off the mound was my first, up-close, impression of a youth in possession of that mysterious language that occurs when the deceptive gravity of a pitch moves in direct opposition to the natural grace of a great hitter.

Fast forward, 41-year-old Freitas held up pretty damn well against the Stars stellar lineup. It wasn't until the bottom of the fourth when Tony barely managed to retire the side that the Solons manager, Del Baker, decided to sent in a pinch hitter for him at the top of fifth.

For the last few years, Cobb had authorized an additional dragging of the field between the top and bottom of the fifth. The idea was to give the vendors, outside of the seventh inning stretch, another window of opportunity to increase their sales.

The grounds crew was on the field and the vendors were loudly hawking their wares when Angel, who was carrying a walkie-talkie hooked up to Cobb in his office, received a communication from him. There had been a shootout between Jenks' Feds and three members of the Nazi Fifth Column at the site of the radio tower in the Ventura Hills. The three Nazis were dead and Novak was nowhere in sight; however, his truck was still there. Though Jenks and his crew had stopped the Nazis, in the middle of them receiving a radio transmission from the south, it appeared that Novak had escaped into the woods.

Angel turned off the walkie-talkie and hooked it back onto his belt. We looked at each other and then at the large powerful flashlights we'd been awkwardly carrying around all night. We couldn't help but smile.

"So, you think it's over?" asked Angel.

"Until Novak shows up."

"Why don't we just sit down, enjoy the game, and keep our eyes and ears open."

"Sounds good to me," I said.

We hadn't quite reached our seats when the lights on the field, and throughout the park, went out in one electrical vooooommmm. The fans gave out with a big simultaneous "Ohhhh!" Angel and I, as well as the rest of security, instinctually turned on our flashlights.

Here and there, spectators shouted for "Light!"

"How about some lights! Let's have a little light!"

The shouting for light was building into something close to a chant when I heard the crackling sound of a record needle being placed on a 78.

"That's it," I said to Angel. I hurried in the direction of the Solons dugout. "Novak is here! He's in the electrical room!"

Angel and I had worked out the time and distance between several stadium locations and the electrical room. There was only 200 feet that separated this room from the visitor's dugout by way of the basement corridor.   From there, Novak controlled all the electrical switches to the ballpark's lights and the main audio feed to the entire stadium.

Once inside the dugout, I shoved past a couple of the Solons.   My flashlight was full blast as was Angel's who was trailing right behind me.

"Security!" I shouted.

Racing down the three steps to the dark basement corridor, Angel and I turned left. Separating to the left and right of the corridor, I pulled out my .38 and Angel got on his walkie talkie and ordered the rest of security to block off any access from the field to the electrical room. Communications off, he paused to draw his knife from under his cuff.

Using our flashlights to penetrate the dark that engulfed us, we were now in search of the source of the slow stirring march-time version of "*Deutschland Uber Alles*" that could be heard over the PA system above us. My only prayer was that we could reach the electrical room and take out Novak before the Fat Lady – AKA Adolf Hitler – could sing the swan song of an infamous career.

My Meperidine had kicked in about an hour before and I was feeling no pain. I quickened the pace and Angel easily followed.

As we got closer to the electrical room, we could hear the sounds of outrage, above us, growing louder. Every fan was well aware that this little Germanic ditty was number one on the Fuhrer's hit parade. Some began to shout the obvious expletives in protest.

Nearing the electrical room, we noticed the soft light of a kerosene lamp emanating from under the green wooden double doors to our right.   We could hear Novack singing along with the music.   From our survellience photograph, we knew he was sitting to the right of the record player.

With the help of a shaft of moonlight, from the grid above us, we quickly turned off our flashlights and placed them on the ground behind us. While Angel advanced to the far side of the left door, I took aim at the doorknob of the double doors that I assumed to be locked from within.

With Haydn's infamous theme beginning to fade, I took my two shots at the locks. Novak immediately returned fire rapidly shooting several shots through the door.

As Novak continued to fire, we rushed to the doors, kicking them in. They flew open, swinging inward into the room. Angel took cover, and I moved between the two doors, squatted, and fired toward Novack. I missed. Novak, with two bullets left in the clip of his Luger, caught sight of me and took his shot. He missed. My next two blasts went right through his throat and forehead. The impact forced Novak's left arm outward over the top of the turntable, scraping the needle across the record.

Taking out Novak when we did, we were able to cut the Fuhrer's speech off right at its beginning: "My dear and precious Americans, this is your leader…!"

The Fed's electricians showed up on the heels of the shootout. They immediately entered the electrical room and restored lighting to the stadium. Players, on both teams, who thought they'd heard gunshots echoing through the corridor were told that it was the sound of fuses blowing.

Everyone on the electrical crew and working security that night was sworn to silence at the threat of losing their jobs. The green doors were roped together. An "Absolutely No Entrance" sign hung from a wooden sawhorse in front of the doors.

The game started up again, played out, and came to an end. The stadium emptied and the players left for home. The Solons won the game 4 to 1.

The dead body of Novak – AKA Hoffmann or Holderlin – remained in place until Longdown showed up with his homicide crew around 11:30. Angel and I were able to leave the scene by 12:30. "Good work, gentlemen," Longdown said to the both of us as we turned to leave Gilmore for home.

Before we retired to our rooms that morning, Angel and I shook hands and embraced. Once again, we'd survived a moment of combat together.

I was about to hit the sack when I got a call downstairs from Jenks. He apologized.

"We were both right," I said, in a cordial manner.

"Novak must have spent the night in the ventilation system," he said.

"Go figure."

"We still don't know exactly who left Gilmore disguised as Novak."

"It was probably the same Nazi who drove the Gilmore maintenance truck north," I said.

"But Novak didn't leave Gilmore in the truck. My men pinned him leaving in his own car and driving it to his apartment downtown."

"And the truck…?"

"Wasn't reported missing until yesterday morning. I got a hunch there's more of them."

"Still, could have been the same guy in both cases, one of them killed at the tower." I said.

"From your mouth to the devil's dreams," Jenks added cynically.

He ordered me to call Bob Hunter and crack a deal. If Hunter would write a good cover story for what had gone down at Gilmore, I would eventually give him a bigger story on the Fifth Column.

"So I'm free to let him in on what's been going on?"

"Sure, but only enough to wet his shiny Fourth Estate whistle."

"Sounds good to me!"

When I got off the phone with Jenks, I immediately called Bob. Ravenous for the full scoop on the Beverly Boulevard murder, he agreed to provide a cover story for the shootout. That morning, Bob's column was able to whitewash the blackout and Hitler's attempted public address as a coincidental combination of an electrical overload and a failed commercial for a German bakery. Thank God Bob had the clout to get all the other sport's writers to follow suit.

I finally got to bed around 2:30 and told myself I was going to sleep into the afternoon.

Boy, did I get that wrong!

I woke up a little after six to take a piss when the phone rang. It was the Colonel. I had barely said "Hello" when he gave me an address and ordered me to be there as quickly as possible.

I knew the address to be Reich's home and had a bad feeling about why I was being ordered there, especially when I saw Richie Goodman standing outside, as I pulled up. He filled me in on what to expect inside.

"Total Dutch Act, Jake."

The iron door was opened wide, as well the carved wooden one. Reich's home was as I remembered, a shelter of contrasts and contradictions, all magically brought to light under the masterful guidance of a unique cinematic eye. Reich had a vision that was capable of juxtaposing the abstract virtues of an unquestionable morality in perfect opposition to the earthly canine wisdom of playing a dirty game.

Longdown was nowhere to be found, but one of his young detectives was interviewing Maurice on the third level of the enormous interior. Maurice caught sight of me as I made my way toward the pool. He stood up and walked in my direction.

"Hey," exclaimed the detective, "I'm not finished with you!"

I gestured to the detective and said, "It's all right, I know the gentleman." I turned to Maurice and said, "I'm so sorry for your loss."

"There were legions who misunderstood him, but to the few who really knew him, he was a great artist and man."

I shook his hand and embraced him. He turned and walked back to the detective. I continued in the direction of the pool where I could see Coleman and the other detectives.

Reich was slumped over the poolside table where I had interviewed him. Coleman filled me in on the details. It was cyanide in his Bloody Mary. Having dusted Reich's suicide note for prints, he handed it to me. It read:

Ask my fish, Rodrigo, why he refused to leave the pool.
Leave the River as you found it.
"Thy word is a lamp unto my feet and a light unto my path,"

Detective Sergeant Morgan, who I'd gotten to know over these last several weeks, was waving me over to the pool.

"You gotta help me out with this, Salazar!"

As I walked toward Morgan, I looked down and noticed Rodrigo in the pool taking laps.

"I've already begged this Latino flit to get out of the damn pool. What's the matter with him? One thing I know, I'm not going in after him. He says he isn't getting out of the pool until you show up."

I bent down on my good knee and offered Rodrigo my hand.

A look of relief came over his face. Just for Reich's sake, he had endured hours in the cold water awaiting my arrival.

I helped him from the pool. He emerged a shivering wreck. Maurice, having finished his interview, suddenly appeared with a fluffy white beach towel, the size of Rhode Island, and placed it gently over Rodrigo.

"I thought you would never come, Officer Salazar," said the freezing Rodrigo.

"Come now, Rodrigo, nothing a hot shower, some dry clothes, and some breakfast can't fix," suggested Maurice as they turned to enter the house.

"Why did Reich make you swim those laps until I arrived?"

Rodrigo stopped short and sneezed. "Oh yes, I almost forgot. I am to remind you of how impossible it is for a fish to survive out of water?"

As they entered the house I turned east toward the rising sun and whispered to myself, "You've got some perfect morning light here, Caesar. Just a hair above the magic hour. Just a hair, mind you."

Over the last few months, I'd gone through several possible definitions of "lights out!" I had reflected on the expression all the way from my perfect game to Novak's failed attempt to shackle the electricity of America's national game in order to spread the word of an over-the-hill dictator. Still, I wasn't figuring on Reich's version of "lights out."

I didn't drive home, but over to Melrose. Nothing like a dirty spoon early in the morning, to calm the nerves. There were only a few early birds in the joint. I sat in the same duce as I had after my visit with Jenks. As I sipped at my coffee, I kept asking myself why had Reich killed himself, when he was about to get off with a slap on the wrist. It had to have been guilt, right? But not some big time regretful look over his shoulder; no, his "lights out" was far from some morbid reflection on how he'd screwed up his life by joining the Bund in the '30s. Furthermore, the old man's ultimate act wasn't just the result of the death of Story; no, something closer to coming clean with me as to what von Geist had to do with the Fifth Column. And what the hell was that reminder about a fish not being able to survive out of water all about.

I took my last sip, left my quarter tip, exited the coffee shop and drove home.

Chapter XI

Diamonds, Squares and Inside Straights

Returning home from Reich's suicide, I fell into bed and didn't wake up until Sunday afternoon. When I dressed and came downstairs, Angel and Hilo were making breakfast. Once we sat down for some bacon and eggs, Angel gave Hilo the blow-by-blow of the shootout at Gilmore. Hilo turned to me and offered his congratulations.

"Thank you," I said apprehensively, knowing there was probably more to come.

"And how does the pawn feel after his first successful gig with the LAPD?"

"Like it's time we all took a vacation in Vegas."

"Now, that's the old Jake Salazar talking," said Hilo.

"Unfortunately, my FBI friend, Jenks, seems to think there may be more of these Nazis around."

"I say we forget about them and go to Vegas for a good time," said Angel.

We all had a laugh.

Despite the fact that there was some mention of the doubleheader that day, I think we all had had enough of baseball for the moment, certainly Angel and I had. Hilo went upstairs to work on his songs while Angel and I practiced our Tai Chi Quan along the canal.

The way I looked at it, this was going to be a carefree Sunday afternoon.

After our practice, Angel confided in me that he made an appointment to see Dr. von Geist.

"Good for you," I said.

"It's not until next month; she is a very busy doctor."

"And very knowledgeable. You're in good hands and..."

I'd barely gotten the words out when a car horn beeped in the alley.

"That's Carlo. He says there's a space downtown that would work for my Tai Chi studio."

"Carlo. Isn't that the guy you had a thing for?"

"Not to worry. We have an understanding."

"You're sure about that?"

"Look, I told you I'm going to your doctor!"

"Sure you're not trying to get in a little something before confession?"

Angel gave me a stare that could have cut through my heart.

"Only you, my brother, say such things to me."

"Only you, my brother, know if they're true."

He put on his black hat at a cocky slant, turned, and exited through the back door to the awaiting car in the alley.

Late that night, sitting on the porch with scotch in hand, I couldn't help but mull over Reich's parting caveat regarding the impossibility of a fish surviving out of water. Off the top, the question elicited an obvious answer. Reich was implying that homosexuals can only survive among themselves. But thinking about Reich, the man and creator, I couldn't help but believe that he was referencing a fish story much bigger than his relationship with other homosexuals. No, his admonition came from the bottom of the deck, a calculated laugh from the purview of the dead. After all, we had talked politics in one of the most confidentially corrupt and peacefully organized cities on the face of the earth. Having taken in Reich's tuneful dissertation on quid pro quo, I could be damn sure his final warning came directly from the sacrificial heart of this electrified industrial silence. A fucking Pinocchio shouting from the belly of the beast, itself. More than likely, Reich's final message was nothing less than a rebuke against believers in fish surviving out of water and pointed in the same direction as Jenks' intuition. There were more of these Nazis out there! But where were they, who were they? It was somewhere between the gradually blurring moonbeans on the canal and my fourth scotch that it came to me. That photo on von Geist's desk, the one with the father flanked by his sons: The fishes covering their faces were dead.

I was late for work that Monday. I figured Longdown would cut me a little slack.

When I walked into headquarters, I was surprised to find no one but Sergeant Morgan and Longdown's secretary looking over some records.

The sergeant turned in my direction and asked, "So how's Richie doing?"

"Richie?"

"Christ! You just arrived didn't you."

A chill went up my spine. "You talking about Richie Goodman?"

"Jake. Richie was shot last night down on Skid Row off Main Street."

"How is he?"

"Last I heard, he was in critical condition. They got him over at Methodist on Hope Street."

I turned and hurried out the door. Morgan yelled after me, "You know where you're going?"

"Yeah," I yelled, as I started down the two flights. Then, taking the stairs to the basement garage, I hopped into the Plymouth and headed south for the hospital.

I was too late, Richie had been dead for an hour by the time I arrived.

His wife and their two boys were there. I introduced myself and embraced Richie's wife. "I'm so sorry," I said.

"Jake Salazar," she said, holding back tears from eyes that had been weeping for well over an hour. "Richie spoke of your friendship so often." As if in a strange nightmarish trance, she took her children's hands and walked to the bedside of her dead husband.

Now, Richie was just another dead cop. Just another strong family man sent to the grave. Another good man with a caring face covered with a sheet.

After some awkward moments of standing around with the other detectives and uniformed officers, Longdown grabbed me by the arm and led me down the hall to a medical supply room. He closed the door behind him, locked it, and turned on the light.

"What the hell happened?"

"Around 3 a.m., a sniper, with a silenced Remington M30, took him down at street level."

"Any eyewitnesses?"

"If any rummy out there saw it go down, I can guarantee – for the moment anyway - he's keeping it to himself. It's pretty desolate on the Row around that time. So much so, the assassin brazenly crossed the street and placed this next to his body." He reached into his coat pocket and pulled out and unrolled a strip of brown paper bag similar to the one found near the window of Cobb's office on Beverly. There was something written on it.

I hesitated to take it from him.

"No problem. Coleman dusted it for prints. Nothing."

I took the strip of paper from him and read what was written on it.

> Dear Officer Salazar.
> Shoemakers and tailors count hours.
> Yours Truly,
> Hoffmann the Shoemaker

"It seems our FBI friend, Hill, had it right," the Colonel said.

The note was obviously a threat to me and my family. I rushed to the nearest phone but quickly put it down and drove directly home. This call was too important to be made from a doctor's office or a phone booth.

When I got home, I immediately called Oakland. I was sitting at my desk and pouring myself a scotch when Mom answered.

"Hi Mom. Just sitting here thinking about you. How are things?"

"Maybe I'm dreaming and my favorite son has actually called to talk to me."

"As a matter of fact, Mom, I'd like you to ask Frank to ring me here in L.A. Tell the operator to reverse the charges…"

"That's not necessary…"

"No, really Mom, I don't want you to have to pay for…"

"I mean," she said, "Frank's right here, enjoying some of my healing chicken soup."

"What? I thought the bum was a working man."

"Caught some flu from one of the lugs he works with. Here, I'll put him on." I could hear Mom yelling across the living room into the kitchen, "Frank, it's Jake, he wants a word with you."

When Frank came to the phone, I took him into my confidence and insisted that he was not to share what I was about to tell him with any member of our family. He tuned in immediately and was all ears. "If anyone asks why I called you, just tell them I needed your insights about the nature of a horse so I can interpret a clue concerning this Fifth Column thing." He agreed. I filled him in on all the details, especially regarding the other night when we thought that killing Hoffmann, and what we believed to be his entire gang of Nazis, had put an end to our problem. "Turns out, we just realized there are more of these bastards. Not only that, they murdered a friend of mine and left a personal note next to his body threatening me and my family." I wanted Frank to keep an eye out for anything strange or out of the ordinary, like a car circling the block. Honestly, I doubted these Nazi creeps had the resources to enable them to attack our family in Oakland, but I wasn't taking any chances. Again, he agreed. I told him that it would probably be best to include Tommy in on the situation. I was leaving the when and where up to him.

Before I hung up, Frank informed me that he owned a .45. I already knew this since Millie had written to me about it when I was overseas. She also told me he was a heavy boozer and they were having marital problems. All of this information scared the hell out of me. With all of this behind them now, the fact that he still owned a firearm for protection could prove to be a handy advantage considering the present situation. I told him to never leave home armed and only to make use of it if Mom's house was invaded. He agreed. Lastly, I asked him to have Millie give me a ring.

"Thanks for trusting me, Jake."

When we hung up, I felt a lot better about the safety of my family.

That afternoon, Hilo told me that Angel spent the night with his longshoreman friend and that Carlo would drive him to work in the morning. When he gave me a knowing look, I felt I had to defend Angel and said, "He promised me he's going to see a doctor about his situation, and I believe him. All said and done, it's really not our business."

Around three, I called Longdown. I told him I was headed up to Oakland on the Coast Starlight to meet an old friend of mine who had lived across the street from Hoffmann during the war. I thought he might have some information that could throw some light on the remaining members of this Fifth Column.

"Jake, we're all at our wit's end trying to figure out who these remaining Nazis are. I don't see how a trip to Oakland would hurt."

Millie phoned me early evening. I told her I was going to catch the Starlight at 8:15 because I needed to meet with Eephus, after all. I asked her what she thought might be the best time to catch up with him on the Cal campus. She said he was there as early as 8 a.m., took a couple of hours off around 12, and returned after 2. When she asked me if I'd be dropping by the house, I told her some things had come up in the Fifth Column investigation and I had no time for a visit. She could tell I felt lousy about not stopping by. When I made it clear that the family couldn't know I was there, she remembered that we'd agreed that my meeting with Eephus wasn't to be a family visit.

"You know, Jake, it was really nice of you to ask Frank's advice on this case of yours."

"Frank knows horses and I needed some advice."

"Thanks for including him, Jake."

"He's a good man, Millie, someone that I'm sure you can depend on."

"I'm so glad you feel that way."

"How's Charlie doing?"

"He keeps asking about when you're going to visit again and arguing with Tommy about the Oaks not catching the Stars."

"Looks like I've created a Stars fan. Give my love to Mom and everyone."

"Love you, Jake."

"Right back at you, Millie," I said.

Around 6:30, Hilo and I were having an early dinner when Angel came home. He went straight to his room without even saying hello. As we finished dinner, I told Hilo about Richie's murder. It really shook him up. I had planned to tell Angel, but the way he was acting I thought it best not to even bother.

With a bit of a heatwave up and down the coast, I decided to travel light. Sport shirt, jeans, tennis shoes, shades, and my Borsalino Panama. I threw my Modern Library copy of Jeffers' poems in my knapsack and that was that. I was ready for my nine-hour redeye journey.

Before I left for Union Station, I sat out on the porch sipping away at yesterday and doing my best to hold back my rage and need for revenge over Richie's murder. Assassination was closer to it! I recalled the times I'd gone berserk in the Pacific, like when I emptied a clip into that unfortunate Jap who had had the bad luck to kill a kid I'd befriended. I was about to cut off his ears but Angel stopped me just in time.

By the time I got on the Starlight, I knew I was in desperate need of some real R&R, even if that was the mere distance between L.A. and Oakland. My trip north would provide me with some time to read. Maybe one of Jeffers' poems just might do the trick. A good way up the coast, around Salinas, I dove into Jeffers' "The Torch-Bearer's Race."

Arriving at the 16th Street train station in Oakland, a little after 5 in the morning, I caught a cab to an old flop on Shattuck where I used to crash when I'd come in for shore leave. It seemed to always provide me with a comfortable space to transform from the edgy seaman into a civil and loving member of the family located only a couple of blocks south. The desk clerk remembered me from the old days. There he was: the same job, same face, a few more wrinkles, and a few less teeth. I got a room at the day-rate, bought a *Tribune* from a rack next to the counter, and went upstairs to my room to read Emmons Byrne's coverage of the Oaks taking a day-night doubleheader from San Diego and Lee Dunbar's sport's editorial, *On the Level*. Lee was providing some fearful Oaks' fans with his realistic opinion that Casey Stengel was bound to bring Billy Martin up to the Yankees next season. Though I'd slept some on the train, after a half hour of reading the paper, I fell off and awoke about 7:30. I washed up, went downstairs, handed the *Tribune* to a fellow who looked like he could read, and walked to the UC campus.

Millie and I had often walked the campus and dreamed of obtaining a higher education, Jimmy and Tommy, not so much. It was our mutual interests in ideas and literature that set us on the path of dreaming of college. Millie got as far as working a secretarial job at Cal and hoped to audit some classes. But, she got too close to her boss, an associate professor of psychology, and began to look upon their relationship as far more important than an education. To further complicate her shaky college ambition, she met Frank. After he gave her a couple of whirls on the dance floor, Cal and the good professor were kaput.

As I entered the turnaround off Oxford Street, I remembered that this very spot was where we would often begin our twilight walks amidst UC's grove of giant, aromatic eucalyptus. It was the thrill of our youth to live so close to one of the most beautiful campuses on earth. But, at the moment, I was far from the musings of twilight and the dazzling ruminations of our hopes and dreams. Today, I needed to walk around the periphery of these alluring miracles of nature to visit an old friend of profound intelligence and worldly wisdom.

For close to 20 years, Eephus Pitch had occupied the sidewalk side of a concrete walk-around that encircled a 100-year-old, thickly gnarled oak tree. There, he had served as UC's reigning streetcorner chess master proudly enthroned on his departmental rocking chair. His board and chairs were set up just southeast of the University's West Circle where Highway Walk entered what my sister and I called "our sacred gathering of eucalyptus." The Walk, I fondly remembered, met up, deep within the grove, with the majestic Grinnell Pathway.

As I turned right onto Highway Walk, I noticed that Eephus was just finishing up a game with an older heavyset worker type. I figured it would be best not to approach them and interrupt their game. I decided to give Eephus and his opponent a few more minutes to themselves, so I walked north. I wanted to have a look at my favorite building on campus.

Prior to lectures on architecture in high school, the construction of Cal's Life Sciences Building had been my first encounter with the art form. Between 1928 and 1930, Millie and I had watched this columned, classical revival building being constructed before our very eyes. What made it so fascinating was its embossed facade of cellular, plant, and animal representations of living things. In two years time, a hillside, that my sister and I had known to be a simple path through our childhood garden, had gradually and magically transformed into something akin to the splendor of ancient Greece.

In the tenth grade, when I was introduced to the eight taxonomic divisions of the living, I shared this knowledge with my sister. I always remember us, at the deepest crossing of Highway Walk and Grinnell Pathway, hammering out from memory the species Canis Lupis. We were able to recite all the taxonomies from the *Domain* of eucalyptus, paramecium, earthworm, snake, seal, human, horse, wolf, coyote, fox, and dog to the *Species* of the innumerable dogs and the living breeds of wolves from which they evolved. As I turned back and walked toward Eephus and his chess game, I thought of the unforgettable flaming eyes of twin wolves pacing back and forth in the dark forest of a dream I'd had one rainy night in the Pacific, Corpora anima: two bodies, one soul. The primal love for one's progenitors remains equally present in the obedient mind of a faithful dog and the diehard intelligence of Mother Nature's own, the wolf.

As I walked across the street to greet Eephus, I noticed that the broad-shouldered, middle-aged working man was taking his leave. He had just lost his black king to the black man's deadly white endgame and was shaking the master chessman's hand. He, then, turned to depart the campus via University Drive. I took a closer look at the unmistakable dress of the tradesmen who Eephus had been engaging with in mental combat. The white cotton, low on the forehead, flat cap (the so-called West Coast Stetson) perfectly complimented his black, baggy "Frisco" Bens and short-sleeved – *green and white* – Mariniere-striped

Telnyashka tee. The getup pinned him as a longshoreman. The only thing missing was his ever-handy hook. In fact, alongside Eephus, in his snug "Old Goat" blue-white, hickory-stripe bib overalls and Oaks cap, the two could have passed for a couple of stevedores, freed of their drays and gang, hard-timing their dock bosses in an idle game of chess.

Eephus was turning back towards his chairs, table, and chessboard when he noticed me approaching him.

"Good Lord! If it ain't the prodigal, perfect game pitchin' Jake Salazar, returned unto the arms of this old black Eephus Pitch, Himself," he proclaimed, as we embraced. It was going on three years since I'd felt the strong, enduring solace of his mighty arms.

Once the great black bear had released me, I looked him straight in the eyes and said, "Diamonds, Squares and Inside Straights..!"

Then together we said, "...Young Man Beware!"

"For you and me, and I'd include your Pop, bless his soul, ain't nothin' better for a gamblin' man but to learn the games from the ground up. 'Cause, no matter what you playin at, it all comes at you hard and fast."

"From Tinker to Evers to Chance," I added proudly.

"Like I always say, 'You out to join the *tinkers*," he placed his right forefinger to his right temple, "'it's best you for-*evers* out to take a *chance*.'"

"Especially when you think you're fast enough to outrun the throw to first."

"Or, once you're on the square, you take the time to learn the value of your pawns," he said, with a knowing smile and wink.

"Or at the table, the guts, heart, and cash to play out the 11 to one odds of an inside straight," I said, concluding the threefold logic of a gamester.

We had a good laugh.

"Come on. Let's sit and have a game. Your sister tells me you out to do in my London with your Caro Kann."

We sat down, the board between us, and Eephus placed the pieces onto their starting positions.

"So who's the Hook?" I asked.

"Name's Eric Hoffer. He came out of a Frisco fog, one night, a couple weeks after the Japs hit Pearl. We sat down and shared a couple of beers. He tells me he's just landed himself a job on the docks. Gonna join Bridges, and his commie boys, workin' the aprons out of Frisco. So, I tell'em how I earn my shackles. Nowadays, he ferries over, on his day off, and pays me top price for a game."

"He any good?"

"Not anything this black ass can't put an end to," he boasted.

"Where's he from?"

"Swears he was raised up in the Bronx, New York. Sounds like a goddamned Kraut to me."

Then it came to me. I suddenly remembered when I had come across that green and white striped Telnyaska tee. "That's it!"

"What's that?"

"I just remembered the last time I saw your friend's green and white stripped T-shirt."

"Yeah, you usually see blue and white stripes."

"Must have been '33," I said. "We had freighted some of Ford's tractors, bound for Russia, south from Frisco to Manzanillo. The cargo was to be loaded on to a Russian freighter headed for Vladivostok. A shipmate points out these Russians, in green and white striped tees, says they're part of Stalin's Soviet Border Troops Secret Police in charge of inspecting the cargo."

"So you figure this Hoffer dude's some kinda real commie, dressin' on the sly, so as to let Harry Bridge's boys know who's really boss," he said, barely holding back his laughter.

"Dealing with what I've been dealing with lately, I can't tell a commie from a fascist."

"A Hoffer from a Hoffmann," he said with a smile.

I reached into the watch pocket of my jeans, pulled out that 20 I had put there, and offered it to Eephus across the board. "That is what I'm here for, Eephus."

"Yeah, I figured, after talking with your sister, you and me gettin' together wasn't gonna be as simple as an innocent game of chess."

"Go on, take it," I said.

"Don't mind if I do," he said, putting the 20 in the top pocket of his overalls.

"Tell me everything you remember about this shoemaker, Hoffmann."

"I'd best be straight with you, Jake. My memory ain't close to what it used to be," he confessed. "I swear, I look down at the board sometimes, right in the middle of a game, and I have to say to myself, 'where the hell am I!' God damned brain goin' fast and sure as hell not in the righ⁺ direction!"

"Just think back as best you can."

He took a long deep breath into the large nostrils of his flat snubbed nose and stroked his chin like some wise old African king with huge fat hands. "Well, as I remember, he wasn't a bad shoemaker and…ah… then, one day, he up and disappeared altogether."

"That part of the story, I know," I said.

"How's that?" he asked.

"Pop caught him, one night, on a shortwave radio sending messages to a Jap sub off the coast."

"You tellin' me, this Hoffmann was a Nazi spy!"

"Nothing less."

"I knew there was somethin' fishy 'bout that guy. I just knew it!"

"...But all you remember is that he was a pretty good shoemaker who disappeared one day?"

"Tell me the truth, Jake, you workin' for the FBI these days?"

"LAPD. I'm working between them and the Feds."

"Well, I'll be damned. Jake Salazar's taken on the biggest gamble of his life and gone and become a cop."

"'Service above self,'" I said.

Eephus bellowed out a great bass laugh, that could have come from the center of the earth, and said, "I never figured I'd be hearing that old saw from the likes of you."

"Back to the subject at hand. There's nothing else you remember about Hoffmann?"

"Well, let me think," he said. Eephus stared down at the chessboard as if it were some crystal ball of 64 black and white squares, and key to the then and now.

He suddenly snapped his fingers and said, "Now I remember, he was married!"

"Married!"

"Yeah, well...not exactly. More like they was separated. But every once in a while his wife and son would show up for a visit."

"He had a son?"

"Yeah, he musta been 12 or 13. Always came to visit in his uniform. Seemed like his parents kept him out of sight in some military school. Every time he visited, he had his mitt and ball with him like he wanted to play catch with his dad. But his old man, obviously, never played ball in his life. One day I crossed the street, with my old mitt in hand, and offered to play catch with the kid. He had a damn good arm on him too. Told me they was startin' up a Little League team where he lived with his mom during the summer. Ahhh…somewhere in the L.A. area, I think it was. Told me he wanted to pitch. We got together a couple of times when he visited. I was even able to give him some pointers, just like I worked with you before you pitched your perfect game."

I was thinking back to the night that Novak went crazy as Bachman entered the game.

"And what about Hoffmann's wife?"

"I ain't seen her but from a distance, when she left the boy off. But as I recall, she was slim and a bit of a looker. She was always wearing a hat, but I think she was a blonde."

"The kid, was he blond as well?"

"Oh yeah, he was blond, all right. Blond on blond," he said.

"Bachman!"

"Who's Bachman?"

"Nothing less than the rest of the Fifth Column," I blurted out. I pulled out my wallet and reached in for another 20. I handed it to Eephus. This was more information than I could have ever imagined. I kissed him on the forehead, turned, and headed in the direction of University Drive.

He shouted after me, "Just remember, Jake, if it's a nothin' pitch, then it damn ain't nothin' till it's in your catcher's mitt!"

Turning back to him I yelled, "I'll keep that in mind, Mr. Pitch! And take a rain check on that game of ours!"

It was Eephus's parting words that encouraged me to feel that, perhaps, Richie Goodman was now spirtually with me. The same guy that had caught my perfect game had become, once again, an intangible bridge between me and the unknown.

Chapter XII

A Fascist's Revenge

I exited the campus and reached Oxford Street. For a moment, I had the urge to continue towards Shattuck Avenue and Mom's house, a familiar walk that could have ended with some new and comforting information for Frank and the family. But since it was only my hunch that Bachman killed Richie, there was no reason to go home because I wasn't sure if he was the only remaining member of his old man's Fifth Column.

I hopped a cab, about to enter the turnaround, and headed straight for the Clay Street Ferry Terminal. There, I made a long distance call to Longdown. He was out of his office. I tried Cobb but Haney answered the phone. He said Cobb was gone for the afternoon. I knew I couldn't say a thing to him concerning the situation, but I thought I might take a shot at gaining some information from him, indirectly.

"You know, I've been very impressed by this kid, Bachman," I said.

"You and me both, Jake. He's done some damn good relief work for us this season."

"So I assume you'll be using him as you guys come down to the wire."

"I sure would if I knew where the hell he was."

"What do you mean?"

"Since the lights went out the other night, he's vanished into thin air."

I took a long pause then said, "Well, good luck with that."

"I'll tell Bob you called."

"Yeah, tell him to give me a ring at home. I'm in Oakland, at the moment; I'll be back later this evening."

"Will do," he said and hung up.

So that was the deal. One minute, an innocent cup of coffee hoping to gain a position in the rotation, the next, an invisible assassin determined to take out god knows who.

I made it across the bay in time to catch the Noon Daylight and arrived home around 10:30 in the p.m.

I poured myself a scotch and was about to get hold of Cobb or Longdown when Hilo came through the back door with a bag of groceries.

"Evening, Jake, how'd it go in Oakland?"

"All right. Say, did I happen to get a call from Cobb this evening?"

"Not that I know of. But then, I just got in about an hour ago and went right out for these," he said, as he crossed to the kitchenette to put the groceries away. He put the bag down and turned to open a cabinet door when he looked at me and said, "Oh, that doctor called you…what's her name?"

"…von Geist?"

"Yeah, she sounded really scared. She said "please tell Officer Salazar to come here as soon as he gets in."

I gulped down my scotch, but it wasn't enough to stop that damn jungle chill from running up my spine. Bachman was nowhere to be found and von Geist was in need of my help. This whole damn situation was moving along faster than I could have imagined. I had her number in my wallet and called her, but no answer. I ran up the stairs to my room.

"What's going on!" shouted Hilo.

"I wish I knew."

I strapped on my loaded .38 and covered up with a blue sports coat. Eephus' description of Hoffmann's wife being blonde wasn't enough for me to conclude that she and von Geist were one and the same. Still, I couldn't help but feel that the pieces of this puzzle were coming together. Could it have been von Geist, not her sister, who misstepped and fell to her ruin by marrying an SS Officer? On the other hand, had I jumped the gun in thinking that Bachman was their son!

For a moment, I thought I should call Longdown. But who was to say I wouldn't be sending him on a wild goose chase. Could be, von Geist's cry for help had nothing to do with Bachman's disappearance. I had to be absolutely sure that Bachman was linked to von Geist before I called in Longdown and the crew. No, this one was on me from beginning to end.

As I hurried down the stairs, Angel came out of his room.

"Jake, I have to talk with you."

"Later Angel," I said, rushing toward the alley door.

"But you're the only one I can talk to!"

I stopped at the door, abruptly turned and said, "Look, I'm clearly not the person to be giving you advice about who in the hell you should have sex with!"

Hilo was shocked at my outburst and stood frozen with a can of beans in his hand.

"But I told you I go to the doctor! I just need some advice…"

"That's exactly where I'm going now. I have to get out of here!"

"You got trouble? I'll help you," he said.

"Don't worry. I can handle this myself." I was out the door.

As I drove out of the alley, I caught sight of Angel in my rearview mirror. He had followed me out of the house and was staring at me with a look of confusion and concern.

I caught some traffic on La Cienega, but beyond Sunset it was smooth sailing into the hills. Once I reached Hillside Avenue and snaked my way to von Geist's mailbox, I parked and made my way by foot up her gravel driveway.

Week's back, in the pouring rain, von Geist's psychiatric citadel had appeared an inviting and brightly lit shelter. But now, veiled in darkness and illuminated in eerie moonlight, it looked powerless to heal the ailing emotions and intellects of those below.

Halfway up the drive, I pulled out my .38 and released its safety. I gripped the weapon with both hands and continued to climb to the circular parking level of the house. There was one hell of a pain gnawing away at my right thigh. I realized that I had forgotten to take my pain meds when I had arrived home from Oakland.

Once I reached the limestone steps, I noticed that the aluminum doors to the interior of the house were open. Leaving the dominant sounds and fragrances of the night behind me, I cautiously entered the dimly lit interior of the doctor's wooden house.

Once in the vestibule, I took a hard right and slowly advanced into the oblong living room. When I felt the outer edge of the Chinese rug beneath me, I turned in the direction of the plate glass windows and was blinded by the tinted blue light emanating from that direction. The eastern ritual masks, to my left, and the stoic stone fragments of western myth, to my right, momentarily disappeared. I gradually realized that the source of light was a lamp on the doctor's elegant desk. There, as if asleep, was Dr. von

Geist encircled in blood. Although this was the same MO as in Cobb's office, a bullet through the back of the neck, the places in which these unfortunates met their end were worlds apart. Above and below, the Nazis had taken their pound of flesh.

I was reaching for the phone on von Geist's desk when I sensed there was someone behind me.

"Good evening, Officer Salazar," said the young male voice.

I was about to turn around when he said, "Just put your gun down next to my mother's body, and fold your hands together at the back of your neck."

I did as I was told.

"Now, if you please, face me and walk towards me, away from the desk."

I turned to look at the murderous cup of coffee and did as I was told. The bastard was wearing his Stars cap and pointing a C96 Mauser at my heart. I was, no doubt, staring at the gun that had killed both Howard Story and Eartha von Geist.

"You were one hell of a pitcher. Why, on earth, did you get involved with your father's Fifth Column of Nazis?"

"Shut up!" he shouted. His gun hand was beginning to shake.

"So, to please your father you murdered Howard Story and my friend, Richie Goodman! But why, your mother?"

"She was undermining him!" He stepped back, pointing the Mauser directly at his dead mother. "She would just go on and on and on and on....!" A look came over his face as if he suddenly realized what he had done. Both of his arms fell limp. He dropped the gun and cupped his ears. "That despicable socialistic feminist!" he screamed. I made a grab for the gun, but, quickly coming to his senses, he beat me to it. Standing and pointing it at me, he was about to let me have it. Suddenly, a familiar, high-keyed, steel-winded sound whizzed through the air ending in a crackling of bone.

Bachman's eyes opened as wide as a drunken rummy struck by lightning. His gun-hand quivered as his trigger finger froze to a rigid horizontal. With his Mauser, swinging back and forth like the separator of some pool hall scoring beads, he landed face down in front of me. His backbone had been snapped in two by the impact of Angel's Bowie knife.

"Thank you, my dear friend," I said contritely, staring at his shadowy image.

"I always have your back."

Thank God Angel ignored my indifference to his troubled soul.

I phoned Longdown and did my best to explain the situation. He said he was on his way.

I sat on the white swivel sofa, and Angel tried his best to get comfortable on La Corbu's chaise lounge. With dead bodies lying behind us, we looked out onto the movieland's illuminated cityscape.

After several moments, of remaining silent and taking in the view, Angel said, "By the way, I didn't sleep with Carlo last night. I wanted to, but I didn't."

"Okay."

"We just talked all night. He thinks it is good, my dream to have a child."

Longdown, Morgan, and a few others from Homicide arrived around 12. I pulled Longdown off to the side and filled him in. I explained how I came by my information about Hoffmann being married and having a son. I went on to say that from my contact's description of his son, I could only conclude that he was Joe Bachman, a successful reliever for the Stars. Furthermore, Eephus's description of Hoffmann's wife was damn close to Dr. von Geist. When I arrived back in L.A., I found out that Dr. von Geist had called me. She was in a state of fear and wanted to see me immediately. Rushing here, to her home, I found her dead. Moments later, Bachman confronted me. He would have killed me if Angel hadn't followed me into the hills and killed him first.

"If you ask me, Colonel, it was Bachman who killed Officer Goodman. Find where he was holed up, and I'm sure you'll find the sniper rifle that killed Richie," I concluded.

Longdown told me to have a full written report on his desk within the next day or so. He congratulated Angel and me and said he'd take it from here.

"It looks like you've gotten to the root of this Fifth Column crap."

He told us to go home and get a goodnight sleep. We happily did just that.

Just as the death of Novak – AKA shoemaker Hoffmann/SS Holderlin – had been explained in the press as a hunting accident, the demise of Dr. Eartha von Geist and her sadistic son, Joseph, read as the sad death of a renowned Jungian psychiatrist at the hands of a home invading thief. Perhaps, these public obits weren't all that far from the truth in all three cases.

On Sunday, the 11th of September, after the Stars had taken the better four of six from the Padres at Gilmore, Haney was asked, in an interview with Bob Hunter, why he hadn't used Joe Bachman in relief for close to two weeks.

To my mind, his answer was a result and a credit to the silence maintained by the LAPD and the Feds in the name of our national game.

"Find me the damn kid and I'll pitch him!"

Chapter XIII

Epitaph in Terror

By Thursday night of that week, two days after the bloodbath in the Hollywood hills, the three of us attempted to get things back to normal. Taking our seats, third base side, we were determined to enjoy every game with the Padres, straight through to the weekend Sunday doubleheader. The Stars took the better half of that series, one more in their pocket on their way to the pennant.

In a congratulatory phone call from Jenks, he expressed a hesitancy to believe that the death of Bachman had put a period on this Nazi situation. His insight reinforced my decision that it was best to hold off on the *all clear*, as far as Frank and the family was concerned. In fact, something was gnawing at my spine, telling me that there could still be a loose thread to this Fifth Column operation.

At the moment, Longdown had no case for me to work on, so he suggested I return to my security job at Gilmore until his plan came to fruition to make me the LAPD's official liaison for both the Stars and Angels.

It felt great to get back to some baseball, easy going summer nights, and good friends. I was whole again, at one with myself and my surroundings. I really wished Richie Goodman was sitting beside me.

I attended Richie's memorial service and funeral on the 8th. Every cop in L.A., as well as other parts of California, showed up. I spoke proudly of our days in the sun. I recalled the pass I received from Richie's bullet arm that led University High to the city championship in '30. I went on to say how, in the following year, it was Richie who had gently guided me through a terrifying gauntlet of possible defeat to my perfect game.

It was during the doubleheader, on Sunday, that Hilo brought up the idea of us having another party. He had a new girlfriend and some new songs. He was anxious to try out both. Angel was all for it. He already had his talk with Carlo, and a party among friends would be the perfect atmosphere for him to meet Ai. From the look on Hilo's face, I could only conclude that he and I weren't completely in agreement with Angel's idea of them meeting up.

I agreed to the party if the Stars took the pennant.

To the delight of all us fans, our heavenly Hollywood Stars didn't clinch the PCL pennant in Frisco, which meant, more than likely, they would clinch it at home. However, as a great Sunday team all season, the Stars did manage to take a pair from the Seals, 10-3 and 2-1, on the 18th of September. Their number one challenger for first place, the Acorns, having taken five of a seven game series with the Angels, dropped their Sunday doubleheader to the Stars hometown rivals. Now, hopelessly trapped in the cellar of the PCL, the Angel's 9-8 and 5-1 wins over the Oaks was described in the *Long Beach Press Telegram* as "a case of civic pride." Upon their return to Gilmore, the Stars, with a four game bulge over the pursuing Oaks, only needed three wins out of seven, in their final series of the season with the Seattle Rainiers, to achieve their goal.

Having won their first two games with Seattle, by the morning of the 22nd, every damn Stars fan was holding their breath and looking forward to a final win that night. Even if the Twinks dropped four of the seven to Seattle, Oakland would still have to sweep all seven games from Portland even to tie for first place.

Considering what he'd been through in the last three months, nobody was holding his breath more than Bob Cobb.

Though Cobb had attended both home games with the Seattle Rainiers (a club that battled the Padres, all season, for fourth place and a shot at the playoffs), rather than be present at the park to endure a nail-biting third, he decided to spend the night somewhere else.

Now, if I were to describe Bob Cobb in terms of things close to my own heart, I'd simply say, here was a man always willing to take a chance. Hell, he took a chance on me. In other words, aside from being a successful restaurateur and the managing vice president of a popular minor league ball team about to take their first pennant in years, Bob was driven by the heart of a gambler. Every now and then, when Bob longed to escape the pressures of a VP in charge of champions or catering to Hollywood celebrities, there was nothing that suited his fancy more than an intimate high-stakes poker game among friends.

Despite the fact that Cobb had hooked me up with Wilkerson, who staked me for some of my initial high-roller games in Vegas, I'd only heard whispers of my boss's infrequent ventures into stud poker that secretly took place in his office above the Hollywood Brown Derby's Bamboo Room at 1628 North Vine. Honestly, notwithstanding my successes at the Flamingo, I had never received an invite to these rare turnouts. That is, until the morning of the 22nd when Bob invited me to a last minute diversion that would provide his mind with a buffer from the very thought that another night might pass without a pennant.

I was figuring on attending the Stars game with Hilo and Angel, but I accepted Cobb's invitation. I could always chance a few bucks in the pot for more in my pocket. I explained my change in plans to my compadres; they understood. Their only complaint was that I was going to miss the Stars clinching the pennant. My only hope was that they were right.

Around 7, the three of us left the canal for our destinations. We wished each other luck. I reached the Derby on Vine, a little after 8, and drove into its arched drive-through. I parked in the restaurant's rear parking lot and immediately caught sight of Longdowns's black bucket. He was obviously in on the game. I walked through the arch and took a right on the sidewalk. I was about to ascend the stairs to Cobb's office, to the left of the Bamboo Room, when I ran into Gus Constance, Cobb's head Maître d'. He was guarding the stairs, clipboard in hand, like some stone lion at the entrance to a library. We had previously met one afternoon, early in the season, at a Sunday doubleheader.

"Oh yes, Mr. Salazar. You're late," he said, as if I was the new dishwasher tardy for my first day of work.

"Sorry about that."

He checked my name off. "The rest of the gentlemen are upstairs *awaiting* your presence."

"Good to know," I said, attempting to make a quick escape up the stairs.

"Have a delightful evening and a pleasant game, Mr. Salazar."

"I'll sure try."

"Mr. Cobb tells me that you're quite the poker player."

"I've had my moments."

"I understand it's not just the cards you're dealt, but how you bet the money you have on hand."

"You can bet your ass on that, Mr. Constance. It's how you choose to *raise* to the occasion, especially, in a high-stakes game. It seems you have an interest here. Why don't you just ask the boss if you can sit in on a game?"

"Oh, I don't know…," he said.

"'Service above self'…right?"

"Something like that."

I turned and continued up the stairs.

Cobb's office was located on the third floor of the Brown Derby complex above the mezzanine level of the Bamboo Room. I knocked on the door. A young waiter in charge of looking after the players' needs, from drinks to beer nuts, opened the door and gestured in the direction of the circular oak table to the right of the room.

The office was as I remembered it, a stylish and smart combination of oak furnishings, walls of oak, and shelves of unvarnished cedar. At the moment, the unvarnished cedar was fighting off the odor of cigar and cigarette smoke like a scented garden of roses fending off a surfeit of skunks.

"Would you like a drink, Mr. Salazar?" asked the waiter.

I had already had a couple that afternoon and declined the offer.

There was only one individual at the table who I was unfamiliar with though I was sure I'd seen him somewhere. He was a slim, handsome, stern-faced, middle-aged man with a pencil moustache, slightly thicker than Wilkerson's. This stranger, seated to the right of Billy, was wearing a light blue denim blazer and a plain white shirt tied at the neck with a southwest bolo. Its repousse, a silver concho, was mounted with a teardrop turquoise stone, denoting him as a westerner of wealth and power.

Upon my approach, he was shuffling a deck of cards and finishing off some small talk in a colorful manner with his undeniable Texas drawl. "There are strong producers that can gush to the edge of heaven and, then, there are worthless dry holes that squirt no higher than a coyote's balls."

This regional witticism was met with laughter from everyone around the table.

Cobb stood up and said, "Jake, I think you know most everybody here, especially this gentleman." He pointed to the Colonel, seated to his right, who'd just lit up a fresh stogy.

"Two cops at one poker game," I said. "Be warned, gentlemen, it'd be best you keep both hands above board at all times." We all laughed.

I thought about what Pop used to say: "Enter the Joker, leave as the Ace!"

Pointing to Wilkerson, Cobb said, "And, of course, you're acquainted with the devil in town."

I laughed. "We're lucky his rag doesn't cover the Stars on the diamond," I said sarcastically.

"I only un-cover those in the Hills," Billy fired back, taking a drag off his holder.

"And, of course, you've met our visiting celebrity, Bill Powell."

William Powell was one of the Hollywood elite who'd invested in the Stars and frequently attended the games. We had actually sat in the stands together several times.

"A visiting celebrity under protest," said Powell. "I'm sure you would agree, Jake, we'd all prefer to be at a certain ball game tonight, but I'm here because I was unable to convince the owner of that ball team to get off his skittish ass to attend that game."

"Well, Mr. Powell," I said, as I sat down across from the stranger, "if you're asking me would I prefer to be at a ball park tonight, I'd have to say no. I haven't had the pleasure of a good poker game in quite some time."

"You see, Bill," snapped Cobb, knowing damn well why I hadn't had the pleasure of a game in sometime, "you're not about to find your mutineer in one of the best damn poker players between here and Vegas."

"More's the pity, Captain Bligh," said the eloquent movie star, lighting his cigarette. "More's the pity."

It was during this repartee that it hit me. The elegantly dressed Texan, sitting across from me, was none other than the biggest wildcat multi-millionaire oilman of them all.

"Jake, I'd like to introduce you to…," began Cobb.

"I recognize Mr. McCarthy from the photo of him and Mr. Hughes in the *Examiner*," I said.

"Yeah, I'm in town trying to get that cheapskate to go in on a sure-thing with me. It's a drilling operation just south of Houston."

"Any luck?" I asked.

"Well now, that…ah…Mister…?"

"Salazar. Jake Salazar."

"That, Mr. Salazar, is my own damn business!"

Realizing my faux pas, the Colonel jumped in. "Jake's a veteran, Glenn, picked himself up a bronze and silver star in the Philippines."

The expression on McCarthy's face changed immediately. He smiled, stood up, and offered me his hand from across the table. "Please accept my apologies for my abruptness, Mr. Salazar…"

"That's *Officer* Salazar, Glenn," interjected Longdown.

"Officer Salazar," said McCarthy, offering the correction in a most cordial manner.

We shook hands.

"Call me Jake," I said.

"Glenn," he replied.

We both sat down. A sigh of relief snaked its way around the table, from movie star to devil to restaurateur to cop, like the merciful verdict of innocence in a murder trial.

"I understand that, unlike the majority of successful oil men in Texas, your story of success is the hardscrabble life of a self-made man. I can certainly relate to that," I said.

McCarthy folded his hands over the deck of cards. He stared at me with the same life weary eyes as the ex-pug who had once bought me a cold beer after beating the crap out of me in a Vancouver dive for a wisecrack I made about his toothless mouth. "You're right, Jake. I came to terms with my poor man's ambition to make some big bucks at the corner of Main and McGowan Street, in Houston. That was where I worked my tail off for the woman I loved and intended to marry. Owned and worked a franchised Sinclair Gas Station on that busy corner. With hard work and determination, I grew into a *force of nature* and learned one thing."

"And what *in hell* may I ask was that?" Bill Powell's question was so perfect in it's delivery that you'd have thought we were all in a movie.

"Ain't one damn American, in this blessed country of ours, going anywhere without an auto-mo-bile!"

Here, of course, came the biggest laugh from the table thus far.

"Which brings me, gentlemen," he began to shuffle the cards once more, "to our present moment in time and what I can't help but look upon as the backward state of this beloved game that we're here to play tonight. Just as every red-blooded American needs an automobile to progress into this fast paced post-war world of ours, so, too, poker needs a *vehicle* by which to drive into the future. Gentlemen, I'm here tonight to introduce you-all to a little game we play, in the Lone Star State, called Texas Hold'em."

"It's not enough that you talked me into babysitting you tonight, Bob, but now I'm being forced to learn a new form of poker," argued the dapper Powell to the immaculately groomed Cobb.

"Trust me, Bill, one form of poker is just like another. You only have to use your imagination to find the similarities between them."

"You mean like in all those *Thin Man* movies when everybody in the audience believed I was going to bed every night with Myrna Loy when in truth, I never slept with Myrna Loy. Never! Ergo, I never *really* got to *poker.*"

"Exactly my point," responded Cobb. "It's the same in making movies as it is in playing this game. One imagined form of *poker* is another imagined form of *poker.*"

"So, my dear Socrates, theoretically-speaking – in moviemaking or gambling - one never really *gets* to poker."

"Unless, of course, one is committed to a form of Stud that *really gets* to poker," admitted Cobb, biting his tongue.

Powell, currently a married man, left it at a knowing smile and a drag on his cigarette.

McCarthy had begun to deal the cards and illustrate some of the game's specifics when the phone on Cobb's desk rang. The waiter walked over and answered it.

I'd played some Hold'em, when I was in the service, and was damn sure I had a good chance of coming out on top at the end of the evening. I was listening carefully to Glenn's refresher course when the waiter walked to me and whispered in my ear.

"There's a call for you, Mr. Salazar," he said.

"For me?"

"She says she's your sister in Oakland."

I immediately thought that something horrible had happened. I excused myself from the table.

I reached Cobb's desk and lifted the receiver to my ear.

"Millie…?"

"You have no idea how difficult it was to get this number," she said. She really sounded rattled.

"Did something happen at home?"

"No, we're all just fine."

"Then what…?"

"Eeph…came over this afternoon."

It was a bad connection, breaking up here and there.

"Who…?"

"Eephus came by this afternoon. Said he remembered something about Hoffmann."

"Hoffmann! What did he remember about Hoffmann?"

"He had…," again there was interference.

"He had what…?"

"Hoffmann had twins!"

"Twins!" I exclaimed in disbelief.

"The shoemaker had twin boys! And they both wanted to be a pitcher," Millie said.

I stood frozen, for a moment, as if I'd just walked in the winning run. "Thanks for the information, Millie. I have to get right on this. I'll get back to you…ah…tomorrow sometime."

"I love you, Jake. I only hope this helps."

"Oh, it helps all right. I love you too, Millie," I said, hanging up the phone.

Walking back to the table, I whispered the bad news in Cobb's ear. He put down his cards and looked up at me with the same look of consternation that, I'm sure, had appeared on my face when I got the news from my sister. I whispered that Haney and the boys at Gilmore, completely unaware of the Fifth Column situation, still believe Bachman just disappeared. Furthermore, tonight's game would be perfect for him to reappear with god knows what in his duffle.

Cobb stood up with the determined look of a general at a regimental dinner who was just informed that his troops had been ordered to immediately advance to the front.

"Gentlemen, I'm afraid we're going to have to take a raincheck on our game." He turned to McCarthy. "Glenn, please accept my apologies."

"Well, what on earth could possibly come between you-all and such a sacred event?"

"Jake, here, my head of security, just heard from a reliable source that…ah… some rowdy Angels fans are out to start rioting if the Stars clinch it tonight. The axe is sure to fall on my neck if any such outrage even comes close to happening. We've both got to *hightail* it over to Gilmore as soon as possible."

"You mean I'm released!" Powell shouted.

"You are, indeed, my dear Aristotle. So run downstairs, jump in that Caddy of yours, and head for Gilmore. That's an order."

"Gentlemen, it's been a pleasure. But at the moment," he said, checking his leather- banded Rolex Air King, "I have a date with some Hollywood Stars about to capture the PCL pennant." Looking in the direction of Wilkerson and McCarthy, he asked, "Now, if either of you are not interested in driving over to the game with the Riot Squad, you're welcome to join me…"

"The truth is, Bill, I was damn well up for a game of poker tonight," said McCarthy.

"Tell you what, Glenn, let's go downstairs and have a big fat Angus T-bone on Bob, here. You can teach me all about Texas Hold'em," responded Wilkerson, picking up the deck of cards.

"Absolutely. Drinks, dinner, everything's on the house," confirmed Cobb.

"Gentlemen," said Powell, pointing to the Colonel, Cobb, and me, "I'll race you to the ball park." And with that, he started out toward the parking lot below. Stopping momentarily, he snapped off a 20 from his silver money clip and handed it to the young waiter. "That's for you, my lad," he said, and he exited the room.

Walking around opposite sides of the table, Wilkerson and McCarthy started toward the door.

"Just tell Gus to put it on my tab," said Cobb.

"I'll do just that," said Wilkerson. Turning to the waiter, he pulled out two 20s from his wallet and handed it to the young man.

"Here, now, I'll…," said McCarthy.

Billy raised his hand in protest. "Not to worry, Glenn, that'll cover both of us. Now, tell me again about this community layout of cards in this Texas poker game of yours."

"Well, like I said, Billy, it's nothing short of the reason why Hold'em's gonna be the vehicle that'll put the

Stud world to shame," McCarthy said, as they both exited for the Bamboo Room below.

Longdown turned to Cobb and said, "So what the hell's up, Bob?"

"We'll fill you in on the drive over," said Cobb. He walked to the waiter, pulled out a

c-note, from his wallet, and handed it to him.

"Gee, thanks, Mr. Cobb," he said, taking the bill gently in hand. He stared at it as if he'd just been handed a fragment of the true Cross.

"That's for the three of us. When you finish cleaning up here, go downstairs and tell Gus that I said you could take the rest of the night off."

"I was sure looking forward to that poker game," said the young waiter.

"That makes two of us."

Cobb, Longdown, and I rushed downstairs only to catch up with the slow moving conversationalists about to enter the Derby's Bamboo Room. Wilkerson had just opened the restaurant's door for McCarthy when he turned and whispered to Cobb: "Tell me the truth, Bobby, this sudden rush to Gilmore has something to do with…"

"Keep your goddamned scandalous nose out of this, Billy, or you're not getting my advertisement check this month."

Billy took a sudden pause and quickly backed off. "'Right you are, when you think you are.'"

"More so when you know you are!"

Wilkerson was still holding the door open as two young women in high-heels, dressed to kill, giggled their way past him into the restaurant.

"By all means, ladies first," said Billy.

"Damn straight!" said Cobb.

Wilkerson smiled at Cobb and entered the Bamboo Room for his free meal and poker lesson.

We were walking through the archway to the parking lot when Powell drove past us in his Cadillac. He waved, copped a left, and headed south on Vine in the direction of Gilmore Field.

As we hurried toward the Colonel's unmarked police car, I shouted to both of them that it would be best that I leave my car in the lot and we all head south in the squad car. The Colonel took the wheel, I hopped in the backseat, and Cobb rode shotgun. Switching on the rotating red light, temporarily mounted on the dashboard, the Colonel rolled down the driver-side window and slammed the magnetic gumball light onto the roof of the vehicle.

He turned on the siren and we were off.

Heading south on Vine, I filled Longdown in on the information my sister had given me concerning the existence of the twin Bachman brothers. He agreed that this would be the perfect night for the living brother to reappear…with a bomb in his duffle. Longdown got on his car radio and called ahead to Officer Wolfer, the LAPD's demolitions expert, to meet us at Gilmore.

Within a couple of blocks, weaving in and out of traffic on Vine, we caught up to Powell. Like the rest of the vehicles, he was forced to pull over and give way to our siren and red light of the law. I waved to him from the backseat. He smiled and delivered a mock salute.

Once we'd taken a hard right on Fairfax, I began to mull over the things I'd missed when it came to realizing that there were two Bachmans. First, there was that bizarre photo on von Geist's desk of an alleged Jewish friend with his sons that was obviously Holderlin and their twins. The concealment of their faces, I now realized, was symbolic of their early baptism into the treacherous depths of the SS. And then there was the dropping of one n, in the spelling of Bachman, identifying Joe Bachman as Jewish, obviously concealing the fact that he was German. This led me to wonder just how involved the liberal minded von Geist *had been* in this Fifth Column operation. Still, there was more. Much more. Like that first day, the day of Howard Story's murder, when I noticed Bachman had left his glove on the top of the dugout. Believing that it was he who was still on the mound, I concluded he had changed gloves because of his injured forefinger. In fact, this Bachman had been replaced, in the latter innings, by his twin brother who had arrived with his own glove. Martin's interview with Finch, after the game, only confirmed the fact that one brother's fastball was sliding outside (to the right-handed-hitting Martin) and the other's was cutting inside. Yes, it all made sense. While one twin 'cut away,' and the other 'cut in' on righties. But why would their father, Holderlin, the professional SS spy who had slithered his way from one alias to another, have taken the chance of switching twins in the middle of the game? Unless, of course, it was that Holderlin wanted to prove, to his wife, that his favorite son was the twin who was most capable of killing a man and pitching the Stars to victory on the same day. I thought, again, about that green maintenance truck, barreling down Genesee Avenue when Cobb and I were crossing the parking lot. All of this had to have been prearranged. That afternoon, when Joe Bachman (the twin who played with his left trigger finger outside his glove) was called in early for relief, provided the right set of circumstances for the other Joe Bachman (the twin who left his trigger finger in his glove) to kill Howard Story and then be driven to Gilmore to finish off the Oaks. No doubt, it was Novak's electrical room that had served as the appropriate space for the magical quick change. As insane a deduction as this may have been, it appeared that SS Holderlin's favorite son was handed the opportunity of being a killer in life and on the mound. Ironically, the Stars lost the game.

A left on Beverly and we arrived at the stadium's parking lot. Longdown killed the siren, pulled in and turned off the rotating light. As we slowly drove around to the back of the stadium, I rolled down the back window and listened to the roar of the crowd. With Gilmore's lights illuminating outward and above us, we came to a stop in front of the large sliding maintenance door at the rear of the field. Longdown reached into the glove compartment and pulled out his .38 and a pair of cuffs. Officer Wolfer, holding a large black suitcase that obviously contained his protective vest and gear, was waiting for us. Cobb had a key to the door and opened it.

As we all entered the cavernous, semi-darkened basement corridor under the stands, Longdown detailed what each of us was to do in regard to the operation. Cobb and I would enter the Stars dugout. If Bachman was present, Cobb was to pull Haney aside and inform him of the story we'd made up about the rookie pitcher on the drive over. Simultaneously, I was to locate Bachman's duffle and hand it to Wolfer in the corridor. All of this was to proceed as unobtrusively as possible. Once in the corridor, Wolfer would search Bachman's duffle for any explosives or weapons.

As we neared the dugout, Longdown handed me the cuffs and said, "If there's any heat to be used, I'll be in charge of the fire. You cuff'em."

"Roger that, Colonel."

Reaching the tunnel to the dugout, we took our designated positions. Officer Wolfer removed his coat and put on his upper body bombproof protection and modified football helmet with visor. Cobb and I stood, at the ready, on either side of the short semi-lit passage. Longdown, standing behind Cobb, his right hand on his pocketed .38, was poised to move in, if necessary.

Once inside the dugout, it took a moment for our eyes to adjust to the brilliance of the lights as we stared out onto the field. When we realized what we were looking at, Cobb and I turned to each other with a look of shock on our faces.

On the mound was Joe Bachman.

Cobb immediately walked over to Haney who was crouched with one foot up on the edge of the dugout.

"Looking at the scoreboard, things still look a little tentative," said Cobb.

Haney turned, embraced him, and assured Cobb that after tonight the PCL pennant would be theirs. Then he remembered. "Wait a minute, you told me you were going to shy away from the game tonight and play some poker."

Cobb quickly changed the subject and asked about Bachman. Haney said he had showed up out of the blue before the game. When Schallock ran into trouble, in the top of the second, he decided to put in the kid for a couple of innings. If that didn't do it, he would put in Ramsdell.

Glen Moulder, the Stars pitching coach, was sitting on the bench closely observing Bachman.

"Say, Glen, which one of these duffels is Bachman's?" I asked. "I gave him a ball to sign for my nephew in Oakland. Kid's crazy about this cup of coffee's success. I was wondering if he signed it for me. You think he'd mind if I take a look?"

"Hell, why not. But it's none of the duffels, it's that backpack over there," he said. He was pointing to the camouflaged army issue, propped up in the corner of the dugout opposite him. "Sounds like there's an alarm clock in there. The kid must have needed something to remind him to show up." He was obviously pissed off at Bachman's unexplained absence over the last few weeks. "On the other hand, maybe it's a bomb," concluded Moulder, breaking into a great guffaw. "There's the ticket. This patch of farmers innings away from a pennant and a promising cup of coffee blows us to smithereens."

"No capital gains there," I said.

"Frickin' Aaaa...merica!"

Jack Albright, Seattle's leadoff shortstop, hit a high fly ball down the left field line and Moulder rushed to the edge of the dugout. I carefully picked up the ticking backpack and quickly made my exit. Entering the corridor, I handed it to Wolfer.

"There's something ticking inside."

"Christ!" he said, looking at me like some vice cop about to hook the working girl at the end of the bar.

When I re-entered the dugout, despite the fact that Albright's fly ball had obviously gone foul, Moulder had remained at its edge, keeping an attentive eye on Bachman. From the look on Haney's face, I assumed that Cobb had provided him with the cover story we'd contrived. He was to tell Haney that Bachman was wanted for armed robbery in Nevada, and there was a cop in the corridor waiting to arrest him.

At that very moment, Bachman struck out Albright. The stands went wild and Glen Moulder, a proud coach, smiled and gave his prize cup of coffee a thumb's up.

"What do you say we give the kid a chance to retire the side," suggested Haney.

Caught between the dreadful world of intrigue and the love of his team that was about to win a pennant, Cobb sighed and said, "Sure, sure, why not."

Cobb, Haney, and I joined Moulder, at the edge of the dugout, to watch young Joe Bachman work his magic.

The kid had it all. He worked fast, accurately, and could change things up. Working between a two-seam and four-seam fastball – the two seam sliding mysteriously away – Bachman struck out "Wild Horse" Sheridan, Seattle's right fielder, in four pitches. Next up, top of the order, was Hillis Layne, the Rainiers third baseman. Layne threw right, but batted left. Bachman's first pitch cut in so hard that it broke Layne's bat. His fastball, that cut in on lefties, was obviously a variation of his sadistic brother's ability to cut in on righties. After Layne caught a piece of a change up and fouled it off, Bachman threw him a couple of curves, striking him out in five pitches, and retiring the side.

Bachman caught sight of me when he turned from the slab toward the dugout. As is customary, the Stars fielders left their gloves on the grass of the playing field. As Bachman and his catcher, Mike Sandlock, were placing theirs on top of the dugout, the Stars ace, who had been staring at me all the way from the mound, walked directly to me.

"I figured you might show, Officer Salazar," he said.

With a finger on the trigger of his concealed .38, Longdown peeked into the dugout and said to me, "Ask Mr. Bachman to please step into the corridor."

His teammates looked confused, especially Sandlock, who was planning on a detailed conversation with the kid as to how they were going to face the rest of Seattle's order.

"Don't worry about me, guys," said Bachman. "Just concentrate on winning the pennant."

Haney looked at the young pitcher and said, "I'm really sorry about this, kid."

"Thanks for everything, Mr. Haney." Then he turned to Moulder, "You too, Glen."

Cobb wasn't so sympathetic. "You had a lot to give, Joe, but you blew it."

Bachman looked toward the corner of the dugout where he'd left his menacing backpack. He moved closer to Cobb and whispered some parting words for him alone. "Tell your capitalist investors I'm just sorry I couldn't blow all of them to holy hell."

I took Bachman by the arm and led him into the corridor.

"Cuff'em, Jake," said Longdown, his hand still in his coat pocket with a finger on the trigger of his .38.

Holding up several taped together sticks of military dynamite he'd taken from Bachman's pack, Officer Wolfer said, "Our Star pitcher, here, was about to blow himself and a good portion of Gilmore Field sky high."

I cuffed Bachman's hands behind his back then turned to Longdown. "Mind if I have a word with him before you take him away?"

"Sure, Jake."

"Why Joe, for what…?"

"For my mother," he said softly.

"She was a communist, wasn't she?"

"A communist who lived everyday of her life in fear of the iron boot of my father."

"I take it, you both lived in fear."

"Mark my word, Officer Salazar, there'll come a time when the women of this great country of ours will no longer be under the suppression of rapists, philanderers, and wife beaters. They'll – at last - be free to initiate socialism at your nation's motherly core, and then, only then, will true international communism find its way into the hearts and minds of the American people."

"It sounds downright *fashionable*. But what about those who don't *fancy* joining the urban proletariat? What about those who prefer to remain farmers, beekeepers, or just wish to take a chance on making a living by playing games?"

Bachman looked at me like I was some smartass in class, on parent-teacher's day, interrupting his mother's dissertation on socialism.

"My mother taught me a rhyme when I was a child. It went like this:

'When Lenin took the train
All dapper and restrained
And left Berlin for the Finland Station
In hope of forming the Soviet Nation
'Twas on the journey east
In a confidential feast
He traded with a banker chap
His bowler for a workman's cap.'"

My mind immediately flashed back to the note left next to Richie Goodman's body: "Shoemakers and tailors count hours." I wasn't all that sure of what to make of the poem, but damn sure our conversation had come to an end.

"I just want you to know," he said, "that I didn't kill your friend Goodman, nor, for that matter, Howard Story."

"I figured as much. You started that game against Oakland, the day that Story was murdered, and your fascistic brother finished it."

"Enough with the gab," said Longdown. "Come along, son; your pitching days are over."

The Colonel took him by the arm and, together with Officer Wolfer, led him toward the maintenance entrance.

"Is your name Joe Holderlin?" I shouted after him.

He turned in my direction and said, "Yes, I'm the real dreamer. I'm Joe Holderlin. My brother's name was Hans."

The Stars took the PCL pennant that night in a 7 to 4 victory over the Seattle Rainiers. Haney sent in Willie Ramsdell in the top of the fifth and Willie knuckleballed his way to his 18th victory. Needless to say, the fans at Gilmore went wild. They carried Haney to centerfield where he hoisted a makeshift pennant. Ironically enough, there was no wind that night and the flag wouldn't fly. In the papers the next day, Haney, who played with Ty Cobb's Tiger's in '23 and hit a homer in Yankee Stadium, reflected on the lack of wind that evening. "Proving again, that in baseball, nothing is ever completely perfect."

That night, after the Stars victory, the Colonel drove me back to the Brown Derby. From there, I drove home.

I entered the alley, on the canal, and parked. I took a deep breath and a moment to myself. It was then that the image came to me like some naïve triptych I had seen once in a silent movie of my youth. To my right, was a wild green meadow illumined by the blaze of the Klan's burning cross. To my left, a perfectly manicured Hollywood lawn served as the backdrop for a televised, bespectacled feminist promising a Vogue in every mailbox. And projected between these extremes, the never "completely perfect" game of baseball, a humble field of dirt and grass, designed in the pattern of a diamond, demanding that life exists simply for the purpose of being lived and not in the name of some half-assed ideology.

For the moment, all looked well. With a pennant in hand, a nation intact, and a thriving economy that offered plenty of capital above and jobs below, what more could an honest American politician, businessman, or hardworking member of the middle class expect from life. Sure, at the end of that summer of '49, all was as well as could be expected.

Chapter XIV

Hilo's Giant Flea and Its Song of Love

The morning after the pennant win, I got a call from Jenks. He congratulated me on my outstanding work on the case. He assured me that, after a thorough investigation, both the FBI and the CIA could find no evidence indicating that anyone other than Holderlin, his twin sons, and the operatives who were killed in the Ventura Hills, had been involved with the Fifth Column of Nazis. As for the surviving twin, the Feds were shipping him to New York City to stand trial for treason with several other commies that had been arrested on the East Coast. "There will be no whisper to the press or authorities as to his true identity and relationship with his father and brother." Before we hung up, I told him that we'd have to keep in touch. He promised to get hold of me the next time he was in L.A.

Needless to say, I immediately called the family in Oakland. Frank answered the phone and I sounded the all clear. Thinking it was best to handle it himself, he told me he never let Tommy know about the situation. I asked to speak to Millie. I wanted her to know how much she'd helped in providing me with Eephus's last minute information and how important it was in finally resolving the Fifth Column intrigue.

"And the shoemaker, Hoffmann…?" She asked.

"Dead as a doornail."

"Oh my God, I was so worried about you, and I couldn't tell a soul because I didn't want to worry Mom and the others."

"Everything worked out just fine."

In the background, I could hear Mom insisting that she wanted to speak with me. Millie put her on and the first words out of her mouth were, "When are you going to visit? It seems like every day Charlie's asking about you." I promised her I'd be home for Christmas and, without missing a beat, asked her to put Tommy on. I could hear her yelling upstairs to his room. After a moment, he picked up the second floor phone.

"So, how about those Stars," I said.

"Congratulations. You know, Jake, Charlie's still an Oaks fan. I convinced him there's always next year."

I couldn't help but take a deep breath. "Yeah, and we can sure as hell thank God for that. Thanks for your original lead, by the way. It really helped us track down Hoffmann and the entire Fifth Column."

"So that all worked out, did it?"

"It sure as hell did."

Our conversation ended with my telling him to give my best to Theresa and a promise to be home for Christmas.

The moment I got off the phone with Tommy, I thought of the perfect Christmas gift for Charlie. I'd ask Haney if he could get the team to sign a Louisville Slugger. I was determined to turn him into a Stars fan.

That year, the Stars won the pennant and the playoffs. After the first round, with the Twinks taking four out of five from the Solons and the Oaks dropping four out of seven to San Diego, the Stars took on the Padres in the Finals. They lost two out of three in San Diego then came home to win the last three games, capturing the Governor's Cup. Adding the $35,000 playoffs' prize to the $15,000 for the pennant and Cobb and his boys of summer were pretty much in the chips by October of '49.

Hilo, Angel, and I listened to all the away games on radio. We were in attendance at Gilmore for the three home games with the Solons and the last three with the Padres.

Knowing in our heart of hearts that the Twinks were bound to wrap things up on that Sunday of October 9th, we agreed that the following Saturday would be the perfect night for our party. The guest list was of prime importance. For the most part, it would prove to be the usual suspects from our last party with, of course, exceptions.

Fact is, I ran into Stuart Perkoff at the old Townhouse Bar a week or so after the Stars had taken the pennant. We even sat down and had a few drinks together. He apologized for the way he had acted that night, and I said I was sorry for Angel's savage overreaction to Ginsberg's come-on and poetry. At one point, I thought about inviting him to our party but decided against it. If I was going to invite any writer, it would be Bob Hunter from the *L.A. Examiner*. Anyway, I owed him an explanation – to some degree – concerning the whole Fifth Column thing. As far as I was concerned, Bob's well-written prose and observant baseball reportage was more to my taste than some psychotic jerk, howling down the street at midnight, in search of a fix or a blowjob.

With the exception of Emilia and Aleksy Kowalczyk, who showed up early to find a place to set out their delicious desserts of makowki, paczki, and mazurek, everyone arrived around eight.

As for as the main course, the three of us agreed that the menu from our last party was far too elaborate. So, Angel came up with the idea of whipping up a big batch of his mom's adobo, a Filipino culinary favorite that he had made for us several times. This incredibly tasty dish of pork belly stew, marinated in soy sauce, vinegar, and garlic, would prove to be a delectable meal for our friendly gathering. With our borrowed dockside coffeemaker and an impressive array of beverages from hard liquor to coke, we were set for quite a feast.

The bar girls that Hilo invited arrived about the same time as Angel's friends from the docks, Carlo was among them. A few remembered each other from our last party. They began to dance to a 78 album of Ella Fitzgerald and the Ink Spots that Ben and Willie had brought by for the evening. Angel introduced Ai to Carlo. They would spend the rest of the evening getting to know each other.

I invited Cobb and Longdown, but neither one could make it. Cobb, however, sent over one of his top bartenders with a case of Dom Perignon as an apology. Although I was given permission to inform Bob Hunter about what really happened, Cobb may have been a little shaky about coming face to face with him at the party.

The minute Hunter showed and after we both filled our paper cups with Champagne, I asked him to follow me out to the porch so we could speak in private. I filled him in on some of the specifics of Holderlin's Fifth Column operation that could have culminated in Hitler addressing the American people from Gilmore Field. I explained how it all started with the murder of Howard Story and ended with the death of my buddy, Richie Goodman. I left out details concerning the Bachman twins. After hearing my version of the story, Bob did exactly what I thought he would.

"For the love of the game, I'll just tell the muckrakers across the hall that there was nothing more to it than two more unsolved murders in this wicked metropolis of ours."

"Think they'll buy it?"

"Oh, they'll buy it all right. Trust me, with a new supply of dirt every day, these brooding scandalmongers haven't got time to investigate yesterday's murders."

When Bob and I returned to the party, I introduced him to the Kowalczyks who were already deep in conversation with Smitty Teste. Aleksy was doing his best to explain to Smitty his reasoning for the Red Sox losing the American League pennant and Ted Williams losing his bid for the triple crown. According to Aleksy, it all came down to Boston's final game with the Yankees. Oddly enough, the Yanks had gone on to beat the Dodgers in the World Series on the very same day, October 9th, that the Stars took the PCL playoffs. The Dodgers loss of the Series put Smitty and his boss, Rickey, in one hell of a win-lose situation. Who knows, maybe if Smitty had been doing his job, instead of reading East Coast newspapers and worrying about outlawed pitches and stealers of home, and suggested that Baxes or Noren be called up to the Big Show, it might have been the Dodgers that had taken home the gold. As Hunter, with his journalistic expertise, took command of the conversation, Smitty excused himself and motioned me off to a corner of the living room. He apologized for bad-mouthing Pinky Woods the day he'd been taken out for the kid, Bachman. Angel had been right, Pinky would win 20 games. As a matter of fact, he won 23. I would have enjoyed getting Smitty's apology for other nasty things he'd said to me over this last season, but my attention was averted to Healani and Leonor who had just walked in.

Hilo was introducing them to his new girlfriend. I don't think I ever got her name. I was sure, before the night was over, he was hoping to get her and Healani in the sack. While this little romantic intrigue was going on, I walked over to Leonor and asked her to dance. Ben had just put on Billy Eckstine's "My Foolish Heart." We had danced through several of Eckstine's songs when Hilo took the microphone on our makeshift stage. He introduced the two other members of his trio and provided his audience with a few words concerning his new approach to songwriting and performance.

"As most of you know, my first instrument was the ukulele. The story of how the ukulele got its name is important if all of you are to understand the reason I've named my new electric guitar my *Giant Flea*. You see," he began, "when the Portuguese sailors first arrived on the shores of my Islands they brought with them a small guitar they called the machete. With my forefathers so anxious to play and sing songs of love on this new instrument, it jumped from one Islanders' hands to the next and was quickly renamed the *ukulele*, Hawaiian for 'jumping flea.' It has been argued, by many well-meaning and learned scholars of this historic event, that this gift of a flea, brought to the Islands by the Portuguese, was something far less delightful than a new means of playing love songs. But this question, I'll leave to the historians of social diseases."

This one got a big laugh.

"So then," he said, lifting his newly obtained Gretsch, "Tonight, I offer you my Giant Flea and its songs of love."

"My dog has *fleas*," sang Angel.

"Yes, and now that you mention it, I think I know why," said Hilo.

Again, a laugh.

Everyone began dancing or listening to Hilo's new songs. They were fresh, contemporary, and modern. His style was no longer limited to that which he'd been nurtured on when he came up with Harry Owen's band.

Hilo's compositions and their lyrics were competitive, and I was sure that he could find himself a record label that would be interested in giving him a shot at a recording contract. There was one song, in particular, that I'd heard him composing and practicing in his room. I thought it was one of his best. It was entitled, "Tell You the Truth about Love."

> "Though it's written in the stars
> And hustled on the street
> And yes perhaps it twinkles in that soul
> You long to greet
> First let me say my friends
> I'm out to put an end
> To all those myriad questions
> And endless intellections
> And tell you the truth about love...
> And tell you the truth about love..."

After dancing through several of Hilo's tunes, it was this song that was giving me the courage to kiss Leonor. I was about to do just that when Aleksy interrupted our dance.

"I know that you are quite obviously interested in dancing with this beautiful young lady, but Emilia and I are about to leave and I didn't want to go until I saw your progress with that novel of yours."

Excusing myself to Leonor, I walked to my desk. I opened the top drawer and brought out the first chapter of my detective novel held together by a paperclip. I handed it to this old Polish librarian who'd given me so much encouragement to continue my efforts at writing. He read no further than a glance at the title page. "*Epitaph in Terror*, a most intriguing title," he said. He set the typed sheets of paper down on top of the desk. "Frankly, I need no more than that. It was one of the ancients, I can't remember who, that insisted a true prophet is never obscure nor in need of explaining too much."

"I don't see myself as much of a prophet," I said, "but I'd sure as hell like to *make* some profit."

Emilia suddenly appeared between us. "Jake, this is a much better party than your last one."

"Certainly a hell of a lot less dramatic," I said.

She nodded in agreement. "Despite your delightful party, I'm afraid we're going to have to leave. We old ones need our sleep."

"I was just about to explain that to Jake," said Aleksy.

"But not before you explain, to Smitty, your position on the Soviets possessing an atomic bomb," she said, poking her husband in the chest with her right index finger.

"Yeah, I read about that. It was in the papers the day after the Stars won the pennant," I said.

"If only the entire world was baseball and had no interest in these insane international politics," the old man sighed.

"Tell me about it," I said.

"Come, come now," Emilia said, as she started across the room toward Smitty sitting on the sofa.

"Smitty thinks it's the end of the world now that the Russians have the bomb. I'm trying to convince him that it's the beginning of détente," said Aleksy.

"You might do better by explaining to him what he could have done to help the Dodgers win the Series," I suggested sarcastically.

"Oh, no, politics I understand, traveling back in time I leave to H.G. Wells. Lovely party, Jake," he said, shaking my hand and turning in the direction of Smitty and his wife.

I noticed that Leonor was dancing with one of Angel's friends from the docks. I decided not to cut in on them. Instead, I turned toward the double doors leading to the porch and the canal. I had a sudden desire to be alone. I walked outside into the night. I didn't need another drink. I just needed to reflect.

So, here I am starting my first novel. A retelling of my involvement in tracking down a Fifth Column of Nazis. I'll certainly have to leave some things out. For example, there was Reich's ironical commitment to the "as above, so below" culture of Hollywood's silent world of quid pro quo, a state of affairs that he considered an essential ingredient to a peaceful and forward looking take on true liberty. He had argued this *conservative truth* to be the hidden key to an amicable evolution of the middle class. Does "something for something" simply translate as an honest day's work for a decent day's pay?

So lost in my thoughts, I didn't notice Leonor until I felt her arms around me. I turned to face her.

"I missed you," she said.

I kissed her, placed my arms around her waist, and she leaned her head back on my shoulder. Staring out onto the canal, we were a perfect fit.

Maybe if I played my cards right, I could ta'k her into staying the night.